To Bill,

MICHAEL CALHOUN TUCKER

Welcome to Tuckertown

Tuckertown is the second novel in THE CRACKERS series. *The Legend of Jessie B. Tucker* began the story of how Jessie fought in and survived the Civil War with the help of his new-found Creek Indian family and then drove cattle across the wilderness. Paid for cattle in gold, Jessie bought up the land surrounding his homestead, fearing the carpetbaggers from the north would purchase his land.

Traveling to Georgia for ex-slaves to help him build his empire, Jessie unknowingly begins an unstoppable force that will end in *Tuckertown*. With men to share crop the land, a preacher, a new church, a blacksmith and new commissary, the seeds of this new town are planted. All the new families will come to depend on Jessie and his wisdom to help them grow and prosper.

Two Worlds, Jessie's spiritual advisor, guides Jessie through difficult times, when as a man, a husband, and a father, he is tested. Lawless greedy men travel the landscape of Florida causing terror in the new residents. Having defied the law by sheltering the Creek Indians, Jessie now has to become the law to protect the people and the land he loves.

Filled with adventures, love, loss, and promise, *Tuckertown* will not disappoint you!

Amazon.com Reviews

Here are two of the reviews for Book One of *The Crackers*.

"The Crackers" The Legend of Jessie B Tucker a GREAT Story, A wonderful read! A wonderful Florida frontier story. Historical references to the Civil War, Florida settlers, Creek & Seminole Indians, homesteading, including the outstanding flora-fauna & environment of South Florida. Characters are quite believable and very interesting. I truly enjoyed reading this book.

The story is very well written, captures your imagination, you just want to keep reading page after page to know more about the people, the land and where the story will take you next. I REALLY hope this author writes the next story soon. This book would be a wonderful start to a series of Florida stories that are historically driven and all the interesting characters we know were absolutely essential in the development of Florida. A note to Michael Calhoun Tucker. . . please keep writing!!" *Bubble J.*

"Wonderful journey to a time when a man's word was his bond, and his loyalty was to his people!!"
"I just finished reading and traveling back in time with The Crackers. What an awesome journey it was. One of the best written books of these proud southerners and the Indian tribes of a bygone era. Life was hard in those days but, yet it was much simpler. The cover artwork takes you back in time as well as the story line. I am so looking forward to the next book on this by this author. Yes, (Wyatt) the read was worth the wait." *Alice Rowland*

THE CRACKERS

Tuckertown

THE CRACKERS

Tuckertown

MICHAEL CALHOUN TUCKER

Copyright © 2019 Michael Calhoun Tucker
All rights reserved.

Editor Raven Dodd
Preserving the Author's Voice
www.ravendodd.com

Cover art by Brenda Tucker
Photos by Brenda Tucker

ISBN: 978-1-947678-12-5

Imprint: Independently published
by Preserving the Author's Voice

Published and printed in the USA

Dedication

To my wonderful wife, Brenda.
She keeps our life in order while I write.

Acknowledgements

My daughters Callie and Meghan for their encouragement. My grandchildren Aylah, Nate, and Lily. My friends who reviewed this novel and for their input. My editor Raven Dodd; she stays with me until I get it right.

Prologue

It was the third day. The old medicine man Two Worlds had been drawing with his gourd of dye and pens made from the stems of the palmetto, bringing the history of his people up to date on the memory hide. He knew his final journey to join his ancestors would come soon. Needing to stretch his old muscles, he rose slowly to his feet. Steadying himself, he started with small steps and began to walk in a circle. His companion the large panther rose with him and followed him around the giant cavern.

Several caves dotted the wall. Some were large enough to stand and walk in, and others were so low, you had to crawl to enter. Two Worlds walked to the cave entrance and saw the shelf that had been dug into the wall by his only son. This would be his final resting place. He knew it would not be long now as he made his way back to the small fire and the hide. He had to finish soon before he had no more energy to stay here in the present; the ancestors' voices in his head were calling to him to join them.

Two Worlds sat with his legs crossed once more in front of the small fire that kept the chill from his fragile body and added a few small branches to the embers. He lifted his drinking gourd and the leather bag his wife Woman of the Wind had sent to help on his journey. He shook a little powder from the bag, poured a swallow of water, and mixing them together, he raised the gourd and swallowed in one quick motion. He took the long stem pipe, filled the bowl with his tobacco mixture, and with a twig from the fire, he lit the pipe. After several puffs, he laid the pipe aside and spread the hide with the history of his people across his lap. Taking the palmetto stem, he paused a moment to decide where to begin again. Two Worlds chose to start with the part when they almost lost Ed and his granddaughter to the outlaws.

One

THE OUTLAWS

Belle and everyone in the small schoolroom heard the rifle cracks of the whips in the distance as the men drove the cattle. The men had spent over three weeks north of the lake because they had found and rounded up most of the cows they could locate to the south and east over the past five years. Jessie and the others were pushing over five hundred head, moving them south past the lake into the eight hundred acres of salt marsh where they would feed. Jessie had six hundred or more branded cattle waiting, and this herd would join them until they could pen and brand them to get ready to push to market.

Jake and Hawk were the first ones off the bench and running for the door. Horace was next, hurrying to see his best friend Snake Handler, to talk to him and find out how his first cow hunt went. They were both seventeen now, and Snake Handler couldn't wait to join the other braves and become a true cowhand. Race, as Horace was called now, had no interest in either cows or farming. His passion was reading and writing stories of the things going on in his life around the lake. He had been keeping a diary since he was ten years old, and he loved helping his ma teach the Indian children to read the white man's words and to count as the white man counted.

Earlier, when the weather turned warm enough, Belle restarted Horace and Jenny's schooling under the shade of the giant live oaks using books she had brought from Georgia. After a few days, she saw the Indian children standing in the distance watching.

Belle called them to her, "Would you like to stay and learn with Jenny and Race?"

The kids excitedly joined them. It wasn't long before Little Otter asked Belle to teach her and the other women of the village to read the white man's words. Belle had Franklin build her several benches and knew that when the rainy season arrived, she was going to need a building to house all her students.

Belle asked Jenny if she could help with the beginners, which she was happy to do, while Race helped the faster learners. Belle watched her children with pride; Jenny was patient with the children and a genius with numbers, and Race was a great organizer. Race became the manager of all the supplies for the ranch, and that included everyone's personal needs. Belle had never met anyone who was as good with numbers as Jenny, and she was a great help making a list for Ed who would purchase the supplies when they reached the market with the cattle.

Spirit Snake saw Hawk and Jake running as fast as their little feet would carry them, racing each other as they had been doing since they were big enough to walk. Thinking back about it with a smile, he wasn't sure if they had ever walked! Turning the small Marsh Tackie he rode, he cantered toward the boys until he met them. He reached down and lifted his son Hawk in front of him then reached for Jake's hand and helped him straddle the horse behind him with his little legs sticking straight out. Spirit Snake saw Ed riding from the back of the herd toward them and moved to join him. Coming alongside Spirit Snake's horse, Ed reached for Jake and set him in front of him.

As they turned back toward the moving herd, Jake asked, "Where's Paw Paw?" He looked around anxiously and couldn't see him.

Ed lifted him up, so he could stand in the saddle and said, "Look over to the other side toward the back; there's Paw Paw." Jake yelled to get his attention and saw Jessie wave back to him then sat back down in front of Ed.

"Are you going to keep the cows at the lake?" Jake asked, looking up at his pa.

"No, we are going to move them a couple of miles past the lake to the salt marshes."

"Can I come with you?" Jake asked, anxiously looking up at his pa with those crystal blue eyes.

"Sure," Ed answered, patting him on the head. Jake had inherited the blue eyes of his father and the thick black hair of his mother, his skin color falling somewhere in-between his parents, a deep rich brown.

The women came out to watch their men as they drove the cattle past the lake around the top of the valley, listening to the sound of whips long after they were out of sight. Belle watched Franklin walk out to meet Sara Mae as she brought the wagon toward the barn to unload the left-over supplies. Sara Mae had fed and taken care of the men on their three-week hunt for cows. Belle knew that Franklin had missed his wife, just like she had longed for her family; it was going to be a good time now to rest and enjoy each other.

As he moved the herd into the wetlands, Jessie knew they almost had enough to start to market. The cows began to mix with the more than six hundred already feeding on the lush wet salt grass. Jessie cracked his whip twice over his head, the signal to gather up, and sat and waited for the others. Before Ed even got close, Jake jumped down from the horse and was running to a grinning Paw Paw with his arms out. Jessie reached down, took him by the hands, and swung him up in front of him. Then he waited for Jake to unwrap his arms from around his neck, so he could breathe.

"Paw Paw, can I go with you next time? I could ride with you, and you can teach me how to crack the whip. We could get lots and lots of cows; I could find them for you!"

"I bet you could," Jessie responded, his heart about to burst with love. Jessie couldn't imagine loving anything more than he did his family but looking at that worship love in those blue eyes, a feeling like he had never experienced came over him; his love for Jake flooded his heart. "We'll see, little guy, we'll see."

After everyone had gathered around Jessie, he spoke. "I think we are going to have to make one more hunt to drive over a thousand head to market. After we cut out enough to supply Fort Dade, I want to cut out a hundred of the best-looking cows and leave them here with four of the biggest bulls in the herd." He saw the puzzled looks on their faces and explained, "Soon, we are not going to be able to travel far enough to find cows, so I think we should start considering raising our own if we are to stay in the cattle business. I don't know much about the cattle business in Cuba, so I don't want to count on them to keep us in business. Every time I go to either Tampa or Brooksville, I see more and more people moving down from Georgia and from as far north as Tennessee. Fort Dade has almost doubled in the last four years. They are all going to need beef so there will be a good market. But for now, I know we all want time with our families, so let's leave these ornery creatures to fill their bellies. I've got other things on my mind," he said, grinning.

Turning the Marsh Tackie and pulling Jake close to him, he kicked the horse lightly in the ribs and started home at a full run. He had not gone a hundred yards when Ed passed him on his big roan as if he were standing still.

Ed yelled as he went by, "I'll pick Jake up later." He grinned as he pulled away. With his grandson in front of him, the only one Jessie outran to the lake was Big Cypress because they didn't have a horse big enough to carry all his weight that fast. Ed dropped the reins and slipped off his horse when he reached the front of the house he built for himself and Little Otter almost five years ago. He was a happy man when his new wife accepted it without a word. She brought her sleeping furs and made them a place where Ed could hold her in his strong arms, and she could feel his love with every touch.

Standing in the doorway watching Ed leap from his horse before it came to a stop, Little Otter grinned, remembering when she had told Ed she was going to give him a child. He had picked her up and carried her all the way to his ma and pa's house, and she saw their surprise and confusion when he came through the door yelling, "We are going to have a baby!"

"Well, are you going to carry her around until she has it?" Jessie asked, grinning.

"I might." Ed laughed, letting her down like she was a piece of fine china.

Belle came across the room and gave Little Otter a hug. Holding her at arm's length and smiling, she said, "I've seen it in my dreams. It's going to be a boy, and you might want to talk to your sister Little Moon because I saw you both in my dream." Belle didn't mention that in her dream the babies were joined together. It had frightened her because she didn't understand what it meant, so she just hugged Little Otter tightly against her, melting her fear away. It was only a dream.

Reaching Little Otter, he grabbed her around the waist, lifting her off her feet and whirling her around. He informed her with a grin on his face, "Jake's with his Grandma and Paw Paw, and we're all alone." His desire was plain on his face for her to see.

"First things first," she said, laughing. "I'm not sure I will even let you in smelling like you do, the stink of those cows is pretty bad."

Still carrying her in his arms, he started through the door. "How are you going to stop me?"

"Well, you can just carry me right on through the house to the back porch!" Little Otter smiled and held her nose.

Stepping out the back door, he saw that the bathtub, which he had brought home from Tampa as a surprise after she had Jake, was half full of water. "Well, do we have to go to Ma and Pa's for supper right away?" Ed grinned and put her down, as he hurriedly began to unbutton his shirt.

"No," she said and smiled as she watched him finish undressing, step into the tub, and sit in the cool lake water.

"Maybe you should get in with me to make sure I get clean enough," he said, trying to look serious.

"That's not going to happen," she answered, shocked as he grabbed her arm and pulled her into the bath with him. Little Otter struggled for only a minute until she relaxed in his arms. Smell or no smell, she was glad he was home.

Belle watched through the kitchen window as Ed and Little Otter approached the house. They were holding hands and had that special smile you carry when you are overcome with loving someone, and her heart swelled with love and pride.

They were sitting at the new longer table that Franklin had built, along with the extra chairs he made as their family had grown, and everyone was stuffed from eating a good home cooked meal. Little Otter smiled and announced she had a surprise for everyone.

Looking at Ed, she was beaming as she told him she was with child again. Ed sat staring with the words stuck in his throat.

"I love you," he blurted out. Not knowing what to say next, he stood up and lifted her out of the chair. Squeezing his wife to him, he burst out again with, "I love you!"

"Well, put me down," she said and smiled, "before you squeeze it out now."

"Your right, your right," he said as he gently lowered her feet to the floor.

"God bless; I was so hoping Jake was not going to be the last," Belle said as she came around the table wrapping her arms around Little Otter and patting her stomach. "Maybe this one will be a girl."

"I hope so," Jessie added, beaming. "We need another little girl around here. The one we had has turned into a young lady." Jessie smiled, looking at Jenny.

"Can she be my little sister?" Jenny asked excitedly.

"Well, I guess I had better talk to Franklin about getting the baby crib from the barn," Race spoke up.

Jessie and Ed were in the barn sorting out the gear they were going to need for the cattle drive to Tampa, when Ed suddenly blurted out, "I need to talk to you, Pa!"

Jessie saw the strain on Ed's face and asked, "Are you OK? Is Little Otter OK?" He felt his stomach tighten up, waiting for an answer.

"We're fine, Pa, it's nothing bad."

"Then tell me what can make you look like it's bad."

"Pa, you know I've never liked messing with those ornery cows. We have all this land now, and I know you want to start raising your own cows, and I think it's a good idea, but I want to start farming part of my land. This is some of the richest soil I've ever seen, even more so than the land we farmed in Georgia." Ed stood still, waiting for his pa to say something.

Jesse looked at his son and realized he knew what Ed was saying was right. He had wondered if Ed would ever accept being a cow hunter, and looking at his face, he knew the answer. "You can't farm this land by yourself, and I don't know where you can get enough help to do any real farming. Dave and Bill work together to turn enough land to plant their tobacco, and they have about turned all the land they can handle."

"I could go back to Tampa, where Franklin and Sara Mae came from, and see if I could get some help," Ed suggested.

"Where will you put them?"

"I don't know right now, but maybe we can build them houses like we did Franklin," Ed said, starting to get a lost look on his face.

"I know how much you don't like messing with those cows, even though it is very profitable, but it won't last forever." Jessie knew his son was looking to him for answers. "If you are serious, there is only one place we might get people who know how to farm, and that's back in Georgia, where we came from. There just isn't enough people in Florida yet to get that kind of help."

"I'll go there then, Pa."

"We'll go together, son. I still know some people who might can help."

"But you will be starting the drive to Tampa soon with the cows," Ed reminded him.

"Red Sun and Justin can handle the drive without me; we now have Warrior Spirit, White Crow, and Snake Handler. Snake Handler is excited about making his first trip with the others and proving himself a brave. This farming idea is going to take some thought and planning. They have to have housing and food along with equipment to clear the land and turn the soil."

"I know, Pa, but I can do it."

"I'm sure you can, son. I'll talk to Red Sun and Justin and let them know what we are going to do." Jessie watched Ed's face as excitement replaced the look of uncertainty. "You've been thinking about this for a long time haven't you, son?"

"Yes, sir, I just didn't know how to tell you; I thought you might be upset."

"You are your own man now with your own family; you make your own choices, and you live with them—right or wrong." Ed stood a little taller as he nodded to his Father.

Belle watched Ed squirm in his chair as he picked at his food, while everyone else pretended they didn't notice.

"Alright," Belle said, "is anyone going to tell me what you're pretending not to notice. I assume it is about Ed since he's the one sitting here with that look on his face when he has something to say but can't get out."

She saw the smile come over Ed's face and knew there was going to be a change, but not a bad one when she looked around at the grins on the other faces. Ed and Jessie explained to Belle and Little Otter what they had decided and that they would start preparing for their trip back to Georgia.

"Where will you put everyone?" Belle asked.

"I was thinking of building their quarters on the southwest side of the lake where the creek flows to the Little Withlacoochee River. I'll talk to John about cutting enough lumber and delivering it where we will build when we get back," Jessie said. "Race, you are going to have to take Franklin with you to Tampa and start storing food."

"I can do that Pa, but I need a place to store enough food and supplies for all of us and whoever you and Ed bring back. Do you know how many that will be?" Race asked.

"No," Jessie answered, "not until we get there and find out what's left if anything. I will have John send lumber, so you and Franklin can start a commissary."

"Where do you want to build that?" Race asked.

"Somewhere between here and where the quarters will be built," Jessie answered. "Until we get back, use the barn for storage, but if things go right, we are going to need a lot of food."

Little Otter sat listening to the conversation, not knowing anything about this development. Ed saw the puzzled look on her face and asked if something was wrong.

"Does this mean you are going to be gone longer than when you are on the cattle drive?" Little Otter asked Ed.

"No." Ed grinned at her. "This means I won't have to follow those stinking cows to Tampa anymore."

"That is good," she said and smiled for the first time. "I like you being home more now that we are going to have another child."

"Maybe I shouldn't go until you have the baby," Ed said, looking concerned.

"I think there are enough women here to take care of Little Otter until you and Jessie get back," Belle said warmly.

Jessie and Ed rode into the village as the women were lighting the cook fires to prepare the morning food for the men. Jessie didn't miss the smiles on their faces as they went about their chores. It was always good when the cows were feeding; it gave the men time to rest and be with family before they started the push to Tampa. Jessie saw the men down by the lake, taking their morning swim before beginning the day. It was time to set off on their hunt for meat and hides, and they were excited. In another two weeks, they would start the drive to Tampa, gathering more cows on the way, but for now, they would enjoy their families and the hunt.

Jessie and Ed reached the lake and turning their horses loose to feed, they both removed their clothes and ran for the lake. Dripping water from their swim, they put on just their trousers and joined the other men as they all started back to the village to eat. Sitting on a stump, eating the food the women had brought them, Jessie began to explain to them what he and Ed were going to do.

"I could come with you," Justin said. "It may not be safe out there with just the two of you."

"No," said Jessie, "you will be needed on the drive and to handle the business in town. Ed and I will be fine."

"The cows will miss you," Spirit Snake said and laughed.

"I won't miss them," Ed laughed back.

Later, Ed sat at the table sipping hot black coffee with Little Otter. She had come to love the taste of the white man's drink that Belle had taught her to make. He spoke between sips of the hot liquid.

"I have to go to Brooksville for some supplies, and I want you to come with me; I want to buy something pretty for you and the new baby."

"I don't think that would be a very safe thing to do; I am not supposed to be here, and I am afraid," Little Otter answered with fear in her voice.

"You are my wife now, and no one will bother you. I'll see to that," Ed assured her. "I want you to come with me, I want to show you off."

Little Otter felt the beginnings of fear in the pit of her stomach when they reached the edge of town, and she saw all the wooden buildings. Instinctively, she covered her belly with both hands as she sat upright on the seat, so Ed could not see her fear. Little Otter saw the excitement in Ed's face as they started down the main street. Ed wanted to make her happy by buying her something special, and she didn't want to spoil that.

Ed guided the smaller of the two wagons pulled by Dolly, the calmest of the two workhorses, to a space in front of the sign, "J & C Department Store." He jumped down to wrap the reins to the hitching post and paid no attention to the three men coming down the wooden walkway until he turned and helped Little Otter down.

He heard someone behind him say, "That's a pretty little squaw you got there."

Turning, he faced three of the most dangerous looking men he had ever seen. Turning red in the face, Ed spoke to the three of them. "She is not a squaw; she is my wife!"

Bill Dalton reached out and took her by the arm. "I'll give you ten dollars for an hour with her," he said and laughed.

Ed broke Dalton's nose as his fist slammed into his face. Then Ed's head snapped back as Shawn Johnson's fist caught him on the jaw. He felt the bone break and staggered back against the wagon. Hands grabbed both of his arms and held him there, and he felt the air leave his body as Bill Dalton's fist slammed into his stomach.

Ed heard her angry voice as she screamed, "Leave him alone!" Little Otter grabbed the man closest to her, who was holding Ed, and reaching up, she clamped down on his ear with her teeth. Turning Ed loose with one arm, he swung his elbow into her face, splitting her lip, but she kept her teeth clamped as she was knocked to the ground with half of Steve Baker's ear still in her mouth. Still holding Ed with one hand, he turned and kicked her in her jaw then kicked her a second time in the stomach. Everything went black as she curled up into a knot and lay still. Steve turned back to Ed and using one arm, he slammed a fist into Ed's rib cage and watched as Ed tried to fall. He and Shawn held him up against the boards, so Bill could work him over before they threw him into the back of the wagon.

Then Bill told the other two, "Throw that damn squaw in the wagon with him." Bill held the sleeve of his shirt to his nose to try to stop the bleeding as he untied Dolly from the hitching rail and turned the wagon back the way it had come. He slapped her on the rump with his hat, he had picked up off the ground and placed it back on his head. "If that horse is any dammed good, it will take them back where they came from, and I'll bet he don't bring that damn squaw back with him," he sneered.

"I've got to get to the doc; the little bitch bit half my ear off," Baker whined as he held a dirty handkerchief to his head. Watching the wagon already at the edge of town, Bill turned and headed to see the doctor and get his nose put back in place.

Jessie felt someone pulling at his sleeve and heard a sob. Opening his eyes, he saw Jake standing next to the bed holding his stomach with both hands as tears ran down his face. Swinging his feet off the side of the bed, he lifted Jake off the floor and sat him on his knee. Belle was up and coming around the bed when Jessie, holding him close, asked, "What is the matter, Jake?" His first thought was that the boy had eaten something he wasn't supposed to, like green berries or something.

"Mama," he said as Belle knelt next to him and patted him on the knee.

"Mama is not here right now; they will be back tomorrow."

Shaking his head from side to side, "Mama," he said again, rubbing his tummy.

"Something is wrong," Belle said as her face turned ashen. "Something has happened to Ed and Little Otter." Looking up at Jessie, she said in a panicked voice, "You have to go find them; I have a terrible feeling."

Jessie knew Belle felt things that only a mother could sense, and that put him in a panic. Handing Jake to Belle, he grabbed his pants and shirt and fumbled trying to put both on at the same time. When dressed, he tied his boot laces in a knot. Turning to Belle, he said, "I'll go to the village and get some men." He opened the door to find Spirit Snake holding a crying Hawk in his arms.

"Something's wrong," he said. "I woke up and saw Hawk running this way crying. Is Jake OK?"

"It's not Jake," Jessie said, "something bad I am afraid has happened to Ed and Little Otter."

Belle came to the door and saw Little Moon hurrying to the house where she took Hawk from Spirit Snake's arms and stepped inside.

Turning to Belle, Jesse said, "I'll be back when we find them." As Jessie ran to the barn to saddle his horse, Spirit Snake was already running toward the village that had awakened, and men had started anxiously toward Jessie's. As Spirit Snake got closer, he saw Red Sun out front leading everyone else. Stopping in front of Red Sun, he explained what was happening the best he could. Jessie was already headed to Brooksville as the men from the village caught up to him.

As Justin and Red Sun came along beside him, Justin said to him, "If you keep running the horses this hard, they won't make it to Brooksville." Looking at Jessie's face, he saw a rage there as he had never seen in all the fighting they had done together. He knew there was no talking to him right now. Jessie would ride his horse until it fell, and he knew the other braves wouldn't slow down until their horses fell out from under them.

They had been riding for hours when Jessie realized Justin's words were right, and he slowed down to a fast trot, keeping that pace until there was just enough light for Jessie to make out the horse pulling the small wagon in the distance. Kicking his horse hard in the ribs, the horse lunged forward and in three steps was running as fast as possible until Jessie pulled him up short next to the wagon. He saw the bodies of Ed lying still and Little Otter curled up in a knot. Dolly had come to a halt and stood waiting while Jessie and Red Sun crawled into the wagon. Red Sun shook as he turned his daughter over. She looked up with eyes full of fear, a sight Red Sun would see the rest of his life. He knew someone was going to die as he sat down next to her, putting her head in his lap and starting a low chant to keep his daughter alive until he could get her to her mother to heal. Little Otter slipped back into unconsciousness as Red Sun chanted. Jessie put his hand on Ed's shoulder. Ed had opened his eyes and tried to speak.

"Hold still, son, we are going to get you home now, and you will be alright. Your mama is waiting with Jake for me to bring you home safe." Stepping over the seat, he took the reins lying on the floor and flicked them across Dolly's rump. "Finish taking them home now," he said to Dolly.

Belle was waiting at the village with the others as Jessie drove the wagon to a stop in front of Woman of The Winds' lodge. Spirit Snake had ridden in the wagon with Ed, assuring him he was going to be fine, and they would find the men who did this and get their revenge. Turning, Spirit Snake squatted down to help Red Sun, still sitting with Little Otter's head in his lap. He lifted Little Otter and handed her to Big Cypress who carried her to the opening of the lodge. There, her mother Waiting Owl and her Grandmother were waiting, and they would work to keep her and Ed alive.

Next, Spirit Snake lifted Ed's legs as Jessie lifted his head and shoulders, and they handed him over the wagon side to Justin and Warrior Spirit. Ed's eyes were still open, never leaving Jessie's. He lay limp as they carried him and placed him next to his wife. Jessie knew that whatever happened, Ed would bear the blame the rest of his life. The thought brought chills up his spine, and the anger almost overwhelmed him, but he saw the anguish in Belle's face and knew there were more important things he had to do right now. Jessie didn't have time to dwell on revenge now, he headed to Belle and took her in his arms. "They will be alright," he assured her with all the truth he could put into words. "Where is Jake?" Jessie asked, looking around but not seeing him.

"He is with Little Moon and Hawk; she has taken them to the lake to play and try to get Jake to stop crying. He needs to see his mother; he knows she is hurt."

"As soon as Woman of The Wind and Waiting Owl let us know she is stable, we will take him to them," Jessie said.

"Oh, Jessie!" she cried. "What happened out there?" Jessie caught her as her knees gave way; they both went to their knees, and Jessie held her as she prayed to her God to save her son and his family.

Jessie lay in their bed with Jake in-between him and Belle, listening to the drums and the chanting that had been going on all night. As the sun turned the darkness into light, Jessie dressed quietly, not to wake Belle, who had cried herself to sleep sometime in the early morning. Stepping softly through the door, he headed for the lake where he knew Two Worlds would be bathing in the clear water. The ancient medicine man was the grandfather of the twins, Little Otter and Little Moon, the daughters of Red Sun. Jessie saw the thin silhouette of Two Worlds, sitting chest deep and smoking his pipe, and he knew the old man had been visiting his ancestors all night and had not slept yet. This was his way of returning to this world. Two Worlds waited, knowing Jessie would want to talk to him.

Removing his boots and clothes, Jessie waded in and sat next to Two Worlds. Sitting for a minute, he waited for his head to clear, then leaned forward and pushed himself under the cool water. There, Jessie let it wash away the chatter that had been going on all night in his head until he had no clear thoughts. Coming up and taking a gulp of fresh air, he turned and pushed his body under the water, swimming back toward Two Worlds, again sitting next to him. Jessie asked the question he hoped the man, who had saved his life only a few years ago, would answer.

"Will my son and his wife live?"

Two Worlds removed the long stem pipe, and after a brief silence, he answered as the sun slowly warmed their backs. "I did not see this in my visions, but I felt the change of energy in their lives. Their innocence is lost forever; only the love of their children will give them back their peace. Their love for each other will be tested until Ed can find what has been taken away from him."

"What is that?" Jessie asked.

"His warrior spirit that gave him the knowing that he would always keep his family safe as his father has," Two Worlds stated, putting the pipe back in his mouth. Jessie sat for a while longer letting the fresh water take away some of the pain he felt for his son, knowing that the old medicine man was right. Jessie walked slowly from the lake to Woman of The Wind and Waiting Owl's lodge, hoping he could go home and give Belle some comfort, in knowing that Ed and Little Otter would live. Reaching the lodge, he pulled back the hide covering the opening and stepped inside.

Jessie froze as his breath caught in his throat; he hardly recognized Ed's swollen face. Little Otter was lying next to him with her face swollen, her eyes closed, and her lips split. He knew it would be almost impossible to stop Belle from seeing her son and the woman whom she considered to be her daughter lying here like this. He was going to hear the anguish and tears as he lay holding her in his arms at night. Looking at Ed's swollen face once more, bitter bile rose in his throat as he turned to leave and get Ed's ma.

Justin was sitting in front of his lodge drinking coffee that White Dove had learned to make over the fire, although she never learned to drink the hot black liquid. She wanted to please Justin, who had moved her and her two-year-old son into his lodge with the approval of her brother Big Cypress. Three years ago, White Dove gave him a daughter that they named Shining Star. Justin had found peace here with Jessie and his Indian family. Sipping his coffee, he watched as Jessie stopped in front of him.

"Have a cup of coffee while it is still hot."

"No thanks," Jessie answered. "I want to talk to you."

Watching the anger that covered Jessie like a blanket, he knew what it was going to be about and waited for Jessie to start.

"I am going to find the bastards that did this and kill them. I'm not asking you to go with me, I just want you to take care of the cattle drive and take care of business in town when you get them to market."

"What about Ed?" Justin asked. "Don't you think he will want to avenge what happened to him and his wife?"

"It will be a long time before Ed will be healed enough to do anything, and I don't want those bastards to get away," Jessie said.

"If it's who I think it is, they won't go anywhere, they think they are safe now. We have fought a lot of men in the past but never without knowing things were in our favor. I am sure you can go there and find them, but by the time you find out who they are, they will know you're coming and be waiting on you. Maybe you can kill one or two of them, but your family will have to bury what is left of you. Are you sure that is what Ed would want? I know Belle wouldn't," Justin said, keeping his voice calm.

"I have to do something," Jessie stated with some frustration.

"Do you trust me?" Justin asked.

"Of course," Jessie answered, "my life has been in your hands more times than I can count."

Handing Jessie a tin cup, he said, "Then sit down and have some coffee, and let me tell you what I have been thinking since we found them. I will go to Brooksville for a few days and find out who did this and where they hang out. More than likely, they will have their own bar where they drink, get drunk and brag about teaching you a lesson."

"What do you mean, teaching me a lesson. What does this have anything to do with me?" Jessie asked, confused.

"Those men are killers like the ones we met on the trail coming from Fort Myers; they could just as easily have killed Ed and Little Otter and got away with it. They wanted to send you a message, to keep your Indians on the ranch. Everyone knows about you letting the Indians live here under your protection. They are letting you know what happens if you don't. They don't represent the whole town, but enough of them don't like Indians or are afraid of those men. They are hardened men from the war, and the bigger the town grows, the more powerful they get."

Jessie took another sip from his cup as Justin waited. "You are right. I will wait for Ed to heal, but I want to know who they are and if they will still be there when Ed can ride again."

"I will go today," Justin answered, and sipping the last swallow of coffee, he rose to get some things together.

Jessie was almost out of the valley when he saw the riders on top of the ridge turn and head toward him. Riding on to the top, he stopped and waited. As they got closer, Jessie knew who they were. One was a head higher than the other two he rode with, and he knew when he saw the shotguns lying across their saddles, that his friends had come to fight with him once again.

As the riders pulled up, John spoke first. "Justin came by on his way to Brooksville and told us what happened. That pack of wild dogs has roamed this country killing whole families of settlers and other men that were driving some of those scrub cows to market—men who were trying to get money to feed their families, only to be ambushed and killed for their cattle, which were sold to that low life butcher in Brooksville for whiskey money. If we don't stop them now, none of our families will ever be safe."

John's oldest boy Frank spoke up. "If they hurt Ed's wife, they would hurt Dancing Sun and our daughter also."

"They have to be stopped," Bill Walsh added.

"We can go rid ourselves of those outlaws now if you are ready," Dave confirmed what the others were thinking.

Jessie hesitated before speaking, looking at these men who came to this country with him to get away from the violence of war. He wasn't sure anymore if they could ever get away from the brutality the war had brought to this country.

"I was ready to go the moment I saw Ed and the mother of my grandson, but Justin is right; we need to know more about these men, and I won't go after them until Ed can be there."

"Is there anything we can do to help in the meantime?" John asked. "If not, send word when you are ready. This is our fight too, and we'll be ready!" Jessie nodded his head in acknowledgment as he watched the men turn and head for home and their work, to wait for his word.

Jessie was helping cut the newer cows out and moving them to the holding pen to be branded and readied to make the slow drive to the Tampa stockyards. From there, they would be shipped to Cuba, but first, they would cut fifty cows out to be delivered to Fort Dade. This time, he would have to deliver the cows along with Race since Ed was still recovering. Jessie and Red Sun were heading to the pen where Big Cypress was grabbing horns, throwing the cows to the ground, and waiting for Spirit Warrior and White Crow to brand them with the Double "T" hot iron.

Red Sun spotted Justin in the distance riding toward them and waved to Jessie. Jessie cracked the whip over the heads of the cows and made them lunge forward to get them to the pen, so he could meet Justin. It had been close to two weeks since Justin had gone to Brooksville, and he was anxious to talk to him. Jessie and Red Sun pulled up a couple hundred yards from the pens and waited as Justin stopped just in front of the men. Justin saw the tension in both Jessie and Red Sun's faces and spoke first, telling them both what they had been waiting to hear.

"They are still there; I would like to tell you the rest over some of Sara Mae's cooking. I left before daylight, so no one saw which way I was headed and have been riding all day."

As Jessie turned his horse toward the wagon, he said; "I'm sure she has food left over, and I know she has been worried about you like she would over her own child. She will be glad you are back, so she can stop worrying."

Sara Mae saw them headed her way. She knew it was past eating time and wondered who the rider was with them. They's bringing company for me to feed, she thought as she got out the pot of venison stew. Sara Mae placed it over the fire to heat it a little bit and make it even better then added the covered pan of left-over biscuits. Looking up from her work, she caught her breath when she recognized Justin.

"Thank you Lawd! Thank you Lawd!" As she hurried to get a bowl, she felt like her heart was going to jump out of her body. As far as she was concerned, the "Lawd" had sent him to her and Franklin, for she knew if it were not for Justin, they would not be here among her new family. Justin stepped down from his horse, walked over and gave a hug to his smiling second mother.

"Lawd I'm glad you saw fit not to get yourself killed and come on back home," she said as she took the bowl, filled it with stew and carried it over to where the men squatted on their heels and talked. Handing Justin his bowl, she turned slowly back toward the wagon, so she could hear bits of the conversation. Sara Mae was anxious to know what was going to happen; she knew there was going to be killing. Even Franklin had talked about going with them when they went to take care of those outlaw men. Sara Mae felt the blanket of sadness that surrounded the whole valley, and she knew there would be no peace or laughter until those evil men were gone. She had even supported Franklin when he said he wanted to go after the men that had brought all of this on with their evil.

Sarah Mae didn't think God would think they were bad for sending those men where they belonged. There is no place on God's earth for those kinds of men, she thought as she listened to Justin explain what he had learned in town.

"The ones that jumped Ed and Little Moon are the leaders of a gang of thieves that robs settlers moving into this country and take any cattle they can steal. A week ago, they killed two settlers with over twenty head of scrub cows and took them to Brooksville to sell to the local butcher, who doesn't care where the cows are coming from as long as they are cheap, and he can sell the meat at a high price. Those three men along with some other lowlifes that do what they are told, have everyone in that town afraid to say anything after they beat a couple of people almost to death who had stood up to them. They live at the end of town in a rooming house above a bar where they eat, sleep and drink.

"The owner was a guard at Anderson Prison Camp for captured Yankee soldiers in Georgia. After the war, he rode with a gang, robbing Yankee banks throughout Georgia and Alabama. Then he was shot in the knee by some hired guards during a bank robbery and can't ride anymore with a stiff leg. He's still wanted in Georgia and Alabama, but nobody wants to come looking for him in that rattlesnake nest."

Before they went any further, Justin asked, "How is Ed and Little Otter?" He could see the anger in Jessie's face as he spoke.

"They are beginning to heal. The swelling has gone down in their faces, but they can't walk yet with those broken ribs, and they are not sure the baby will live. Little Otter still has pains where she was kicked in the stomach."

"What do you want to do about driving the cattle to Tampa?" Justin asked, looking at Red Sun.

"We will have all the cattle branded in a few days, and then it is up to Jessie when he wants to start moving them to market," Red Sun answered.

They waited for Jessie to answer as they watched the uncertainty in his face. He struggled to find the right answer. Jessie wanted to go with the herd to market, but he knew he was needed here for now. He stood up and walked in small circles. When he stopped, he turned to speak to both men.

"After we get the herd on the move, I will take Race, and he and I will drive the fifty cows to Fort Dade. Race is big enough to help me now. Justin, you and Sara Mae will have to do the shopping for supplies. Race will make you a list for the women, and I will have him make one for the village. I will not be going with you on this drive; there are too many things happening here that are going to have to be dealt with before we could get back. I think we would push the herd too fast and not give them time to fatten on the way to market. As Ed gets better, we are going to have to deal with him. Anger is what's healing him now, and sooner or later, that anger is going to get him up and back on his feet. We all know where he's going to want to go."

"I think you have made the right choice," Red Sun spoke up. "I too want to be here when it is time to avenge what has been done to my daughter and your son, but I know it will be many moons before he is well enough to go after the men who harmed him and the mother of his child, possibly killing his unborn baby. I know how I feel now and know the anger of the husband who could not keep his marriage promise, to keep his wife safe."

"You are right, Red Sun," Jessie said. "I know the anger I feel doesn't come close to what Ed is feeling right now. It will be hard, like Justin said, to keep him from charging in and getting himself killed. Even if I went with him, we could possibly kill the men who did that, but we would wind up making Belle and Little Otter widows. I don't think either one would have that if it was their choice."

"We can handle the cattle drive, and I agree with Red Sun; you have made the right choice," Justin stated.

"I will help get the drive going, and then Race and I will move the cows to Fort Dade," Jessie said as he stood up to leave.

"You are doing wonderful," Belle said to Ed as she changed the bandages on his face. The swelling has almost gone away, but the cuts and the scars will be there forever, she thought as she listened to his silence. What worried her most was the blank look in his eyes that showed no emotion or any indication of what he was thinking.

"How is Little Otter?" Belle asked, looking across at Waiting Owl as she stirred the powder and liquid in the small gourd. They heard the anguish in Little Otter's moan as she pressed on her stomach, trying to hold back the pain. Waiting Owl lifted her head, poured the liquid into her mouth and waited for her to swallow.

"She will sleep now," Waiting Owl answered. "We will have to wait to see if the child she carries wants to come into this world."

Jessie sat next to Two Worlds in water up to their chests as they enjoyed the silence of the early morning and felt the sun on their backs as it rose above the treetops.

"I am puzzled. It has been weeks now, and Ed will not speak to anyone. He won't sleep with his wife; he won't even let her come home. She has been with her mother all this time even though she asked Ed to take her home. When he comes to sit with her, he just stares without saying a word. I have watched over him as he roams the woods at night, never letting him know I am there. The other day, he sat in the lake with his clothes on for hours. I was afraid he would walk out over his head and not come up. I don't know what to do," Jessie said, confused.

Two Worlds puffed on his long stem pipe, enjoying the flavor of his tobacco mixture then spoke slowly, "Your son is still lying in the back of that wagon. All he can hear is the pain of his wife who he had promised to protect. Until he can get revenge on the man that hurt her, he cannot be a man. He no longer believes he deserves a wife or to be a father."

"We will have the revenge he wants," Jessie said with anger in his voice, "but not until he is better. He still cannot strain or lift anything of any size because of the broken ribs. Red Sun and the others should be back from the drive to Tampa within two weeks. By that time Ed should be able to ride, then we will rid this country of that pack of dogs that roam at will, hurting people and taking what they want."

Jessie watched as Jake ran from the village toward the house to see his grandma and to be spoiled by Jenny and Race when Belle wasn't fussing over him. Belle hated that he had to stay with Hawk and that he cried at night for his ma, who remained with her mother. Jake followed Ed for hours and wondered why his father didn't want him anymore. He stayed with his Paw Paw during the day when he could, but mostly he played and stayed with Hawk and his Hunka mother Little Moon at night. Sometimes, he would slip out of the lodge and sneak in to lie next to his mother. If she could, she would pull him close and keep him in her arms all night, or he would lie next to her and cry silently as he listened to her moan in pain, curled up and holding her stomach. Jake didn't understand any of this, only that he didn't have a mother or pa anymore, and he wondered what he had done wrong.

Franklin was in the barn that he had expanded to make room for his wood shop. Whenever he had a chance, he made tables or chairs for the ever-growing family. He heard the whooping and yelling from the village, and his heart started racing as he hurried for the door as fast as his crippled leg let him move. Outside, Franklin saw the riders on each side of the wagon as his woman, he was so proud of, was handling Dolly and Preacher. Preacher, the big stud, and Dolly had already brought three strong foals to help work the ranch; they would soon be clearing stumps to ready the land for farming. The dogs were trotting alongside the wagon for shade. There were four pairs now, and the men loved them. The dogs were real professionals and could outguess the riders most of the time, making the work much easier.

Franklin was surprised when he saw Jessie riding with them but guessed he had run into the others while he was scouting the land. Jesse was deciding where he wanted Ed to plant and what area he was going to use to start raising his own cattle. While at home, he spent his time scouting and watching out for Ed, whose body had healed to where he could cut and haul his own firewood. His body had healed but not his spirit. Franklin offered to help scout more of their land for farming or grazing cattle but was ignored. It sure is puzzling, Franklin thought as he went back to finishing his chores, so he could go meet his wife.

Justin and Red Sun followed Jessie to the barn where they placed the bags of gold coins with the other bags. The gold from the sale of cattle was kept in the barn, and all of it had been recorded by Jenny as it was divided between the ranch, Two World's village, and Justin's share. Putting the heavy bags away, Justin looked at Jessie's strained face and knew things were still not right.

"How is Ed and Little Otter?" he asked, then waited for Jessie to pick the right words. Jessie explained as much as he could understand to Red Sun and Justin, and he knew they didn't understand any more than he did.

"We are back now, and it is time we ended this evil that has been brought to our families," Red Sun said with anger in his voice.

"I will go tomorrow to make sure they are not gone on one of their raids to get whiskey money. It won't take but a few days, and if I am not back right away, it will be because I will wait until they return," Justin stated.

"That sounds good," Jessie responded as they left the barn.

Spirit Snake was surprised when he rode into the village and saw Little Otter sitting with her mother outside her lodge. Jumping down from his horse, he forgot about everything but his wife Little Moon coming out of their lodge. He reached her and lifted her off the ground, whirling her around.

She smiled at him, saying, "I love you, and I am glad you are home safe."

Sitting her down, he asked, "Where is Hawk, and why is Little Otter here with her mother?"

"Come inside," she said. Little Moon explained all that she understood about Ed. "Little Otter has healed from her wounds, but the baby is causing her great pain. It's like it is punishing her for what happened and it's very confusing to everyone. Little Otter will hardly talk; she only answers when you ask her a question. She feels that she has lost a husband and maybe the baby. She has not spoken to her son since she was hurt. I have lost my sister." Tears ran down her face as Spirit Snake pulled her to him and held her close until she stopped crying.

Hawk and Jake ran through the opening, and both grabbed a leg and held on to Spirit Snake until he walked them around the lodge with them sitting on his feet holding on and giggling. He stopped in front of his smiling wife, reached down and lifted both boys up into his arms.

"I will go and see Ed," Spirit Snake told his wife and saw the smile leave her face.

"Go and see him. I am afraid we are losing my sister and your best friend if you can't make him want to live."

Spirit Snake had been sitting next to his friend for the last half hour. He talked to Ed about his wish to farm the land and about how he and his father were going back where they had come from and how exciting it must be. But, no matter how long he waited for a response, Ed had not looked at him or spoken a word; it was like he wasn't there. Shaken by the loss of his friend, he left Ed sitting and rode toward Two Worlds, who was sitting on his backrest under the shade of one of the great oaks, smoking his long stem pipe while waiting for Spirit Snake. Two Worlds explained to the young brave what he had to do to help his friend.

Jessie stopped to greet Spirit Snake as he entered the barn, and as he looked at his face, he knew he had been to see his friend.

Spirit Snake explained to Jessie what Two Worlds told him he needed to do. "I am going to take Ed on a trip, and it will be several days before we return."

"I'm not sure Ed will go anywhere, so how will you get him to go with you?" Jessie asked.

"He will go even if I have to tie him on his horse," Spirit Snake spoke with determination in his voice.

"Well, I hope for all our sakes you can get some kind of response from him. No one else has been able to, not even his son," Jessie spoke with sadness in his voice.

"I will do my best," Spirit Snake said as he turned to leave.

It had been easier than he thought. Spirit Snake helped Ed put his foot in the stirrup and pushed on his butt as Ed swung up into the saddle and sat there. Mounting his horse, Spirit Snake took the bridle of Ed's horse and started on the long trip to the caves. They rode for two days, stopping only to drink water from the clear springs, then before the sun took its light away as it set behind the trees, they rested. Ed never spoke, but the determined Spirit Snake had them up and on their way as soon as the sun's light let him see the way. At the end of the second day, they stopped at the spring where he and Ed had camped the first time Ed brought him here. Spirit Snake watched Ed kneel to drink from the spring and then look around as if expecting someone. Ed stood up and started walking in the direction of the caves. Spirit Snake hurried to catch up with Ed, and taking him by the arm, turned him around. Talking slowly, he spoke to Ed for the first time since they had left the valley.

"You know where we are going, don't you? We cannot go any farther today, but tomorrow we will reach the caves." Sitting Ed down by the spring, Spirit Snake removed the saddles from the horses, and after building a small fire for the night, he handed Ed some beef jerky and told him to eat.

As Spirit Snake led the way down the almost invisible path, he looked back and saw a look of recognition on Ed's face. Hope rose in his chest as he led the way to the bottom of the massive hole in the ground and watched in surprise as Ed walked straight to the small spring and knelt to scoop water in his hands and drink. Spirit Snake knew Ed recognized where he was when he started for the oak branches that hid the entrance to the cavern and caves of his ancestors. Spirit Snake helped Ed pull back the branches hiding the opening and was not surprised this time when he saw Two Worlds and the huge panther that lay beside him. Rising in one swift motion, Two Worlds led them farther back into the vast cavern where his small fire bathed the cavern with soft light. The panther settled, watching a few feet from the fire. Spirit Snake watched as Ed turned his palm up and looked at the small scar that ran across his hand. Spirit Snake looked at the scar that ran across his own hand, held it up for Ed to see, and saw recognition in his eyes. When Ed had circled the cavern, looking in the smaller caves and walked back, Two Worlds motioned for him to sit next to the fire.

Two World's chanting became louder, and his voice rose above Spirit Snake's quieter chanting as he danced slowly back and forth behind Ed. The old man suddenly stopped, and he placed both hands on Ed's shoulders, his chanting rising to a fever pitch. Ed's scream caused the birds and small animals to take off in fright. Spirit Snake jumped to his feet as the scream went on until Ed lay back on the ground moaning in pain. The moan came from deep within until he suddenly stopped and lay still.

"Is he alright?" a frightened Spirit Snake asked Two Worlds.

Then he saw Ed's eyelids flutter and open. Sitting up, Ed looked around the cavern and asked Two Worlds how he had gotten here. He suddenly began to sob as the memories started to return. Ed had pushed the images out of his mind by leaving the world where the evil had happened. Two Worlds watched the anger as it took over Ed's consciousness, bringing back the terrible memory of what he had let happen to his wife. Only the anger kept him from escaping back into the world of no memory. He felt Two Worlds hands on his shoulders and heard him saying he would be fine now.

"How can I be OK when I am not man enough to keep my wife and unborn child safe?"

Two Worlds felt the tension moving back into Ed's body and kept his hands on his shoulders, speaking with wisdom that penetrated Ed's mind. "You are no less a man than you were when evil overtook you and your wife and the child she carries. You must take control of your feelings now, while you rid yourself of this evil that has taken away your family and make things right again."

Ed felt the anger flowing through his body and giving him energy as he led the way up and out of the giant hole. Spirit Snake hurried to keep up as Ed mounted his horse and put him in a run, pushing the small limbs out of his face with his forearm. Spirit Snake tried not to fall far behind as Ed's big roan pulled ahead of his small Marsh Tackie. As they left the woods, he saw Ed slow the big roan down to let him catch up with him.

Coming alongside Ed, he said, "We have two days ride before getting back to the valley. If you keep up this pace, we will be walking the last day before we get there. You are going to have to control your anger until the right time comes. Your father has already made arrangements, and he is waiting for you to be his son again."

Jessie and Red Sun were sitting on his porch talking about where they would look for cattle this year when they saw Ed and Spirit Snake start down into the valley. They both stood up and headed for the village. Jessie realized that Ed was sitting up tall in his saddle, riding side by side with Spirit Snake, controlling his own horse. His heart raced when he saw his son dismount his horse in front of Waiting Owl's lodge, pull the hide back from the opening, and step inside.

Kneeling next to his wife, he lifted her into his arms. She put her arms around his neck and heard him say, "It's time to go home now." She laid her head on his shoulder, and Ed felt the wetness of her tears. As he passed his pa, he nodded his head; the anger in his eyes told his father he was back. For Jesse, it was not much of a mystery what had taken place out there after his own experience with Two Worlds and his power. His heart swelled in his chest as he started home to tell his wife her son was back. There was not a lot of talk as they all sat around Belle's table, but she ate her food with a smile on her face. Knowing what was coming in the next few days, she would not let anything take away how she felt at this moment with her son and daughter sitting at her table, talking or not.

Ed slept little that night, holding his wife in his arms until her tears stopped and she fell asleep. The smell of coffee woke him as he lay there watching Little Otter move about in the soft glow of the lamp. By the time Ed put his clothes on, she was sitting at the table with a cup of hot steaming coffee for her husband. Little Otter blew into her own coffee, cooling the black liquid enough to drink. As she watched Ed blowing in his cup, she spoke to him.

"I know what you have to do to make things right but promise me you will be careful. Our family cannot stand to lose you again."

Ed heard the fear in her voice and took her hand. "I am not going alone. Pa and his friends he fought with during the war are going; they are experienced fighters. This type of evil has to be eliminated, or we will never be safe. I will be careful," he promised as he saw the doubt in her eyes.

Daylight approached as Ed met his father in the barn. Jesse was saddling his horse, and he had the big roan saddled next to his, the rifle butt protruding from the scabbard. Jessie saw the pistol in Ed's holster and the sheath with the knife Red Sun had given him at his wedding. Nothing was said as Jessie finished saddling his horse. They rode out of the barn to be greeted by every brave in the village including Snake Handler, sitting proudly with the other braves. Turning their horses, they headed to help Ed take his revenge even though the braves could not be seen. It would interrupt the balance of Jessie keeping Indians on his ranch if they were to fight, but they would be there to see Ed take his revenge.

An hour out, they saw Justin with the others waiting for them to catch up. Justin had started out before daylight to let the others know they were coming. As he joined Jessie and Ed, Big John saw the braves riding behind them covered with war paint on their faces. Their horses were decorated for battle too. The braves had spent hours getting ready for a battle they knew they could only fight in spirit. John looked over at Jessie with questions in his eyes. Jessie explained to him and the others that the braves would not fight but were there for support. The men, understanding the Indians' need to be a part of the revenge, nodded their heads.

It was late evening, an hour before dark when the riders reached the outskirts of Brooksville and dismounted. Justin spoke to the others as he sat his horse. "I will ride in and make sure they are at the bar and will be back by dark."

"Be careful," Jessie said.

"I've said that to you several times in the past, I believe," Justin said, grinning. Then he turned his horse and headed into town.

The moon was just peeking over the treetops, and Jessie saw it would be full in a couple of days. He heard the hoof beats first before he recognized Justin in the moonlight. Everyone mounted their horse and waited for Justin to pull his horse to a stop in front of the men.

"They are in the bar and drinking. Looks like they are there for the night," Justin informed the waiting men. "The men we are looking for are at the bar. The one that hurt Little Otter is on the right side, and the one who beat Ed is in the middle. The other man who held you is on the left."

"I want the man who hurt my wife," Ed said, shaking with anger.

"I want the man who started this," Jessie spoke up.

"I will take the other one," Justin said.

Jessie turned to John and the others and said, "Keep us covered."

"Your back is covered," John assured him.

Jessie turned and nodded to Red Sun and followed Justin as they started circling the edge of town. They would approach the bar from the side where no one could see them coming. Looking back, Jessie saw Red Sun and the other braves circling the buildings from the other direction, where they would wait for any unexpected trouble. Jessie and the others dismounted and tied their horses to tree limbs. They moved quietly to the front door and took a moment to make sure everyone was ready.

Jessie and Justin pulled their pistols and saw Ed pull the knife Red Sun had given him as a wedding gift. Holding it by his side, he stepped through the door first, followed by Jessie, Justin, then John and the others. They were all carrying double barrel shotguns loaded with buckshot. Ed saw the man with half of an ear missing. In four steps, he reached Steve Baker as the three of them were turning to see what the commotion was about. Baker saw Ed and started for his gun, but never made it. Ed grabbed his gun hand before it reached the handle and bringing his knife up with the force of a madman, he buried ten inches of blade to the handle through the breastbone into his heart. At the same time, he heard two shots together. Out of the corner of his eye, Ed saw the two men drop to the floor with a bullet through their chests.

Ed felt Steve Baker's knees give way as he stared in disbelief at the burning anger in Ed's eyes. Ed held him against the bar until he saw the light go out in his eyes. Pulling the knife from his chest, he stepped back and watched as Steve Baker crumbled to the floor at his feet. Seeing movement out of the corner of his eye, Ed looked up and saw a man at the top of the stairs raising a pistol. The flash of a knife blade sliced across the man's throat, then a hand pushed him down the stairs. Ed saw Spirit Snake disappear back into the dark hallway. He stood still, shaking with anger and looked down at the dead bodies.

Jessie saw the bartender as he reached under the bar to pull out a sawed-off shotgun. He whirled and fired at the same time as Justin and saw the gun fall from the man's hand. The bartender fell back against the wall and slid to the floor, dead. Jessie stood, gun in hand until he saw Ed gain control and start for the door, looking around at the few other men and a couple of old whores sitting motionless. They were not sure what just happened, but looking at those shotguns pointed at them, they knew not to move. Jessie started for the door and stopped in the middle of the room.

"If I see anyone of you sons-of-bitches again, I'll kill you." He turned and followed Ed and Justin out the door. John and the others backed out, still covering the men.

The last thing John said before stepping outside was, "If any of you lowlife bastards even think about using one of those little guns you carry, I'll send every one of you to hell." Stepping back out the door, he left the men and whores too stunned to move.

Mounting their horses, they turned and slowly rode through the main street of town, wanting the residents to know who they were. Lights appeared in several windows as people looked out to see the riders; some even said they thought they saw Indians meet them at the edge of town.

An hour out of town, riding in silence, each man thought about what happened tonight, found a place to put it and go on about their lives. Spirit Snake rode his horse alongside Ed. Looking over, held out his hand. Ed saw the thin scar across the palm, reached out with an open hand, and as their hands met, Ed said, "Brother." "Brother," Spirit Snake said with a smile on his face.

Two

THE BLACK PEOPLE

The sun was just topping the trees as Jessie and Ed sat on their horses and relaxed, looking at the creek flowing from the west side of the lake. The land flattened out, and the clear, cool water flowed across a thousand acres of rich bottom land before it reached the Little Withlacoochee River. It had been two weeks since they returned from Brooksville and left those terrible killings behind. Ed was anxious to get started with his new life of farming and get away from the stink of "those ornery cows."

"I think building the quarters along the creek here would keep the workers close to the land you want to farm," Jessie said.

"How many people do you think we will need, Pa?" Ed asked.

"At least ten to twelve families if you are going to work this much land. We will have to see how many families want to leave where they are and what kind of equipment we can find."

"Well, when can we get started?" Ed asked, eager to get to Georgia.

"Well, now that we know where we want to build and what land we want to turn for farming, I think we should ride on over and see John about lumber for the quarters and the material to build a commissary. We need to store all the supplies for the number of people we have coming plus Bill, Dave, John and any other people we may add in the future. I think it would be just the right thing for Race to manage. Your mother needs a school room to keep teaching her students; it has become a part of her happiness these days. She has already told me to see if I can find any school books when we go to Georgia."

Big John saw Jessie and Ed riding toward the mill, and he shut down the big steam-powered engine turning the saw. He walked out to the giant oak and waited for them in the shade of the huge limbs. Frank looked up when he heard the engine shutting down and seeing his friend Ed coming, joined his pa. They all stood or squatted on their heels for the next hour discussing their plans and the lumber they would need. John agreed he could supply that much lumber by the time they got back from Georgia.

"I'm sure Bill and Dave, along with me and the boys, will help build the commissary. We all wouldn't have to go to Brooksville or all the way to Tampa to get food and supplies."

"I think it's a great idea," Frank said to his friend. "I am glad you are going to farm again. What are you going to plant?"

"Tobacco to start with. Bill and Dave have produced great crops, and there is a demand for it," Ed replied.

"When will you be leaving?" Frank asked.

"Within the next couple of days; we need to be back before the winter sets in," Jessie answered.

John looked over at Frank and said, "We better get started!"

The day before they were to leave for Georgia, Jessie finished his coffee and headed for the lake just as the sun started the beginning of the day. He knew he would find Two Worlds already sitting chest deep in the crystal water of the lake, smoking his long stem pipe. Removing his clothes, Jessie waded in and dove under the water, swimming for as long as he could hold his breath. Then he turned and swam back to the ancient medicine man and sat next to him and waited. Two Worlds knew what he wanted, and after several puffs on his pipe, he spoke, giving Jessie the answer he came for.

"I have seen in a vision the black people who came from the beginning of man. They were turning the land upside down, and strange plants grew in this new dirt covering the land. It will be a good thing."

Placing the long stem of the pipe in his mouth, he became silent, and Jessie knew he had the only answer he would get this morning. Wading to shore, he put his clothes on over his wet body and headed home to eat breakfast. He knew Belle and Jenny would be waiting on him to begin loading the saddlebags the packhorse would carry. Tomorrow, they would start their journey for Georgia, not knowing what they would find when they arrived.

Everyone except Two Worlds walked down to the house to see Jessie and Ed begin their journey. They all waved and watched Ed, with the lead line of the pack horse, disappear out of site. The women of the village surrounded Belle and Little Otter. The baby had settled down, and the hurting had stopped. With hugs, the women assured her that Ed and Jessie would be safe. The braves went back to preparing for another hunt. The animals would have extra thick coats of hair and fur for the oncoming winter. They would dry the meat for their people to eat and extra to feed the dogs. They had come to depend on the dogs to help move the scrub cows out of the brush and palmettos, and they took good care of them.

It had been over a week since Jessie and Ed left for Georgia. They took the ferry across the Suwannee River and made their way northwest until they reached the outskirts of Tallahassee. Ed was amazed at the size of the town and the tall buildings.

"Are we stopping here?" Ed asked his pa, looking at the movement of all the horses and more carriages than he had ever seen in one place. They were dodging each other as they made their way up and down the wide dirt road running through the middle of town.

"I want to stop and see the governor if he is at the capital. If not, we'll just keep riding. I don't have any desire to stay in this mess," Jessie answered.

"Is he the same governor that came to our yearly calf roast a couple of years ago?" Ed asked.

"I don't know, but he invited us to stop in to see him if we ever came this way."

"I remember that," Ed said, with some excitement. "That was the year Major Johnson brought the governor and his replacement Colonel Davidson, who would oversee the fort for the next four years."

"Yes," Jessie said. "I had sent the major an invitation, not knowing the governor had come down with the fort's new commander."

"I remember how surprised we all were," Ed said. John had been the first to see the two soldiers riding out front, next to the fanciest carriage they had ever seen with four more soldiers riding behind. As the group got closer, they recognized the major, then Jessie saw the governor sitting next to his driver when they pulled in under the oaks and dismounted. Jessie and Ed went to meet the group, and the governor, pushing the driver's hand away, stepped down to meet them.

"Welcome," Jessie said, reaching for the governor's hand then shaking the major's hand. Watching Ed do the same, Jessie was filled with pride for his son.

"I hope you won't mind the intrusion, but I thought it might be a good time to further our conversation we didn't get to have at the river," the governor said.

Jessie chuckled, "If I remember right, things were a little hectic that day, and we were a little short on time." Turning to the major, Jessie said, "I am glad you brought your guest with you."

"Thank you, and I want to introduce to you the man who will be the new commander at the fort, Colonel Davidson. Colonel, this is the owner of the Double T Ranch who supplies the beef for the fort and the community. He is the man I told you about," the governor added. "I want you to give him, along with the other men you're going to meet, all the assistance they need."

"Ed, why don't you take the colonel's men and get them something to eat and drink while I take the governor to meet the others," Jessie said.

"Yes sir," Ed answered, walking to where the soldiers were still sitting on their horses, looking for permission to dismount and go with Ed. With a slight nod of his head, the colonel signaled his permission and watched as they dismounted, smiles on their faces as they followed Ed to the food.

Jessie introduced the governor and the colonel to John, Bill, Dave, Justin, Red Sun and the other braves, except Two Worlds, who was sitting on his fur covered backrest under the shade of an oak limb. Two Worlds puffed on his long stem pipe watching everything.

Leaving the other men talking, Jessie pulled the governor aside. "I want you to meet the person who is responsible for all of this," he said, pointing toward the village and the houses. Reaching Two Worlds, Jessie squatted on his heels with his head bowed, deferring to the ancient shaman. Jessie saw the governor do the same thing. The governor studied the old man and was taken aback, looking into those eyes of wisdom.

"You are the leader of the white people?" Two Worlds asked the man sitting in front of him.

"Only of the state of Florida," he stated, feeling humbled by the presence of the old man puffing on his pipe. "I am glad you and your people are here. This is a perfect example of how the white man and Indians can live together in harmony; the colonel will see that you are left in peace," the governor assured the old man. Then he rose, leaving Two Worlds to smoke his pipe. He and Jessie walked back to where the other men were discussing with Bill and Dave about planting vegetables to sell to the ever-growing fort and its surrounding community.

"I see your son and John's son both live with one of the Indian women and have a child by them," the governor said to Jessie.

Stopping in his tracks. Jessie turned and asked with a threat in his voice, "Is there a problem?" Governor or no governor, no one was going to interfere with his family.

"It is certainly no problem with me," he answered, quickly calming Jessie's fears, "but I can see a problem in the future if they are not legally married. I can take care of that personally; by using my authority, I can marry them." Jessie thought about what he said for a minute and realized the governor could stop problems in the future for all of them.

"I will talk to Ed and John and his son. It is OK with me, but it is Ed's and Frank's decision." John knew it was the right decision when Frank and Ed agreed and went to get their wives.

Jessie and Ed weaved their way through the crowded street. Jessie stopped a man walking by and asked him, "Where can I find the governor?"

Chuckling, the man pointed to a tall building and said, "See that steeple in the distance? That is where the governor stays when he's in town." Amused at the hicks, the man walked on down the street.

Jessie and Ed followed the busy street until they reached the steps. The sign said, "ALL HORSES AND BUGGIES PARK IN BACK." Riding around to the back of the building, they saw several horses and carriages tied to a long rail. Reaching a low hanging branch of a red gum tree, they dismounted and tied their horses to it.

"Should I stay here with the horses, so no one will take our supplies?" Ed asked.

Jessie walked over to a man in a uniform with a pistol on his side and asked, "Are you here all the time?"

"I am until another officer takes my place, but yes, someone will be here all the time; your horses and supplies will be safe where they are."

Inside the building, Ed saw the sign: "Governor's Office" with an arrow pointing upstairs. At the top of the stairs was a desk set in front of a large door. A woman was sitting behind the desk, wearing a collar that was so stiff, she could barely move her head. She asked them what their business was here.

"My name is Jessie Tucker." He nodded to Ed. "My son Ed. We are here to see the governor," said Jessie, staring at the way she tried to move her head.

"Do you have an appointment?" she asked.

"No, we are on our way through, and he said to stop by if we ever came this way," Jessie informed her.

"Well, you can't just walk in here and expect to see Governor Reed," she spat at them.

"Ma'am, we have ridden out of our way to come here, and if you don't tell the governor we are here, I will," Jessie said. His anger rose, making the scar across his forehead turn red.

Standing and backing away from Jessie's fierce looks, she said, "Fine." She opened the governor's door and stepped inside. A few moments later, she stepped back out, stiffly turning and spoke in as calm a voice as she could manage. "There is someone with him now, but he asked that you wait. Would you like something to drink while you wait?"

"No thanks, I'm fine," Jessie said, noticing the difference in her attitude.

Ed said, "No thanks, ma'am."

Giving just enough of a smile to be civil, she turned and went back to sit behind her desk.

Jessie and Ed stood up when the governor walked out with another fellow, who was all dressed up in a fancy suit, shaking his hand and telling him goodbye. The governor crossed the room, holding his hand out and smiling.

"I really didn't think I would ever see you this far from your ranch, but I am glad you are here, come into my office."

Ed whistled low under his breath and said, "This is some fancy place you've got here, Governor Reed."

"It's only mine for two more years then I'll turn it over to the next governor. Would you fellows like a drink? I have some of the best whiskey made," he offered.

"No thanks," Jessie said.

"Well, tell me what brings you to my office," he said, sipping some whiskey, waiting to hear what Jessie had to say. For the next half hour, Jessie and Ed explained their decision to farm the land and that they were on their way to their old homestead to find families to bring back and sharecrop the land. The governor smiled, set his empty glass down and told the two men about a bill he was trying to get introduced into law. After the governor had come back from his trip to the Double T Ranch, he decided to propose a bill to stop the killing or removing the Indians from Florida. He had a lot of opposition from men who were seizing the land taken from the Indians.

"Well, if you asked me, it should never have happened to start with," Jessie stated passionately.

"You're right," Governor Reed agreed, "but it's too late to give back their land, and all we can hope for is a law to stop the removing of any more Indians. I use what you and your family have accomplished to make them see it's time to stop the madness of war, no matter who it's against." Standing up, he came around the desk, and as Jessie and Ed stood up, the governor said, "We are having a small dinner party tonight with some of my supporters. I want the two of you to come with me. They need to meet the men I have been telling them about."

"Look at us," Jessie said, "we are wearing the best clothes we own now. I don't think you would want us at no dinner party."

"You're exactly who I want them to meet, just the way you are," he said and smiled. "They need to know this country is not built by men in fancy coattails, but men who go out every day and tame the land. People like them don't know who feeds their hungry stomachs. Where are you staying? I'll have someone pick you up."

"We aren't staying anywhere," Jessie answered. "We were going to be on our way after we came by for a visit."

"Please, be my guests for the night. I'll have someone take your horses to our stables and feed and water them. They'll have them ready when you leave tomorrow morning. We will put you in the stateroom saved for visiting guests, and tonight you are my guests. How about it, fellows?" he asked again, putting his hand out.

Ed shook his hand saying, "I would like to if Pa will."

"I guess we are staying for the night," Jessie said, reaching out to shake hands.

Ed watched the man in the brightly colored uniform and silly little hat, that was too small for his head and held on by a string under his chin, set the saddlebags down and open the largest pair of doors he had ever seen. Lifting the saddlebags, he led the way into a huge room and set the bags on a table. Turning, he said, "Follow me please." He led the two of them into another large room. "This is one bedroom, and if you would follow me . . ." He led them through the huge room then to another large room with another bed. Facing Jessie, he handed him a key and said with a stiff smile, "If you need anything, just pull this rope." He pointed to a small rope with a tassel on the end. Reaching the door, he turned and bowed. "Have a good evening, gentlemen," he said, stepping out and closing the door behind him.

"Have you ever seen anything like it?" Ed asked, in awe, walking around trying to figure out all the things he was seeing.

"I've never seen anything that even comes close to this," Jessie answered. Lifting his saddlebag, he started for one of the bedrooms. Before Ed could take his bags to the other room, there was a knock at the door. He opened the door, and there stood six young black boys no older than twelve, holding a bucket of water in each hand.

"We is here to fill up the bathtubs," the boy in front said.

"Well, come on in and fill up that one first," Ed said, pointing to the room Jessie had picked. Ed followed the boys into Jessie's room and smiled at the confusion on his pa's face. The boys marched by, going into a room connected to the bedroom. They heard water being poured and walked in to see what they were doing.

One of the boys spoke up saying, "These two buckets here are hot water; do you want me to pour them into the tub or leave it?"

Looking a bit confused, Jessie said, "Just leave it."

As the boys closed the doors, one of them said to Ed, "We'll be back to fill up your tub." Then he left.

"Well, I can't say I won't enjoy a good bath and get rid of some of this dirt on me," Jessie said.

"Pa, we don't have any clean clothes; you think the governor really wants us to come in these dusty old clothes?"

"Well," Jessie said, "he invited us there as we are, so I don't think we have much choice. We'll just brush them off the best we can and see what happens. We can at least get this smell off us," he smiled, taking his clothes off as he headed for the tub of water.

Following a man into a room at the Capital Building to a table where the governor and four men in suits were talking, Jessie and Ed looked out of place, dressed in their brushed off work clothes, their holstered Remington .44's on one side and knives on the other. The governor and the other men at the table stood and shook hands with the new arrivals. Jessie sat next to the governor, Ed on the other side.

Governor Reed pointed to fifteen more men sitting at different tables and said to Jessie and Ed, "These are the men that can make a difference in the growth of Florida, including the area you and the others have settled with your families, but they have no idea what is happening in your part of this state. That's why I need you to inform them of the realities away from the protection of the law. But first, let's have some food. I can't guarantee it will be as good as a calf roasted over hot coals all day," he said and laughed, "but it will fill you up."

Jessie and Ed sat and stared in astonishment at the black men and women dressed in uniforms coming through a door with dishes in both hands. They served the governor first, then set plates with sliced beef, little round roasted potatoes, and other vegetables, in front of Jessie and Ed. Looking over at Ed, just as he was taking a big bite of meat, Jessie smiled. Then the smell of the food hit him, and he realized how hungry he was. Cutting a piece of steak, Jessie forgot everything else until he had finished. When Jessie finished his meal, he saw the governor waiting for them.

The governor stood and spoke to the others. "You have all heard me speak about the rancher who lives peacefully with Indians. Together they rounded up and for weeks, pushed thousands of the Spanish cattle to market. They've been supplying beef to Fort Dade and the community growing around it. They have also bought several thousand acres of land, to raise their own beef one day, and young Ed here has told me they are on the way to Georgia to seek sharecroppers to farm this land over time. I have asked Mr. Tucker to tell all of us what life is like in the middle of this state, what we face there, and what we can do to help the settlers that are moving down into our state to start new lives. As the governor sat, Jessie stood up, and pushing his chair back, he looked over at the men sitting—waiting. You could have heard a pin drop before Jessie spoke.

"My family and three other families in Georgia, who never owned slaves, decided to leave our homes and go someplace where we could keep our families safe from the war. The war came to Florida, so we had no choice but to fight. I was left for dead and half scalped as all of you can see with this scar across my forehead. I was found by three Creek braves, who took me to their village. There, an ancient medicine man and the people of his small band gave me back my life. I lived among them with no memory of who I was, because of the bullet that caused this scar." He raised his hair back from the side of his head showing the long scar. "I became an Indian for those three months, knowing nothing else except what they taught me. Then I gained back my memory. Nowhere have I been more welcome than I was among those people. Because of terrible circumstances that cost the lives of several of their family members, they wound up at the ranch with me.

"I learned that the Indians of Florida were cattlemen. We needed money for all of us to survive on the ranch, and they showed Ed and me how to round up the cows the Spanish left and push them to market. Ed and I are on our way back to Georgia, to find as many families as we can that will leave there and come with us to sharecrop the land we bought with the cattle money. Pausing, looking down at Ed sitting there with the scars across his face, he turned once again and began to speak. "Florida has been at war with the Indians that tore their families apart and left them fighting to survive in the worst conditions I have ever seen. It has left white families without husbands and fathers, but maybe the worst of it is, it has left friends wounded and filled with hate for the red man because they were told it was the Indians' fault. Then the war started between the states, and it left hatred in the white man, who has been told it was the blacks' fault."

Pausing, looking at the men sitting and waiting to hear more, Jessie started again, "Men are living off this hate, and they don't care who they hurt. They were mean before the war, and now they have the sympathy of the people who are still angry about losing their way of life. They bully or kill anyone who stands up to them. The black people are more afraid now than they were before the war. More men are bringing their families here to get away from the devastation of the war, and they are being killed for the little possessions they have left. If you want this state to grow, you need to protect them. The only law we have now is the military, and they don't seem to want to deal with local trouble. We need the state to get involved; if you are the lawmakers, you need to do your jobs and stop thinking in black, red and white and know all men and their families need your protection." Nodding to the men sitting, he sat down.

The governor rose slowly, letting Jessie's words sink in before he spoke. "You have all heard firsthand what we must do for this state to grow and become great; it is up to us to make this happen."

The following morning, before Jessie and Ed left, the governor shook both their hands, saying, "I want to thank you for staying and telling your story. Perhaps they will listen now that you painted them a picture of the reality of what we must do to protect our citizens. If we are to have a state that can grow and become a major supplier for the whole country, it's going to take people like you and your son to help settle this state. Whatever I can do here, you can count on me," the governor said, releasing Jessie's hand.

"Just send us some law that will protect us and all the others who have committed their lives and the lives of their families to stay and make a life here," Jessie said in earnest.

The Crackers Tuckertown

Justin helped Sara Mae set up the chuck wagon under one of the massive oak limbs, where she would be for at least two weeks, while Justin and the other men explored this part of the hammock for cows. Earlier, Silent Stalker had spent several days scouting farther to the east of the valley to find new areas they had not hunted yet, and he discovered the huge hammock. He rode north a full day and still didn't see the end of the hammock. Riding back to where he had started, he rode another day south and did not find that end either. The next morning, Silent Stalker entered the hammock and was amazed at what he saw by the end of the day. Riding around sloughs, he explored open grassland, which was full of wild cows that spooked and ran as soon as they saw him. After four days of scouting for cattle and a way to push them out into the open grassland, he headed back to tell them about finding more cows in one day than he had seen while on his way to the hammock.

Justin, Red Sun, and the others had finished breakfast and the last of their coffee when Red Sun spoke to the other braves. "We will hunt for the cows in pairs and meet back here before the sun leaves for the day. We have seen this type of land in the Everglades and know the dangers of the soft earth that swallows people. There will be wild hogs with sharp teeth and bears you will not see until they come out of the brush at you. We are here to find the cows where they feed and leave them as they are. We will hunt them with the dogs next spring when the cold has passed."

Each evening, as they sat eating their meal, they discussed the day's find. The men described the herds of cattle by the hundreds everywhere and the type of land they spotted them feeding on. Some told about finding themselves in shallow water where the cypress roots grew above the water so thick, the horses could not walk. They saw cows feeding on water lilies and alligator weed in the distance. The men rode around the roots and tried to follow the cows, but they found the ground kept getting softer, so they turned back and followed the edge of the water for almost a mile from where they had started. The landscape turned into rich soil where grass grew knee-high to the horses then turned into a hardwood forest, where they could see results of fires caused by lightning. The grasses had returned, making the forest a haven for coveys of quail that spooked the horses as they flushed. They saw what looked like more than a hundred head of cows feeding on the same new grass.

After five days, they had seen more than a thousand head of wild Spanish cows and knew they were a just a small part of the cattle roaming this hammock. There were enough cows to keep the men rounding them up and pushing them to market for years to come. Justin and Red Sun discussed how they would have to build holding pens and brand them before some of the crew took the dogs and moved them from the forest into the valley where Ed had gone hunting. Two or three braves and the dogs could keep them together until they had enough to push to Tampa.

The men spent the next two weeks building a cow camp where Ed's land met the hammock, and they added branding pens wherever they found a lot of cows in one area. Warrior Spirit, White Crow, Spirit Snake, and Silent Stalker decided they were going to stay for a few days to hunt for meat and hides for the coming winter.

"You are going to need a pack horse. I'll leave my horse with you and ride back with Sara Mae," Justin said. The next morning, Justin sat on the seat with Sara Mae watching Silent Stalker leading the way as the others followed him into the trees. Turning toward the two horses, Justin held out his hand, and a smiling Sara Mae handed the reins to the only man other than Franklin she would let drive her wagon.

Jessie and Ed had been riding for several days, following rutted roads and searching for the easiest way to bring back several wagons. They would need to find ferries to cross rivers too deep for the wagons. It wasn't noon yet when they came to the edge of town and the road that turned toward their old homestead. Without hesitation, they both turned their horses as if they were going home. They rode in silence until they sat at the front of their old homestead. The house looked the same as they had left it years ago, but the feelings they both felt were new. Jessie and Ed didn't quite know if they should feel sad for the life they left or glad because of what they had now. Ed smiled, knowing he would never have had Little Otter and Jake, who had brought so much joy into their lives, or the baby she was carrying now if they hadn't moved.

Jessie sat feeling both sad and happy. He knew he had made the right decision to move his family. Even though the war had not come here, it had devastated the people who were trying to put their lives back together after losing so many men in the war. Plantations were in shambles and slaves were trying to live free, but they had no idea what that meant. Nowhere to go, most had stayed and kept trying to farm. Carpetbaggers came from up North, buying up land and plantations and treating the ex-slaves worse than their owners had. The new owners gave them a choice, work for them, grow their own food, or leave.

Jessie and Ed decided since they didn't know how long it would take them to find enough people and equipment, they would stay at the old homestead where they would have shelter and a place to cook food. After bringing in their supplies and hobbling the pack horse out back where the grass was halfway to their knees, they decided to ride the country to see what they were dealing with. They headed first for the Dunkin plantation, to see the man who had bought their land for twenty cents on the dollar. Riding across their old fields onto the plantation, Jessie saw the fields had not been turned in years, probably since they had left. He and Ed noticed a few workers with hoes weeding the garden that fed them now. Riding closer to the two-story house, he could see it was run down from lack of care.

They heard the hammer of the blacksmith so rode toward the large shed where the sound was coming from. Rounding the corner of the shed, Ed stopped, staring at the largest man he thought he had ever seen. The man was shaping a piece of red-hot metal with a hammer that Ed wasn't sure he could even pick up. Sweat covered the man's skin. He wore a faded and ragged pair of overalls, and his arms looked like oak limbs. Ed saw what had to be the man's young son, who by his looks was going to be as big as his pa, working the bellows and keeping the coals red hot. The man laid the iron bar he was working back across the hot coals and turned to meet the men riding his way. Jessie and a still-staring Ed brought their horses to a halt.

"Is the owner still living here?" Jessie asked the giant in front of him. Ed was taken aback by the rumbling voice that answered Jessie.

"Yas sir, he do, but I don't know if he sober enough to be up yet; he usually come out before dark to get himself drunk again," he stated without any emotion.

"Why aren't the fields plowed and planted; it will soon be harvest time," Ed asked.

"The fields have been bare ever since the war ended. Most of the freed people headed north where they thought they would find freedom, buts they's been trickling back for the past year, saying it was no better for black people up North than back where they come from. Most of them are back where they started and trying to plant enough food to feed themselves, that's all they's knows. This country is in a mess!" he declared.

"Did you leave?" Jessie asked.

"Naw sir, I's waiting for my wife and young child to find their way back. Mister Dunkin sold her before the war ended, and I don't know where she be now. Mister Dunkin, he won't tell me cause he thinks I will run off."

"Would you?" Jessie asked.

"If I had my wife and child back and another place to be, I shore would. I's keep my distance from mister Dunkin, cause if I's ask him again where he sent my wife and he don't tell me, I's likely to bust that thick head of his wide open. Then I might never find her and will have to stay here and wait the rest of my days."

Jessie rode closer and reached out to shake hands. He felt small when the big hand closed around his, and he felt the hardened power of his strength.

"My name is Jessie Tucker, and this is my son, Ed," he said as his hand was released from that giant paw.

Releasing Jessie's hand, he spoke again in that rumbling voice, "Yas sir, I knows who you are; you had the farm that joins the plantation. My name is Troy, and this here is my son Leroy. You come back to farm again?"

"No," said Jessie. He decided this was not a good time to discuss things and turned his horse toward the big house.

"Good luck finding Mister Dunkin when he ain't drunk," Troy said, turning back to his work.

Jessie and Ed made camp in their old homestead. For three days, they rode the country and saw the devastation of the war. Prosperous plantations were now in ruins with bare fields, except the land that was tilled by freed slaves to feed themselves. Some areas had been taken over by carpetbaggers from up North using the former slaves supposedly to sharecrop the land. They made sure there was never enough money earned to pay them a share, so they gave them a small amount of credit from a local food store owned by one of the carpetbaggers. There, they could buy enough meat and flour to go with their vegetables, which they grew in small gardens.

Jessie saw enough to make him realize he had made the right decision, moving his family away from this terrible aftermath. On the way back to their old homestead, Jessie decided to take Ed's advice and talk to the local preacher like Justin had done when he found Sara Mae and Franklin. The church was larger than the one Ed and Justin had seen in Tampa. As they tied their horses to a rail in front of the church, Jessie saw the open door and someone walking around talking to himself. Ed and Jessie knocked on the door frame and stepped inside. Reverend Ellis stopped short when he saw the two men. Jessie saw fear in his eyes as he stood up straight and faced them.

"Can I help you?" he asked, keeping the fear from showing in his voice. This was not the first time the reverend had been visited and threatened by farmers for preaching to the people about leaving where they were and starting their own farms. The owners always made sure there was never enough money to help them move forward. The reverend stood waiting for the threat, hoping they were not here to burn their church down as others had threatened to do. Jessie and Ed removed their hats and saw the surprise on the reverend's face as they stepped closer, each offering their hand.

Jessie asked, "Could we have a few minutes of your time?"

"Of course. I was just going over my sermon for tonight's prayer meeting. What can I do for you?"

For the next hour, Jessie explained their decision to leave before the war came to their family and told the reverend part of what had happened to him in the Everglades. Jessie talked about how the Indians gave him back his life and how some of them survived the tragedy that brought them to his new homestead and became part of his family. He explained that to his surprise, they were great cattlemen before the Indian wars, and they showed him how to round up the Spanish cattle and move them to market for Spanish gold. Then Ed talked about how they bought the land with the money they made from the cattle sales.

"We have come to find families and equipment to farm the rich land, but I need your help," Jessie said.

"How can I help?" Reverend Ellis asked, taken aback by what he was hearing and wondering if this was his answer from God.

"We need your help speaking to your people. I remember some of the men working the fields on the Dunkin Plantation, but they don't know me well enough to believe what I am saying. Ed and I have ridden the country, and we have seen the shape the land is in; the freed men working from daylight till dark and still seeing their family go hungry, always on the edge of starving."

"Why don't you and your son come to the prayer meeting tonight and meet some of the people who still live here, and you are sure right, people are going hungry. Most of them feel trapped here, after they had gone north, only to find the people up there don't want them either. The ones who found work was only paid enough to keep their belly full, and the ones that came back are stuck here doing anything they can to keep their family fed. I think they will listen to what you have to say, but don't expect too much from them; they have heard promises before that never came true."

"We would be happy to talk to people, and I won't say anything I can't back up," Jessie responded.

"We are going to make this happen, Reverend, and like Pa said, there won't be any promises we can't keep," Ed added with passion.

"I know who you are, and I know you was an honest man who didn't own slaves to plow your fields. There will be others who knew you before the war that will listen to you."

"Thank you, Reverend," Jessie and Ed said, shaking his hand.

Jessie and Ed sat in chairs behind the pulpit watching the church fill with people, some standing in the aisles, all talking at the same time. The reverend walked behind the podium, and as he passed by the two men waiting, Jessie spoke up.

"Are there these many people every Wednesday?"

The reverend smiled and said, "I sent word out this afternoon that there was going to be someone here tonight that could change their lives, and Mister Tucker, there is no one here that isn't looking for freedom that was promised to them."

The reverend walked to the podium and spoke with a voice louder than anyone else, which quieted the crowd until you could hear a pin drop. "Let us bow our heads and pray. Lord, we all know you have never forgotten us as we are all your people."

"Amen!" the shout rose from everyone in the church.

"I know, Lord, you work in mysterious ways, and we pray the words spoken here tonight comes through you, amen."

"Amen!" came the shout again, and then the crowd became quiet and waited.

"I have talked to these men behind me, and I felt you should hear them out; you judge for yourself the truth in what these men have to say." Turning, he nodded to Jessie and Ed then walked back and sat in a chair next to Jessie.

Ed looked at his pa waiting for him to rise and speak to the crowd, but Jessie nodded his head toward the crowd and smiled as if he had played a trick on him. Ed felt his stomach draw into a knot as he rose and walked to the podium. Grabbing the edge of the podium with both hands, he swallowed the lump in his throat, and looking at the expectations on the faces in the crowd, began to speak.

"Pa and I didn't come here to tell you lies. We came here to find help to farm the land we have bought. Some of you knew our family before the war came and know we farmed our own land without slaves. We are not looking for slave labor, just hard-working families who are willing to share-crop and take the risk to make a change in your lives. The lumber for houses is being cut as I speak by John Campbell, another family I'm sure some of you know that never used slave labor. We will have the opportunity to grow with your families' help. When I say you will be paid for your efforts, you will be paid; you have mine and Pa's word."

A voice came from the back of the crowd. "How do we know your words ain't just more lies?"

Ed waited until the murmur of the crowd quieted down before he spoke.

"You don't—you will have to make your own decision, whether you want to try for something better like Pa and the others who left. They took their families to find better, not knowing what lay ahead, in a place they knew nothing about. Or, you can settle with what you have now."

"How many families are you looking for?" the voice in the crowd asked.

"We have enough land now that a dozen families couldn't turn it all under, but we also have to get equipment and animals to take back with us, or it can't happen. Pa and I have seen enough equipment and animals left on run-down plantations to put together enough for what we need." Ed let out a deep breath. "What I am talking about here will not be easy. Besides finding and getting enough equipment, we have a long way to get everything from here back to our place in Florida. Then we'll build houses for the new families, and the land will need to be cleared, turned and planted."

"How do we feed our families till the crops come in?" another voice in the crowd asked.

"You will be supplied the base food like flour, cornmeal, lard, and material for clothes. There is plenty of meat from wild hogs, cattle, and other wild animals. Within a year, you can take a section of land and plant vegetables when the first crop is harvested, which is going to be tobacco. You will start buying your own supplies with the money from your share. We are going to build our own commissary to supply not only you but our neighbors."

"How we going to be treated by the law?" another voice asked.

"We are the law!" Ed answered. "We have spoken to the governor about getting law to protect the people in that area, but until then, we are the law. You will be protected!" Ed emphasized. Hearing no more questions, Ed made one more plea. "Pa and I will be here until we have everything we need. I know this is a strange request, but these are strange times, not only for you but for us also. Thank you for listening, and I hope we can answer all your questions in time." Ed sat back down as the reverend stood up to the podium and spoke to the murmuring crowd.

"There will be no sermon tonight. I want all of you to think on this and pass the word that we'll talk about this again on Sunday after church services. Between now and then we should be praying for answers."

Little Otter was awakened from a deep sleep, from pain so sharp that it made her sit up and cry out as the first contraction hit, bringing with it a wave of pain and nausea. She grabbed her stomach and laid back and curled up in pain. She didn't realize she was screaming until she saw Jake standing in the doorway, tears streaming down his face.

"Jake," she moaned between breaths, "go get Grandma Waiting Owl," She got the words out before the next contraction hit her.

Jake saw the blood on the bed and turned in a panic, running as fast as his little legs would carry him toward the village yelling, "Grandma! Grandma!" He never slowed down even when he heard Grandma Belle.

"Jake—what's happening?" Belle yelled and began to run toward the house and Little Otter, knowing in her heart what was happening. "Lord let me be wrong—don't take the baby, and please, Lord, don't let Little Otter die." She knew her instincts were right as she ran through the door and heard the scream. She ran to the bed of furs. Kneeling and taking Little Otter in her arms, she began rocking her back and forth. "It's going to be alright," she kept repeating to her until she saw Waiting Owl come through the door and place her medicine pouch on the table.

Taking a drinking gourd and shaking some powder from a small bag into the gourd, the medicine woman added water.

Waiting Owl placed her arm around Little Otter's shoulder, urging her daughter to drink, holding her until she felt the young woman began to relax in her arms as the medicine took effect.

Belle started a fire in the fireplace and hung a pot of water to heat since Waiting Owl had taken over. As she waited for the water to heat, she listened to the soft moans from Little Otter as another contraction hit. Goosebumps covered Belle's body when she heard a scream that chilled her to the bone. She ran into the room and saw Waiting Owl holding a small bloody body, Little Otter laying still.

"Oh my God!" Belle heard herself scream.

"Little Otter will live," Waiting Owl assured Belle. "We are going to need that water now." She spoke so softly, Belle barely heard her. Belle knew how much this was hurting the other woman. Waiting Owl wrapped the small form in a fur and set it aside, so she could take care of her daughter—that had to come first. Belle heard soft footsteps, and looking up, she saw Little Moon with Woman of The Wind holding onto her arm. They made their way across the room where Little Moon helped her grandmother kneel on the furs. The old woman placed her wrinkled hand on Little Otter's head and began an ancient healing chant that would go on all night. Belle and Waiting Owl cleaned Little Otter and the furs she slept on while Little Otter weakly allowed the mothers to tend to her.

Little Moon had been sent back to the village to let them know what was happening, and as soon as the women in the village saw the look of sadness on her face, they began to wail. Holding hands, they started to dance in a circle around one of the fires that had been built. Raising their voices to their ancestors, they began a chant that would go on until they heard from Waiting Owl. Red Sun and the other braves, including Justin, sat outside Two Worlds' lodge, listening to the medicine man talking to his ancestors. When the ancient shaman finished his prayers, he left his lodge and walked slowly to Little Otter's house.

Waiting Owl Helped Woman of the Wind to her feet when Two Worlds entered the room, knowing he would want to be alone with Little Otter. The two women followed Belle into the kitchen to wait.

Little Otter cried, "Grandfather, oh Grandfather, why did this happen to me?"

Two Worlds sat next to her, placed his hand on her forehead and began chanting, taking her on a spirit journey into the future. She saw Ed carrying a small child, Jake by his side, and they were smiling at her. Little Otter knew then that another child would be born. A deep feeling of peace enveloped her, and she fell into a deep dreamless sleep. Two Worlds walked into the kitchen where Belle and the others waited. He turned to the others and said, "She will be fine when she gets through her pain of losing this child—she knows now she has a future." Turning, he left for his lodge.

Red Sun carried his daughter in his arms to the family's burial grounds. Waiting Owl walked beside him, bringing the small form wrapped in furs. They would all eventually be buried at this cemetery, except Two Worlds; he had his own burial site. Big Cypress had offered to carry Little Otter, but Red Sun refused; it was his burden. They reached the small hole the men had dug and lined with soft furs from the fox. Red Sun continued to hold his grieving and sobbing daughter until Waiting Owl placed the small body into the grave. As the sobbing became louder, Red Sun carried his daughter to her mother and grandmother's lodge and placed her on his sleeping furs. Her mother would sleep with her until she could accept what had happened to her and her stillborn child.

It was a half hour before the church service started when Jessie and Ed rode up to an overflowing sea of excited people. The people were silent and watchful as they rode closer. One of the men stepped through the church door and waved at the reverend, then waited until he had worked his way through the crowd already in the church. Reverend Ellis was stepping outside just as Jessie and Ed rode to the edge of the gathering and dismounted. One of the men reached out and took the reins from them as the reverend greeted them with a huge smile and a handshake. The surprised look was still on their faces when they heard the reverend speak.

"I was as surprised as you are, but the word has been spreading all week, and these people have come as far as ten miles away to hear what you have to say. Now that you are here, let's get started."

Jessie and Ed followed the reverend through the crowd and into the church to the same chairs they sat in before. They waited until the people filled the small room, standing shoulder to shoulder. The reverend waved his hands, asking them to quiet down so everyone could hear what the two men had to say. It took a couple of minutes to get the people inside and outside to calm down. The reverend explained to the new ones who Jessie and Ed were and why they were here. Turning to Ed, he smiled and sat down. Ed took one look at the grin on his pa's face and knew he was waiting for him to speak again to the crowd. Ed rose and walked to the podium, took a deep breath and looked at the faces, explaining to the ones who didn't hear him the last time why they were there.

"Pa and I have spent the last several days visiting the different plantations within five miles of here, and there are enough plows and equipment along with mules and oxen for what we need, but all the plows and mules in the world won't do us any good if we don't have people to use them. Pa and I have made arrangements for lumber to build housing and food to feed everyone until we can clear the land and get a crop in. We thought about just hiring people to farm, but we believe the ones who are willing to work should be able to make as much money as possible, and sharecropping gives a man that opportunity. If you come with us, it is a long-term commitment, and that is why we need families willing to take a chance on starting a new life somewhere away from the mess we have seen here.

"We are going to need people who can handle a plow, carpenters, blacksmiths, women, and children old enough to help clear the fields and harvest the crops. Those of you who don't work the fields but take care of the animals and equipment will be paid a wage." Ed stood straight then smiled and turned to the preacher. "We are going to need a leader and a church if there is to be a community." Turning back to the crowd, he said, "If we can talk Reverend Ellis into coming with us, we will build him a church bigger than he has ever seen."

Looking around, Jessie saw a non-committal smile on the reverend's face and nothing from the crowd, and he thought Ed had gone too far. Ed stopped there, realizing he had gone past what they wanted to decide on now and quickly asked if anyone had questions.

A man in the front row, who had been sitting in that seat for hours, so he could ask his questions, rose and asked the question several had talked about in their discussions. "If we decide to come with you, how we gonna get there? No one I's knows has a wagon to gets their families there. I's can walk there iffin I had to, but I's can't make my family walk." The crowd stayed quiet waiting for an answer; he had asked the question they all had in mind.

"Pa and I have found enough wagons and animals to haul plows and equipment. There will be wagons to carry every man, woman, and child. Several pieces of equipment and wagons are going to need fixing before we can take them anywhere. We can't do anything until we have enough people to make the commitment to changing their lives and give us enough help to make this happen."

Another man in the back of the crowd pushed his way to the front and stopped in front of Ed. "I gots a wife and three children who stay hungry most of the time. If you tell me there will be enough food to feed my family, I will go with you tomorrow." Looking at the man standing in front of him with a ragged pair of pants held up with a piece of rope and no shoes, Ed realized how bad it had been for these people, trying to earn enough food to feed a hungry family. The war had given them what they were told was freedom, then left them to the mercy of the people who blamed them for the war and their loss.

"I see several people here who know that my pa never had slaves, and he never owned another man. These people know that his word never came into question, so since you don't know me yet, I will let Pa tell you himself." Ed turned to face Jessie.

Jessie stood up and spoke so the people in the back could hear his words.

"You have heard my son make commitments to you, and he has said nothing that I would not have said myself." Looking at the crowd, he pointed to the oldest man he knew and said, "Mister Francis, you have known me since my pa brought our family here when I was just a boy, and you have never seen a slave in our fields."

"Naw sir, I have never seen a slave in your pa's field and iffin I's weren't so old, I would gladly go with you, buts I's so old. Nobody wants me now."

"Mister Francis, it would be a privilege to have you come with us. There isn't a man here who doesn't respect your word and ask your advice now and then, and it would be a shame if you didn't come with us. I'm sure you would never do without any more than your friends let you do without now," Jessie said with a smile. "Think about it, Mister Francis, we'll be here for a while." Nodding his head at the crowd, Jessie sat down.

Ed stood up to speak again. "I will be here tomorrow morning taking the names of those that want to come with us. We have a lot of things to get ready before we can leave, and I'm going to start putting men to work as soon as I know who's coming with us. Thank you for listening, and I will see some of you tomorrow."

The reverend stood and spoke to the people. "We will continue with this morning's service and pray over what we just heard while these two men go and do what they must."

Ed and Jessie were mounting their horses when a strong looking young man approached Ed and asked, "What about men that don't have no family yet. I can work as hard as any married man here."

Ed heard the edge of desperation in his voice. "You be here in the morning; I can always use a good, hard-working man."

"Yas sir, I'll be the first one here," he said with a big grin on his face.

"Then you will be the first one I talk to," Ed answered and turned his horse to catch his pa.

Jessie and Ed had stopped at two plantations to buy any unneeded animals and equipment. There were many other possibilities, but they had one more place to visit before it got too late. Riding up the tree-lined driveway, Jessie saw just how rundown this place had become as they made their way through the knee-high brush overgrowing the path. Jessie and Ed stopped in front of the veranda where Noah Dunkin sat with a glass of whiskey.

"Well, well, if it ain't Jessie Tucker, and that's got to be Ed all grown up. I heard you were back and looked at plantations; you here to buy back your old homestead?" he asked with a chuckle in his voice.

Jessie barely understood his slurred words. "No, but I am here to talk about buying any animals and equipment you want to get rid of."

"Well now, get down and come have a drink with me." Turning toward the front door, he yelled, "Lucy, bring two glasses for my friends and make sure they're clean."

"No, thank you," Jessie said, "I'm not here to get drunk."

"You should have some; it ain't half bad," Noah chuckled, then yelled again. "Never you mind, Lucy!" Taking a deep swallow, Noah asked, "Just what are you after?"

"Everything here you are not using," Jessie stated.

"You can have everything here for five hundred dollars," he said as he took another swallow of whiskey.

Jessie took the small leather bag tied to his belt, shook out five Spanish gold twenty-dollar coins and lined them up on the small table in front of Noah. "I will pay you one hundred dollars for all your equipment and animals, the use of your blacksmith shop for equipment repair, also the use of my old homestead. You can accept my offer or sit here and wait for the Yankee carpetbaggers to get to you. They aren't going to give you anything except a free ride off the plantation. I didn't come here to argue about price," he added, rising from his chair.

"Wait!" Reaching out, Noah grabbed the coins with sweaty hands. "I didn't say I wouldn't take it. Hell, I already got my notice two weeks ago that I had one month to pay their over-inflated taxes, and as you can plainly see, that's not going to happen."

Standing up to leave, Jessie took one more gold coin out, slid it across the table, lifting his hand so Noah could see. With a greedy smile, Noah reached for the shiny piece of gold, but Jessie placed his hand back over the coin. Noah lost his silly grin as he locked eyes and saw the threat in the crystal blue eyes of the man in front of him.

"What do you want?" he asked, a tremor in his voice.

"I want a name."

"Well, hell, I'll give you all the names you want for that kind of money." He tried to chuckle, but it didn't come out right. Noah swallowed the lump in his throat, feeling an edge of fear as he looked into Jessie's eyes.

Jessie was close enough to smell the whiskey; he slid the coin back across the table and spoke, "One name!"

Ed sat at a table someone had brought outside under a large pecan tree, which towered over the church. He watched the crowd of men and women getting bigger and bigger. He felt a little overwhelmed at the number of people wanting to leave this place of sorrow and wished his pa were here. Pa had told him that he had someone else to see while Ed dealt with the crowd of people. It was his job to decide who and how many would go back with them. Looking again at how many people were gathering, he knew it wasn't going to be easy.

Jessie held the lead line of the packhorse and rode across the overgrown fields that at one time were covered in white cotton. He felt the sadness that any farmer would feel seeing the ruins of so much productive land, the fallow fields empty of cotton. Jessie rode up to where he could see a dozen workers, hoeing grass and weeds in a vegetable garden. When he came closer, they all stopped and waited, dread in their faces, to see what this white man wanted. Jessie rode his horse up close to a large woman. She was not fat but large boned, standing close to six feet, a child by her side. He guessed the girl to be about nine or ten.

Jessie felt sure of her answer when he asked her, "Are you Hailey, the wife of Troy on the Dunkin plantation? Sorry to be so blunt."

"She dropped her hoe, pulled her daughter behind her and asked, "What you want with me? Troy no longer part of my life, ever since Master Dunkin sold me and my child before the war ended. I gots to go on with my life. After the war ended, they told us we no longer be owned."

"Why didn't you go back home after you was free to go? Do you have another man now and don't want to go home?" Jessie asked.

"Naw sir, I's had a lot of young bucks knocking on my door at night wanting to take care of me, and I don't mean feeding me neither, but I's never had eyes for nobody but my Troy. I's spect he done got him another woman to keep his bed warm at night. I's never knowd what direction to go or how many miles it be. I's fraid me and my daughter Jasmine's fate is right here. As bad as it is, we still gots plenty to eat. Long as there is nough for the new owners, they say sleeping in his house and living off his land is our pay. Iffen none of us likes it, we can find us another place. What I hears they's all the same. I hears some people are starving, so, mister, why you come looking for me?"

"My name is Jessie Tucker. I had the farm connected to the Dunkin plantation before the war."

"Yas sir, I recognize you now."

Jessie saw her relax some as she recognized who he was and saw the young girl peek from behind her mother's ragged dress and give a little smile.

Jessie smiled back as he continued, "Your Troy is still where you left him with your son, waiting for you to come home, and he don't have another woman."

"I wants my Troy," she said as the tears she had been holding back for years, quietly slid down her face. "But I's just don't know how to get back."

"That's where I come in," Jessie said gently. Stepping down from his saddle, he held on to the lead line and pulled the spare horse closer to where he stood. He asked Hailey, "If I told you I could have you in Troy's arms tonight, would you come with me?"

"Yas sir, I's waited a long time for Jesus to send you to me." Her eyes lit up for the first time in years.

"How long will it take you to get your things together?" Jessie asked.

"Mister Tucker, you are looking at everything I wants to carry with me." Hailey smiled and stroked her daughter's tangled hair.

"Then we will go see the owner and let him know you're coming with me."

One of the waiting men spoke up. "Just take her away from here as fast as you can, cause you go tell the master, he gonna try to stop you."

"You just go," said another, "we'll take care of things here."

Pulling the spare horse to where he could reach the halter, Jessie asked, "Have you ever rode a horse?"

"Naw sir, but I's can learn real fast," she said as she started forward.

"Ride my horse. It has a saddle and will be easier to ride. Just put your foot in the stirrup, step up and over and sit down."

There was an urgency to her movements now. She stepped in the stirrup, pulled her dress up, swung her leg over the saddle, and sat like she had done it a hundred times.

Jessie held out his hand and said to the young girl, "Don't be afraid, sweetheart. You are going right up behind your mother."

She stepped forward, and Jessie saw no fear as he helped put her foot in the stirrup, waiting to help as she swung up behind her mother. She put her arms around her waist and peeked around and beamed at Jessie. They started back the way he had come, and halfway across the open field, Hailey turned and waved for the last time.

It was dark when Jessie rode across the yard and stopped in front of the blacksmith shop, where he saw several wagons in all kinds of shape. He felt pride because he knew Ed had been busy. Ed was probably wondering where Jessie had gone to since he had not told him anything. He watched as Troy stood up and stopped, his hammer in midair. He dropped the hot flat piece of metal, a rim of a wagon wheel, down into the hot coals. Troy stood frozen in place. Leroy recognized his ma immediately and pushed his pa out of the way, running toward the horses.

"Ma, Ma!" he cried out as he reached the horse and grabbed her leg. "You's home, you's home! I knowd you would come home; that's why pa and me wouldn't leave."

Troy gently moved Leroy back and reaching up, he took his daughter from behind her mother. He held her in his big arms and said, "Welcome home Jasmine, I's been waiting on you and your ma." He had held back the tears for years, but when he felt those small arms wrap around his neck, and felt her tears drop on his rough skin, his tears flowed freely.

He felt her tears stop. She leaned back smiling at him and said, "I member you."

Troy kissed her on the top of her head and put her down next to Leroy. He stepped forward, lifted his wife from the saddle and held her off the ground as she cried in his arms. He placed her on her feet when he saw Leroy waiting his turn to hug his ma. Troy turned to Jessie and said, "I didn't know if this day would ever come, and it might not have if you had not come back. I'll be owing you for the rest of my days for this."

"You don't owe me anything," Jessie said, holding his hand out. Once again, he felt his hand entirely covered, and he held on until Troy had said his piece.

"I have been waiting since the war ended to leave this place, but you know why I couldn't until now. Give me and Leroy two weeks, and we will have every wagon you bring us ready to travel."

"Does that include you too?" Jessie asked before he felt Troy give him back his hand.

"Me and my family be ready as soon as you say so Mister Tucker; we can work on the plows when we gets to where we are going."

You could feel the tension and excitement after daylight broke. Some of the men had been checking loads and tightening the ropes while others were bringing mules and oxen, harnessing them to the wagons. Mothers were getting children dressed and fed before the trip began. Ed and Jessie walked up and down the wagons, giving a hand where it was needed until there was no more to do. Everyone gathered in front of the reverend and bowed their heads, waiting for the prayer to start their trip.

"Oh, Lawd," the deep voice began, "keep us safe as you kept Moses and his people safe on their journey until he found a home for his people. Give us your blessing, Lawd as we start this journey to a new land and a new life, in Jesus' name we pray, amen."

A loud "Amen!" came from the waiting group.

Jessie and Ed rode their horses from one end of the wagons to the other until they were satisfied everyone was ready. Riding to the front, Jessie spoke to the reverend who had decided the people were still going to need him where they were starting a new life. "You ready, Reverend?" Jessie asked.

"If the Lord's willing," the reverend answered, feeling his wife's hand squeeze his leg. He slapped the reins across the two mules pulling his wagon and started a new chapter in his life—only the Lord knew his future.

They only traveled nine miles the first day, stopping to fix a loose rope or change out a limping mule, but by the end of the day, everything seemed to settle in for the long ride. The sun had started setting when they came to a bridge crossing a ten-foot-wide creek. Jessie stopped the wagons until he and Ed could check to make sure the bridge would hold the weight of the heavily loaded wagons. Some of the men had left their wagons and were examining the wooden structure as if they had built it. After ten or fifteen minutes, they all agreed that whoever created the bridge, built it to support a loaded wagon. Jessie held his breath as each wagon crossed the expanse one at a time until the last wagon and extra mules were across. Then they set up for the night.

Everyone had finished eating, and mothers were getting their children ready for bed. The men had a fire going big enough to light up the small camp when they heard the hooves of horses and saw men with lit torches approaching from the direction they had traveled. Recognizing the danger, Jessie said, "Reverend, get your people behind the wagons. Ed, get the extra rifles and pistols." Turning to the men waiting, Jessie asked, "Do any of you know how to handle a gun?" Jessie recognized the man coming forward, as the young man with no family.

"I's can shoot as good as most any man."

Jessie didn't question him. As he handed him a rifle, four more men stepped forward and took a weapon. Ed kept the shotgun; the hunting bag with extra shells was hung over his shoulder. Jessie waited until the first four riders were halfway across the narrow bridge and fired his pistol into the air.

"That's far enough," he called out. The men pulled their horses to a stop on the bridge when they saw all the guns pointed at them.

"Where the hell do you think you're going with our nigras? They belong right here where they have always been; two of those nigras are from my farm. You can't come in here and take our laborers; we need them here."

Jessie walked forward and stopped at the foot of the bridge; he was no more than eight feet from the man who had spoken.

"I believe slavery ended with the war. These people belong to no one; they are here by their own choice, and no one is going to bother them. If any of you men want to try crossing this bridge, we will be obliged to shoot you. I have fought all the war I want, but you are not stopping us." Pointing his pistol at the man facing him, Jessie said. "You are one of the Engle family; I know you and the rest of your brothers. You bought used up slaves from the plantations and worked them until they dropped." Speaking loud enough so the men in the rear could hear him, he continued. "If you want to die for this low life, we will oblige you. It comes down to whether you want to ride home tonight or be carried home draped across your horse."

Ed aimed the shotgun at the rider next to the leader his father was talking to. He saw one man turn his horse around, then others followed until there were only four left.

He heard one of them say, "Come on Melvin; you are going to get yourself killed. There are other nigras we can get."

The leader, trying to save face, said, "You come back here again, Jessie Tucker, and I'll be waiting on you!" Jerking his horse's head around and kicking him hard in the ribs, he followed the others. The men with guns stood until they saw the last man disappear out of sight; the others came from around the wagons and joined them. Walking back to the men, he saw Troy and Leroy standing behind them, each holding a large hammer in his hand.

The men tried to hand Ed their guns, but Jessie said, "Keep those handy. Ed will give you more ammo. I hope we don't run into more men like them, but we have a long way to go, and if we do, you'll need them to protect the families."

The wagons moved slowly, never making more than ten to twelve miles a day until they came to the Suwannee River ferry landing. An old man and woman lived in the shack next to the river and ran the ferry. Hearing the wagons coming, the old man walked outside, not believing his eyes at what he saw.

Spitting a long stream of brown tobacco juice, he hollered at his wife, "Come out here; you got to see this." Jessie and Ed rode to where the old man and woman stood. They stared at the wagons loaded with black people. Black people had been here before, but they had refused to take them across the river. They had never seen

The Crackers Tuckertown

anything like this. "What you gonna do with all those negros?" the old man asked.

"That ain't none of your concern," Jessie answered. "We need your ferry."

"Well this ferry ain't for carrying negros across," the old lady spat out.

"You heard her, mister," the old man said, spitting another brown stream that spattered across the old woman's bare foot, which she never felt. Looking into those blue eyes and the scar across Jessie's head now turning red, the old man added, "Now you can just find another way to get your negros across the river."

Jessie held his temper. Looking at the old woman, he saw her bottom lip pushed forward, full of snuff. His eyes followed the brown streak that ran from the corner of her mouth and down her chin, dripping on her ragged dress. Jessie reached into his pocket and pulled out two gold coins. He flipped one to the old man and the other to the old lady. "You take those coins and get out of our way. We will pull the ferry across ourselves, and I'm not going to sit here and argue." Ed watched the old people's eyes light up rubbing their gold coins.

"You'll have to do it yourself because we ain't helping," the old lady said, turning and going back into their shack with the old man following.

"Alright," Troy yelled down the line, "we need all the men up front. We can only carry two wagons at a time with some women and children." Jessie and Ed sat their horses and watched. Troy, with his strength and calmness, had become their leader without anybody saying so.

It took over three hours before Jessie and Ed rode their horses onto the barge for their last crossing when the old man came out of the shack yelling, "I need to go with you if this is your last load so I can bring the barge back. What were you going to do with my ferry when you got across, uh?"

"Leave it, since you didn't want to ride with no negros," Jessie answered.

"You a mean man," the old man mumbled.

Ed, hearing the remark, said, "You're a spiteful old man." Reaching the far landing, he rode his horse off the ferry, glad that was over with. Everyone checked their wagons before starting out. They had about two more hours of travel before stopping, early enough for the men to gather firewood for cooking and a campfire.

The nights were getting cooler now, and the fire felt good as everyone sat around with plates of food on their lap talking and laughing. The further away they got from where they had come, the more confident the people felt they had made the right decision. Jessie brought his plate and sat down next to the reverend. "How do you like Florida so far?" he asked.

"What do you mean?" The reverend asked. "When did we get to Florida?"

Jessie chuckled and said, "Ever since we crossed the river today, we've been in Florida."

"Well it looks the same," the reverend said and smiled. "Is this what it's like everywhere in Florida?"

"No," Jessie answered, "as we go further south, we'll get into land that is covered with clear water springs that fill lakes and overflow into more rivers than you can imagine. The dirt is rich and black, with very little clay, unlike Georgia."

"How much farther is it to your farm?" Reverend Ellis asked.

"If nothing goes wrong that we can't fix, we are two to three weeks away."

Ed rode his big roan up next to his pa. Jessie could see that Ed was excited.

"Pa, I know where we are, and we missed Brooksville."

"Yes," Jessie said, "we should be home sometime tomorrow."

Ed rode down the line of wagons spreading the word; they would reach the valley tomorrow.

Everyone was excited, and after they had all eaten, it wasn't long before the reverend's wife had everyone singing. Ed, recognizing the church songs, joined in the singing. You could hear a harmonica, and then a fiddle joined in. The singing went on long into the night—no one could sleep anyway. The moon had started its descent before everyone was tired enough to sleep.

Big John shut down the steam engine and stared as he watched the wagons roll by, one by one on the way to the valley.

Frank walked over and stood by John. "They did it, Pa," he said. He saw Ed waving at him, and he waved back.

"Yes, they did, son, and sooner or later we are going to have to do the same if we are going to supply all the lumber this country is going to need," John responded. They stood and watched until the wagons were almost out of sight, then turned to go back to work. Frank felt sick at the thought of the terrible news waiting for his friend.

Jessie led the wagons to the lower end of the lake where the creek flowed southwest and saw the stacks of lumber spaced apart on both sides of the creek. Jessie rode up next to the reverend, and with a big smile announced, "You are home."

It took the reverend a few moments for Jessie's words to sink in. Then stepping down from the wagon, he waved to the others to come to him. When they were all gathered around, he announced to everyone, "We are home." Then he went down on one knee. They all knelt, and he prayed. "Oh, almighty God, you have led us like you did Moses to the promised land, now it is up to us, with your help oh mighty God, to make this a safe home where we can rejoice in your presence, in our new house of the Lord, amen!"

"Amen! Praise the lord," he heard the crowd say as they rose, smiling with hope spread across their faces.

Jessie waited with Ed as Troy approached and asked, "What do you want us to do first, Mister Tucker?" Jessie knew it was time to turn this over to his son.

"From this point on, Ed will be in charge of everything. If you have a need to talk, I will always be around too. That's no problem."

Turning to Ed, he asked again, "What's next, Mister Ed?"

Looking at Troy waiting and the other men gathering to hear what was going to happen now, Ed suddenly felt the weight of what he had asked for. He saw his pa waiting to see what he would say. Ed drew himself to his full height and spoke without hesitation, "The first thing you need to do is build temporary shelter, so you can be dry and warm until we can get this lumber turned into houses. I will let you decide who will build where, and if there is a problem, I'm sure the reverend can work it out." Smiling, he told the crowd, "I'm going home now and hug my wife and boy and maybe feel the new one that's coming kick his mother's tummy."

The wives gathered around, and one by one they thanked him and said, "We will pray for your wife and child on the way." Thanking them all, he turned and put the big roan into a gallop toward home, catching up with his pa.

When Jessie and Ed reached Ed's house, a happy Ed turned away and said, "We'll be over to see you later this evening." Ed jumped from his horse, tied the reins to a porch post and walked through the open door expecting to see Little Otter waiting. He was a bit surprised when he didn't see her. Walking to the bedroom door, he stopped, shocked. His wife was sitting in the middle of the sleeping furs crying. She saw the look on Ed's face, bowed her head and began to cry harder. Ed went to his knees, crawled across the furs and took her in his arms. They both cried until there were no more tears.

When the tears stopped, the agony started. They held each other tight until the agony found its home deep in their hearts, where it would stay until only moments of remembering would bring it back to life. Ed slowly released her and stood up. Reaching down, he lifted her into his arms and started to the lake. At the lake, Ed waded in chest deep and went to let her down, but she kept her arms around his neck. He pulled her to him and held her. Once she let go of his neck, she moved back and slipped her dress over her head and waited for Ed as he removed his clothes. As they came together, she whispered in his ear, "I will have more babies, all you want."

"Are you sure?" Ed asked.

"Yes!" They spent the rest of the day in each other's arms until the sun started over the horizon, then they started out to see his ma.

The closer Jessie got to his house, the more excited he became and as he reached the front of the house, he leaped from the saddle and dropped the reins. Belle met him at the door with a big smile and a promise on her face. Jessie reached her and lifted her off her feet, dancing around the empty room. "Where are the kids?" he asked.

Smiling, she reached down kissed him deeply, setting him on fire. "They are at the village and won't be home for a while."

"That will do," Jessie said, grinning and heading for the bedroom with Belle still off her feet.

Jessie was sitting at the table relaxing, drinking a cup of coffee Belle had made, watching her fill her cup, and enjoying that feeling you get from missing someone for a long time. He started to feel uneasy watching her movements; she began to tremble, and a knot started in his stomach. Belle pulled her chair away from the table, sat placing her cup on the table before she dropped it, and when she looked up, Jessie saw her tears. His whole body shut down, he could barely breathe. "What?" he asked.

She could barely bring herself to say it. "Little Otter lost the baby."

"What!"

"Little Otter lost the baby," she repeated.

Jessie knocked the chair back to the floor when he stood up. "I need to get to Ed, he's going to be devastated; he's been talking about that baby ever since we left here." He turned to the door reaching for his hat, but Belle stopped him in his tracks.

"No! You can't fix this, Jessie. They need to be alone right now, so you are going to have to get a hold of your feelings now and let them work this out by themselves. Little Otter knows what to do, and she will make sure Ed will be alright. Come finish your coffee."

Jessie and Ed sat on their horses watching the men working on their houses. They were both amazed at how quickly the houses had gone up once they got organized. They were now building the large work shed where the blacksmith shop would be. Some of the men were sorting plows that needed work, getting them ready for Troy once they got him set up. Others were sharpening axes and laying out chains they would use to pull stumps. The first thing they had done was to build a large corral to keep the animals safe at night. They would let them graze along the creek bank or the edge of the lake with a couple of the boys taking turns watching over them. Ed kept his eyes on the men working when he spoke.

"A few of the men will start building the commissary in the next few days. The others are going to start clearing the first five hundred acres on the south side of the creek; it only has a small stand of red gum trees with some small scrub oaks and palmettos. They should have it turned while it is still cold enough to kill the roots, and by spring, we should have at least a hundred acres of tobacco planted."

Jessie listened and felt humbled by the way Ed had taken over completely. He had asked him for very little advice.

"Well, since I would only be in the way here, I am going on the cow hunt with the village. They have found a new area where they say is full of cows."

"Where would that be, Pa? I didn't know there was a place where we haven't been."

"If you recall," Jessie said, "that section of land you bought. Part of it is a swamp, and apparently, it goes on for miles, running north and south and several miles wide. Red Sun said they saw several hundred head when they were scouting, but there is danger in there."

"What kind of danger, Pa?"

"Red Sun said there are holes in the ground as big as a house with no bottom, places where the sand will swallow your horse with you on it. But, there are hundreds of acres of grassland full of cows, and they are fatter than the ones we've been finding. It is too far away to go and come, so we will build camps where we can stay for a couple or three weeks at a time."

"I'm glad I don't have to mess with those stinking, ornery cows anymore," Ed chuckled.

"I've kind of come to like the smell, getting kicked, head-butted, and chasing after them in a lightning storm," Jessie said.

"What about Race? He is old enough to go. Snake handler is the same age as Race, and he is already hunting with the others," Ed reminded his pa.

"Snake Handler is different. He was born to ride and hunt as a brave. Besides, Race is going to have his hands full running the commissary and keeping the books until Jenny is old enough to help, which won't be long now," Jessie answered.

"Will we see you for supper?" Jessie asked, before turning his horse and heading to see Two Worlds.

"Pa," Ed paused, trying to find the right words. "I don't know how to thank you for your confidence in letting me do this."

"You don't have to, son. Farming is in your blood, the way it was in your grandfather's. You are lucky you have a direction for your future—live it to the fullest, son." Turning his horse, he headed for the lake.

Three

DEATH WALKS ON FOUR HOOVES

It was early spring now, and Jessie and Justin were sitting in front of Red Sun's lodge planning the next roundup. They had pushed over a thousand head of cows from the hammock during the last two years and thought they could get that many more this year. They had cut a hundred and fifty head of the best-looking cows along with six more bulls to add to the herd, they had already set aside, and moved them into the valley of wet saltmarsh with the others. Jessie, Justin, and the men were raising over seven hundred head now including four hundred yearlings added to the herd this year to be pushed to Tampa.

"Are you coming with us again this year?" Justin asked.

"Yes," Jessie answered. "Ed is doing fine with the farming, and he doesn't need me getting in his way. I've never seen anyone as excited about something for as long as I can remember. They have cleared over eight hundred acres these past two years and have close to five hundred acres planted with tobacco. Ed wants to plant a hundred to a hundred and fifty acres of corn to supply our own flour, cornmeal, and grits. I have also talked to him about planting at least fifty acres of sugar cane."

"Good," Justin said and smiled. "That is one of the things I've missed over the years."

Red Sun just listened, not knowing what they were talking about. "I think we should ready ourselves and start out for Tampa two moons from now," he said, bringing the conversation back to the cattle.

Rising, Jessie said, "I will have Franklin and Sara Mae get the wagon ready. I'll be ready myself."

After Jessie left Red Sun and Justin, he headed to the quarters to find Ed. Riding through the quarters, he waved back at the people smiling and waving until he reached the blacksmith shop. There, Jessie saw the big roan tied to the rail and could see Ed inside talking to Troy. Ed saw him ride up and dismount, so he walked outside away from the heat of the furnace to speak to his pa.

"You have time to take a ride?" Ed asked, approaching his pa.

"Sure," Jessie answered as he untied his horse and swung back up into the saddle.

They rode past the large corral behind the blacksmith shop where they kept the mules and oxen, then crossed the creek that separated the houses built on both sides of the clear water.

Jessie and Ed rode no more than a hundred yards from the houses, where they had started clearing the land. Jessie counted seven sets of mules or oxen pulling plows, turning the fertile black soil and felt that urge to be behind one of those mules, guiding the plow straight as an arrow. He watched how the men handled the mules and kept the plows straight, row after row, while Ed explained how he was going to plant all that they had managed to plow with tobacco. Then Ed showed Jessie the ten acres the men had cleared and planted with vegetables for the families. He said that those should be showing in the next week or two.

They suddenly heard the loud ringing of the church bell that Jessie had found in the back of Wooten's hardware store, sitting in a corner covered with dust. The store owner sold it to him for what it had cost him to have it shipped. The preacher he had ordered it for ran off with someone's wife, and the church never got built.

The bell tower had been built and the bell hung in place, but Reverend Ellis would not let anyone ring the bell until Sunday morning. With his watch in hand, and when the second hand came around, and the big hand moved to nine o'clock, he pulled that rope as hard as he could. Then he stood looking toward heaven with his eyes closed, listening to the sweet sound as the bell swung back and forth until it slowed almost to a stop. "Thank you, Lawd," he shouted. Then he pulled the rope again and didn't stop until he saw everyone come running from houses up and down the quarters, waving at him and grinning from ear to ear.

The bell would become a way to communicate the same way the whips had done in the scrubs. It would ring for dinner and again in the evening when it was time to bring in the mules and clean up for supper before dark. There was no working on Sundays. That was God's day to rest, and a couple of times a month, they would have all day sermon on the grounds with lots of food. Now and then there would be a baptism in the lake.

Jessie and Ed had been invited with their families to join them whenever they wanted. At least once a month, Belle took Race and Jennie to the services, so she could sing the church songs she had been brought up singing. Sometimes she could talk Jessie and Ed into going, but only when they had all day services, so they could gorge themselves on all the food Belle and the women of the quarters brought. Ed had taken Little Otter to the services once, but she felt uncomfortable with everyone looking and sometimes staring at her, then all the singing and shouting to their god. But, she didn't mind when Belle took Jake and Hawk with her.

Jessie and Ed saw the workers unhitch their mules from the plows and lead them to the creek, so they could feed while they went home and ate their noon meal. They turned and headed home too, knowing their meal was ready because Belle had started using the bell as a clock. It was confusing to the village, and they all had walked to the church to find out what was making that sound. They stood watching as the reverend pulled on the rope, and he laughed, seeing the looks on their faces as they tried to figure out how the sound was being made.

On the way back home, Jessie and Ed went by the commissary to pick up Race. They passed Oscar, the young boy from the quarters, who had talked Race into letting him work there. Now Race wouldn't do without him. Oscar wouldn't allow Race to hire any more help when the wagon came back from Tampa loaded with supplies. He insisted he could do it all by himself, and he did, with Race's assistance now and then, handling a heavy and awkward piece of equipment someone had ordered. Race was already walking home when Ed rode alongside him and removed his foot from the stirrup to let his younger brother sit behind him.

Belle, Jenny, and Little Otter had dinner ready when they arrived. They brought the food out to the table Franklin had built for them because it was cooler under the oak branches. They waited for Sara Mae and Franklin to join them as they did almost every day that she was not on the cattle round-up or the drive to Tampa. Looking across the table at his mother, Race informed her that the blackboard she had ordered was with the shipment they were unloading now.

Belle's face lit up, and looking at Franklin, she said, "I will need you to hang the board for me when you get a chance." Ever since the commissary was completed with her school room at the end of the "L" shaped building, she had wanted a blackboard to help her teach a room full of people. Her students were every color and age imaginable since she had spotted little black faces peeking through the open windows. While Jenny kept the class going, Belle walked outside and asked them if they would like to come to school. Her heart sank when she realized they didn't know what she was talking about. She knew it was against the law to teach a slave to read or write, and even after the war ended, there was no one to show them. Belle had gone and talked to the reverend's wife about letting the kids who were too young to work in the fields come to her school. The reverend's wife was in tears when she promised Belle she would walk them to the commissary every morning herself, and maybe if it was alright, she could stay too. Belle told her she was more than welcome.

After finishing his meal, Jessie spoke to Franklin and Sara Mae. "We are starting the cattle hunt in the next couple of days, and you will need to load the wagon for at least three to four weeks; then I will send the wagon back for more supplies. The men have built their cow camp further north now to find cattle. They found more cattle, and everyone says how much larger and fatter the cows are than the ones we have found all the years outside the hammock."

"Yas sir, Mister Jessie, I'll start soon as I'se finished with dinner," Franklin replied.

"Mister Race," Sara Mae spoke up. "I'll needs to get with you soon as you can for supplies."

"I'll have the supply wagon unloaded today, so why don't you bring the wagon to the commissary tomorrow, and I'll have Oscar load everything you will need."

"Yas, sir," she answered.

They sat and talked until they heard the church bell ring once, then Sara Mae and Franklin thanked everybody and left to prepare the wagon for Jessie and the others.

Jessie lay on his horse blanket, resting his head on his saddle, wide awake trying to understand this feeling of dread in the pit of his stomach. Everything had been going fine as they had over four hundred head of cows feeding in the bottom of a valley with a thirty-acre lake and lush grass. The cows could find no reason to leave. Not being able just to lay there waiting for daylight, Jessie rose, saddled his horse and rode out where the cows were bunched up for the night. Seeing Big Cypress at the back of the herd, he rode through the cows and met him.

"You have already had your turn, why are you up now?"

"I can't get to sleep," Jessie answered.

"In all the time we have been hunting cows, I have never known you not to sleep."

"I know," he said. Jessie and Big Cypress rode and made small talk until daylight started to break over the eastern horizon. Then they headed for the wagon to get some hot coffee and maybe some biscuits and sausage gravy, before starting out for the day. If they told Sara Mae they were going to be gone all day and wouldn't be back until late that evening, she would make them biscuits with thick cut bacon to put in their saddlebags to eat when they had a chance.

Jessie whistled for the two dogs that hunted with him and taking a couple of pieces of extra bacon Sara Mae always cooked, he fed them to Scout and Zack. Watching them eat, he couldn't help but admire the muscles of both hundred-pound animals. They could take down an ornery cow determined to stay in the brush and fight with them. When his hunting partner Red Sun rode up ready to go, Jessie mounted the Marsh Tackie he liked to work with when hunting in the brush.

They all rode together as they entered the hammock and then split into pairs with their dogs to start their hunt. They seldom hunted farther than hearing distance from the other hunters when they cracked their whips. Then when the sun was straight overhead, someone near a spring or a creek would crack their whip twice over their head. The others would gather and eat under shade by the water and discuss what was happening with each team. At the end of the day, they would come together and drive all the cattle, anywhere between fifty and seventy-five head, to the branding pens until they were full. It would take a day or two to brand them and move them with the other cows, then start the hunt over again.

After their noon meal, Jessie and Red Sun had close to twenty head. With the help of the dogs, they moved the cows to a cypress pond where they would mill around, feeding on lilies and alligator weed until the end of the day. From the sound of Red Sun's whip cracking across a wide meadow, Jessie could tell that he had found more cows. He headed toward the sound to help move however many Red Sun had seen back to the pond to feed with the others. Then he saw movement in the scrub palmettos and decided to get them out before they got too far in the thick scrub.

Whistling for the dogs that had gotten ahead of him as he rode to join Red Sun, he kicked the Marsh Tackie lightly in the ribs and leaned forward. The little horse bolted for the palmettos to do what he loved to do best, match wits with a small group of cows while Jessie sat in the saddle and let him work, using the whip when he needed. Jessie saw the tip of a horn and charged through the thicket. A hundred feet in, he burst into an opening no more than seventy feet across and faced the biggest, deadliest animal he had ever seen. He was magnificent! His blue-black coat of hair shimmering from the sun shining through the opening was mesmerizing. Pulling the little horse to a stop and turning his head at the same time, Jessie knew he was looking at his own death as the bull lowered his head and pointed horns, spanning over six feet, at his enemy.

The world stopped as Jessie wondered why Two Worlds had not seen his death in one of his visions. In all the fighting he had done in the war, he never considered he would die. But at this moment, he knew the little horse could never turn fast enough to get away from the charge of this monster, and they were both going to die. The Marsh Tackie was trying to turn when the bull started his charge. The bull was two steps into the charge when a hundred pounds of fury burst through the palmettos and grabbed the bull by the nose, locking his teeth. The momentum of a hundred pounds turned his head sideways, just as another hundred pounds latched onto the heel of his hind leg. The dog's weight pulled the bull's leg out from under him, and Jessie felt the ground vibrate when sixteen hundred pounds hit the dirt.

Jessie didn't see much after that as the little horse in a panic had made the turn and in two leaps was running faster than he had ever run. Jessie held on until they reached the open grassland, and he began to get some control over himself and the Marsh Tackie. Looking back for the first time, he saw the dogs break through the thicket on a run to catch up, then saw Red Sun leave the half dozen cows he had pushed into the clearing and race toward him. Looking back one more time to make sure that monster had not followed, he pulled his horse to a halt just as Red Sun came to a stop in front of him.

Looking at Jessie's face that was white as a summer cloud, he waited as Jessie tried to find words to describe what had just happened. Instead, Jessie slipped out of the saddle and called the dogs to him. They stood wagging their tails as Jessie patted and praised them. He knew he was alive because of these two dedicated animals. As they drove the animals Red Sun had found and the ones feeding in the cypress pond to the branding pens, Jessie explained what had happened. After a moment's thought, seeing that magnificent creature in his mind, he shuddered at the thought of someone killing him. Jessie told Red Sun to keep what he had experienced to himself. He didn't want the others to get jumpy and start shooting at everything they thought was a large bull.

After spending two more weeks branding, the men were tired and bruised but happy at their success. They now felt they had enough cattle to make their drive when these were added to those waiting back at the ranch, and they started moving the cows toward home and family. There were close to twelve hundred head of cattle when they reached the salt marshes and added the ones they had just branded. Now they were headed home to rest before they started the slow drive to Tampa.

Jessie woke to the smell of coffee and lay wondering if he would ever get the picture of that creature out of his mind. He had come awake a half-dozen times, seeing the bull charge and the dogs dragging him to the ground. Dressing on his way to the kitchen and coffee, Jessie thought about whether he should tell Belle. She was going to know he was different somehow, but how could he tell her how he felt the moment he knew he was going to die. Jessie knew he couldn't tell her how close he had come to death because she would worry every time he went hunting cattle.

Belle waited, watching Jessie drink his black coffee until she realized he was stalling. "Am I going to have to sit here and wait until you decide to tell me what happened out there that could make you have nightmares? I know you, Jessie B. Tucker! What happened?"

Jessie set his coffee down and described meeting the large bull in the thicket that happened so fast he thought he was going to charge him, but the dogs ran him off. That was as close to the truth as he could tell Belle.

"Well he must have been a big bull if he scared you that bad," Belle said, looking skeptical.

"Yes," Jessie answered, looking over his coffee cup. "He was a big bull." Belle rose from the table to start breakfast; the others would be awake soon, and she knew she had all the answers she would get.

It was getting light outside when Jessie finished his coffee. He was glad to be away from Belle for a while as he headed for the lake, where he knew Two Worlds would be. Removing his clothes, he waded to where the old man was sitting, puffing on his pipe, waiting. Pushing himself under the water, he swam as long as he could hold his breath, then turned and swam back to the old shaman to ask his question. Jessie sat gathering his thoughts when Two Worlds began.

"Legend calls them Andalusians. The Spanish brought them here. They are the largest of the Spanish cattle, and they live in the swamps of the hammocks. I saw them when I was young and lived with my grandfather, and he told stories of braves being killed while hunting the hammocks. But I know of no one who has seen one since. Until my vision, I thought they were gone."

Jessie was not surprised that Two Worlds knew why he was here but asked, "Why did you not see my death in your vision?"

"I did not see your death, and there was no way to tell you. There are things in life that cannot be told, only experienced." Two Worlds rose and waded to shore, leaving Jessie sitting confused.

Jessie rode alongside the wagon Sara Mae was driving, listening to the rifle cracks of whips when they reached the herd. He saw the men already gathering the strays together and starting them on the slow trip south. They had spent the last two days cutting out six hundred head of the cows and six of the largest bulls from the hammock, to replace the ones they were raising. Jessie realized why the cows were bigger and fatter from the hammock where the blue-black death roamed and bred. He would keep the rest and sell them to Fort Dade.

James Whitmore called to his wife Dottie, their two daughters, and sixteen-year-old son to get behind the wagon when he heard the rifles firing in the distance. He could tell they were coming closer. Fear gripped them all as they tried to figure out who could be at war in this part of the country. They peered from behind the wagon in shock as they watched what looked like Indians herding cattle and cracking long whips over the cows' heads. James thought they had not been seen as they watched the men on horses drive the cows into the river and out the other side, but then he saw two men cross the river and ride their way.

Red Sun and Big Cypress had been leading the herd south and west for close to two weeks along the same trail they had been using since the first small herd of ornery scrub cows. They all laughed about it now as the herd approached the Withlacoochee River. Jessie watched the cows plunge into the river as Red Sun and

Big Cypress led them up the bank on the other side and started bunching them together for the night. The other men rode their horses into the river, cracking their whips and keeping them together. As Jessie and his new partner Snake Handler pushed the last of them into the river, he stopped before going in with them. He tried to figure out what he was looking at almost a half mile down the river bank. Jessie rode his horse into the dark water, pushing the last cows up the bank to feed with the others. He worked his way through the milling cows to where Justin sat with Red Sun, discussing settling the cows in for a couple of days and letting them feed next to the water.

They stopped talking when Jessie rode up with a puzzled look on his face and waited for him to speak. "Did either one of you see what looked like a covered wagon further down the river?"

"I saw something," Justin spoke up, "but I was too busy pushing cows across to get a good look."

"I was on the far side of the cattle and did not see anything but horns," Red Sun added.

"I'll take Justin with me and find out if you will send a couple of braves to fetch Sara Mae and the wagon."

James Whitmore gripped the wooden stock on his old shotgun. He stood in front of the wagon with his son Robbie, waiting to see if these men meant them harm, while his wife and daughters hid inside the covered wagon. Jessie and Justin came to a stop, ten feet in front of the man and boy. Jessie saw the fear that covered this man and a boy who looked to be sixteen or seventeen. He thought again how badly they needed the law in this part of the country to protect people like these. He knew the fear was for the man's family that was hidden somewhere. Stepping down from his horse Jessie walked forward holding out his hand and felt the sweat in their hands as they each took his.

"I'm Jessie Tucker, and this is part of the Double T Ranch." Turning to Justin, he introduced him.

"I'm James Whitmore, and this is my son Robbie."

"Where is the rest of your family? We are not here to do you harm. We are moving that herd of cows you see there to market in Tampa."

Jessie stood still as James walked behind the wagon and brought his family out of hiding. Jessie waited, looking at James and his family with a wagon that looked as if it was on its last legs and would fall apart if it moved any further. Their clothes were held together with dozens of pieces of different color patches. He saw holes in the tarp that covered the wagon, and only James wore boots, which were coming apart and too big for his feet. He knew there were holes in the bottoms. Even the ox looked about to fall over. He had seen families like this surrounding the fort.

"Where are you headed, and what are your plans?" Jessie asked.

"Well, we have kept the wagon patched together to get us this far."

"Where did you come from?" Jessie interrupted.

"Tennessee. We left over a year ago finding what work we could on the way, but it's been hard."

"Where are you headed now?"

"Mister Tucker, I'm not sure where we are headed. We just need to find a place that has work; I don't know just how much further I can go. I'm thinking with this rich soil and a river right here, we could turn enough land to grow us vegetables. Since its spring now, there is enough time for the plants to grow before the snows come, and I've seen wild animals everywhere. We can build traps for the animals."

Jessie saw Sara Mae driving the wagon toward the river with Big Cypress on one side and Warrior Spirit on the other. Jessie turned and spoke to Justin, "Go and bring the wagon here." Justin smiled as he started out at a canter; he was not surprised at what Jessie was going to do.

"What did you do in Tennessee?" Jessie kept probing.

"I was a farmer," James replied, "until the war came, and by the end of it, there were no farms left. Tennessee was pretty much destroyed by the war along with the menfolk. Womenfolk are turning the fields with hoes alongside blacks. General Sherman burned or destroyed most of Georgia. Folks are having a hard time surviving with what's left after the war."

"Mister Whitmore."

"There ain't no mister, just James will do."

"Well, James," Jessie started, "we not only have cattle on this ranch that we are standing on, but my son is farming with sharecroppers. You are right; this is good rich soil to farm. If you are interested, and your ox is able to pull a plow, I can help you get settled. You and your family can sharecrop this valley from the river north on land I own."

"Mister Tucker, I have never seen more beautiful land as we are standing on right now. I could grow crops on this land that would make your eyes pop out of your head," he answered, smiling.

Jessie heard the wagon as it came to a stop behind him. Walking to the wagon, he spoke to Sara Mae. "These people are in bad shape. How much extra supplies are we carrying?"

Stepping down from the wagon she walked to the back and climbed inside. "I'se got more than enough flour and extra pails of lard, plenty enough smoked hams and bacon to share. I'se got one and a half crates of canned vegetables," she said, looking at Jessie.

"There's plenty food back here we could share, if that's what youse asking, Mister Tucker."

Jessie stepped from behind the wagon and motioned for Justin, Big Cypress, and Warrior Spirit to come help, as Sara Mae handed a sack of flour to Jessie and reached for another. When Jessie started toward the other wagon, the whole family stood motionless, staring at Big Cypress and Warrior Spirit.

"Have you ever seen Indians before?" Jessie asked, smiling.

"No sir," they all said at one time.

"Well, get used to them, because you will see them around as long as you are here. If you see the Indians, you can feel safe. They are fierce warriors, and they are on our side."

"Yes sir," Robbie said and stepped forward to take the sack from Big Cypress.

After unloading what supplies they could spare, Justin and the others started back with the wagon.

"We will be back this way in about four weeks if nothing goes wrong," Jessie said to the family, "and then we will get your wagon to the quarters and have our blacksmith work on it. My son runs the farming; he will get you set up with plows and tools, and more supplies until you get on your feet."

Jessie and the others rounded up more than two hundred head of wild cows and added them to the herd, giving them over fourteen hundred when they reached the Hillsborough River and turned west, two days from the stockyards.

"Mister Marshal," Randy yelled, "here come some crackers with more of those scrub cows." Tom Marshal walked out of his office and stood on the porch listening to the sweet sound of whips as the crackers brought him gold on four hooves. He couldn't help but smile when he realized who was bringing him cows. The Double T had always brought in the best cattle, and he thought Jessie was going to be happy this year because the price of prime stock was sixteen dollars a head.

Randy and Hank started opening gates, then watched again in awe as the Indians worked the cattle with their whips cracking over their heads and the dogs moving back and forth under their feet, turning them as if they could understand what the riders were thinking. Jessie sat in Tom's office discussing the future of cows while waiting for Justin, who had replaced Ed and was counting the cows. Randy, Justin, and Hank came through the door with a big grin on their faces. "They have brought us fourteen hundred thirty-two prime cows," Hank announced.

"The best yet," Tom said as he got a pencil and paper out of his desk and began adding figures. He smiled as he looked up at Jessie and said, "Good news this year—the going price this year for prime beef, which I'm proud to say you have, is sixteen dollars a head."

Finishing his figures, he handed the paper to Justin. Justin took a couple of minutes going over Tom's numbers, nodded his approval, then handed the paper to Jessie. Twenty-two thousand, nine hundred twelve dollars was written on the paper. It took the help of Randy and Hank to lift the gold-laden saddle bags across Jessie and Justin's horses. With a handshake and a promise to be back next year with more cattle, Jessie and Justin headed back to catch up with Red Sun and the others.

It was too late to start back after Jessie caught up with the others and put the saddlebags of gold in the wagon. They were far enough away from the cattle yards to get away from the stink of cows, so they camped by the river after helping set up Sara Mae and her wagon. While she prepared supper, the men went to the river and waded in clothes and all, to rid themselves of all the stink they had been living with for weeks.

When they reached the Withlacoochee River, Big Cypress and Snake Handler turned with the wagon to cross further downstream where it was shallower. As the others crossed, Jessie looked for James's wagon, thinking they would have shelters built until he could get John to send lumber for a house. He would leave the extra food along with an ax, shovel, extra rope and chain they had not used on their trip. Jessie was confused when he didn't see any sign of the family or the wagon.

"They seemed like they wanted to stay," Justin said, seeing the confusion on Jessie's face. They rode closer, disappointed that they hadn't kept their word. Jessie was about to turn back when he saw a piece of canvas from their wagon hanging from a branch, and he got that uneasy feeling in his stomach when he knew something was wrong but didn't know what. As he got closer, he saw part of the burnt wagon, then he saw the bodies scattered as if they had tried to run. Jessie had seen some bad things during the war and the devastation of Two Worlds and his people by the storm, but he had never seen anything as gruesome as this.

James and his son lay in front of the burned wagon where they had tried to defend their family. They had been shot several times. His wife and the two girls lay several feet apart, their clothes ripped and scattered around them. They had been shot several times.

Jessie could barely speak when he told Justin, "Get the wagon and the men." Walking around the wagon, he saw the provisions he had left with them scattered, flour sacks ripped open and dumped. Almost everything that had been in the wagon was thrown about as they looked for something they could use or sell for whiskey money. Walking down to the river to get away from the smell, Jessie came upon the ox bloated and full of bullet holes. The flies were crawling in and out of it, and Jessie figured it had been dead for several days. Hearing the wagon approaching, he started back to the carnage. It was going to be a messy job burying what was left of a whole family.

They dug a hole big enough to hold all the bodies, then removed a piece of canvas left from the wagon and covered the bottom. After placing the bodies in the hole together, they took another part of the canvas to cover the bodies. After covering the shallow grave, no one knew what to say, and they followed Red Sun to the river and waded in clothes and all, hoping they could remove the stench from their clothes and minds.

Everyone rode in silence until they were miles from the river when Silent Stalker rode up next to Jessie and asked, "Do you want me to try to track them?"

"No," Jessie answered, "it has rained several times since they were killed, and the tracks will be gone by now." His anger showed when he said, "Something has to be done to stop these outlaws roaming and killing at will, just for the pleasure of hurting someone. I've had enough living in fear, worrying about my family every time they leave the lake. I buried one unborn grandchild, caused by people just like the ones who killed that family we just left in a grave. He gave everything to find his family a better place to live, only to wind up buried in a place he didn't even know where he was."

It was a somber group that started down the valley home. No one could forget what happened at the river. The women of the village stood silent waiting. They had seen tragedy before, and they wondered who it had happened to this time. Arriving at the village,

Red Sun and the other braves turned to greet their wives as each woman sighed with relief when her husband reached her.

Franklin heard the wagon approach the barn, and his heart beat faster as he hurried outside to greet his wife. He felt his heart stop when he saw his wife hurrying to him. He held her tight until she could speak.

"Oh, Franklin, we have just seen the most horrible thing, and I don't know if I will ever get over it."

He listened as Sara Mae told him what had happened and led the wagon inside the barn to unload.

"Mister Tucker said just to unhitch Dolly and turn her loose to feed with the others, that they will unload everything tomorrow."

Belle saw the wagon about half way down the valley, and she felt the chills as she started readying herself for the man she had spent most of her time waiting for since they came and made him go to war. It was almost worth it as she found herself anticipating being in his arms when he came home. Belle waited until she heard his footsteps get close and threw open the door. The smile froze on her face when she saw the agony that cloaked him like a blanket. Her breath stopped until he stepped forward and took her into his arms, shaking, and then she felt the tears he could no longer live with fall on her cheek, breaking her heart into a million pieces.

Belle felt the shaking stop, and pulling away, she led him to the kitchen and sat him in a chair. She poured them a cup of black coffee, which was sitting on the back of the stove to keep warm. Setting the cup in front of Jessie, Belle pulled out a chair across the table and waited. When he began to speak, she sat silently, tears streaming down her face as she listened.

Jessie and Belle sat drinking coffee and waiting on daylight when Two Worlds would be at the lake. Belle saw the uncertainty in Jessie's face as his mind raced. What she saw in his face frightened her. She had seen this same look after they found Ed and Little Otter in the wagon and knew this was not going to end well. Belle also knew she would always be here when he came home. She gave what smile she could when he came around the table and kissed her on the head before he headed for the lake.

It was just getting light when Scout and Zac came off the porch to follow him to the lake, and they lay at the edge of the water waiting while Jessie removed his clothes, walked out knee deep and dove under the water. He held his breath long past his usual time, trying to clear his mind. It didn't help; even under the water, Jessie saw their faces. Diving back under, he swam toward shore until he had to breathe or pass out. Putting his feet down, he felt the bottom and pushed himself up for air. He stood six feet in front of Two Worlds, who was puffing on his long stem pipe—waiting.

Four

THE LAWMAN

Jessie didn't have to ask directions this time as he and Justin rode down the main street of Tallahassee headed for the capitol. He didn't pay attention to much of anything except the capitol building in front of him, but Justin was awed by all the activity and every kind of shop you could imagine. He saw a men's store with a dummy dressed in the latest style, and he liked the boots next to it displayed in the largest glass window he had ever seen.

"Jessie," he called out to get his attention, "before we leave, I would like to visit that store there." Justin pointed at the boots. Looking at what Justin was pointing at broke his train of thought, and he realized he had never noticed what was in all those glass windows.

Then he saw women's dresses in the store window next to the boots and said, "There's no reason we can't do some looking around before we leave." He thought of Belle in one of those dresses; she always liked to dress her best when she went to church.

It was going on noon when Jessie saw the sign, "ALL HORSES AND BUGGIES PARK IN BACK." He turned his horse and found the tree, dismounted and tied the reins to a branch, watching Justin do the same. Taking the stairs to the second floor, he started to the desk thinking he really didn't want to deal with the stiff neck secretary again. The stiff neck looked up, saw them halfway across the room and stood, giving a real smile this time.

"I'm sure the governor would be happy to see you; however, we have a new governor, Governor Perry, and he's aware of who you are and what you're trying to accomplish. I'll go let him know you are here if you would like to have a seat."

"Thank you, but I will wait here," Jessie replied.

As she closed the office door behind her, Justin looked at Jessie and smiled. "I'm impressed."

"You would really be impressed if you had seen her last time Ed and I was here," Jessie replied.

They were both smiling when the governor came through the door and greeted them with his hand out. "Come into my office," he said, and he turned and led the way. "Please have a seat. The former governor has brought me up to date about what you're trying to accomplish in central Florida and that you have the Indians living with you. He suggested that I give you all the help I can. What can I do for you?"

After introducing Justin, Jessie began to bring the governor up to date. The governor sat quietly and listened to Jessie describe what happened from the time he was bringing Justin from Ft Myers, Ed being shot and left for dead for a few cows to buy whiskey, Ed and his wife kicked and stomped which cost the life of his unborn child, all because his wife was Indian. He told the governor about the family they had tried to help, but before he could, they were murdered for nothing, just pure evil. They were nearly starving and had nothing of value. They even slaughtered the ox and left it to rot.

"Governor Perry, I refuse to have my people become prisoners in our own homes. I had asked for help before and was told I would get help, but I have yet to see a lawman in our territory. I don't want to be stubborn, but I don't intend to leave Tallahassee until I get some kind of commitment from you."

The governor sat for a few seconds taking in what he had just heard. Seeing the determination in Jessie's face, he spoke, "You won't have to. I want you, and Justin of course, to meet with the attorney general, but it will be tomorrow morning before I can schedule his time. If you can stay over tonight, I will arrange a meeting with him for tomorrow morning. You can stay in the stateroom, and I will have your horses taken care of. If you and Justin would be my guests for dinner tonight, I would like to hear more. Will you stay?"

"Yes, we will." Jessie smiled at the governor. "I really enjoyed the steak last time, but we eat a lot of steak year-round."

"You won't have to eat it again," the governor promised. Stepping out of his office he spoke to his secretary, "Maggie, would you please have someone take Mister Tucker and Mister Hannah to the stateroom and find someone to take care of their horses?"

"Yes sir," Maggie answered and picked up a small bell. She rang it back and forth several times until two young men emerged from a room next to her. When they were escorted to their rooms by the same man in his uniform and funny little hat, Justin wondered why they would make someone look silly, just to greet people. Justin was thoroughly impressed as he checked all the rooms. Then he spotted the bar. It looked like it had every kind of whiskey, rum, and gin. Then there were a half dozen bottles; he had no idea what they were. But he did recognize the bottle of fine bourbon and reached for a glass. Filling it half full, he started for the tub of water the young boys had filled. Jessie was just as fascinated as he was last time. Checking their saddlebags, they found clean shirts and pants.

"We need something nice besides these work clothes," Justin said, holding up a pair of worn pants.

"I know what you mean," Jessie agreed, "but they're better than the dusty clothes we had last time."

"Since we have a few hours before supper with the governor, I would like to take a walk back where we passed the window with those fancy clothes and a fine pair of boots," Justin suggested.

"I know the one you are talking about," Jessie said, "and there was a store window next to that one with some mighty purty dresses. I would like to find Belle and Jenny something purty to wear to church."

Jessie and Justin walked the few blocks to the store and stepping inside, were met by two men with their noses held high. The one with his nose held highest spoke even before they had closed the door.

"I think you gentlemen have entered the wrong store."

Jessie turned to go, but Justin caught his arm and speaking to the high nosed one, said, "I guess we will just have to go back and tell Governor Perry he was wrong sending us here. I'm sure he knows other places, that would be happy to take care of a couple of his dinner guests." Releasing Jessie's arm, he turned to follow.

"Wait, wait!"

A small man who had been hiding behind a rack of suits came around almost knocking it over. "We can take care of you—they didn't know the governor sent you. I am the owner. You just tell us what you are looking for, and I'm sure we have what you need. Will this be put on the governors' account?" he asked.

"No!" Jessie answered, and removing the small leather bag from his waist, revealed a hand full of gold doubloons. "We'll pay ourselves."

Justin saw all their eyes bulge when he did the same.

"Please," the little man stammered, "just tell us what you need."

Jessie and Justin stood in the grand living room, looking at each other with smiles on their faces.

"You look mighty fine in those new clothes and boots; I won't be ashamed to take you with me," Jessie said.

"Well," Justin said, "you look like a politician; maybe you should run for governor."

Jessie laughed. "I don't think so. I'd shoot most of them and start over. I don't think that would get me very far."

Justin went to answer a knock at the door. The man in the little hat was taken aback looking at Justin's new clothes. "If you are ready, I will escort you to the governor."

The following morning, they had been up since daylight and were finishing all they could eat from platters of eggs, ham, bacon, pancakes, biscuits, bowls of grits and sausage gravy, which had been delivered to their room when they heard the knock on the door.

A well-dressed man said, "If you are ready, the governor is waiting."

Jessie asked if the paper wrapped packages that held the dresses, and other feminine things that the women insisted went with the outfits, would be alright until they got back.

"Please, don't worry; your things will be taken care of. Would you like boxes to carry your goods in?" he asked.

"No, thanks," Jessie said, "I had them wrapped that way so they would fit across my horse."

They were led through a beautiful lobby to a small foyer, and a man in a uniform, with a pistol on his side, opened the door to the stairs leading to Governor Perry's office. The secretary smiled as their escort led them to the door.

He knocked twice and entered, then stopped and announced, "Mr. Tucker, Mr. Hannah."

Like the governor didn't know who they were, Jessie thought. Coming around the desk, he smiled looking at Jessie and Justin from top to bottom as they removed their new hats.

Shaking their hands, he led them across the room, and their escort backed out, closing the door behind him. A severe looking man stood to greet them.

Turning to the men in their new suits, the governor introduced the man, Attorney General of Florida, Patrick Summerland.

Shaking hands, he spoke to them. "I understand from what Governor Perry has told me, that you have a big problem, and I can surely sympathize with you, but we have the same problem all over Florida. There is only so much money in our budget for law enforcers. We are doing everything we can to get the federal government to send us federal reinforcements or money to hire more men."

"What about the soldiers at Fort Dade?" Jessie asked.

"They are Federal, and we have no control over them," the governor said. "But there is one thing I have the power to do. I can appoint you, Jessie Tucker, a State Marshal and give you the authority over all local law, to carry out the law of the state as you see fit."

"As long as it's legal of course, and we will have to trust you to see to it," the attorney general added.

"You can swear in deputies as you need them, and we can reimburse you and the other men as required, and Mister Tucker, that is the best we can do for now. It is tough times for everyone now with the reconstruction being pushed by our new government; we are all limited one way or another." The governor walked to his desk, opened the top drawer, reached in and pulled out a hand full of badges. "There is only one State Marshal badge. I will swear you and Justin in now if you will accept the responsibility."

It was not what Jessie had come for, but he knew this was the best he would get. Stepping forward, he spoke to the governor and the attorney general.

―⁶―

"I will accept this for now if you give me your word you will keep trying."

"You have our word. Raise your right hand and repeat after me, Justin if you would please do the same." The two men felt a blanket of responsibility covering them, as they repeated the governor's words. Picking up the badges he had removed from his drawer, he handed them to Jessie. "You will answer to no one except the attorney general and me. Is that understood?"

"Yes," Jessie answered.

"Is there anything else I can do for you before you go?" The governor asked. Shaking their hands, he picked up a small bell like the secretary had and rang it. The attorney general rose to shake their hands.

"Good luck out there," he said.

Governor Perry went to the door and met the man who had brought them here earlier.

"I know you men are doing your best, and if you have any questions about the stories that will get back to you, just keep in mind that I am going to take you at your word," Jessie said to both men.

"We understand; you do what you have to do out there. We are behind you, and don't worry about the stories," the governor said and smiled. "Blake here will take you back to get your things and have your horses ready."

Red Mangle sat at a table with his six men, drinking in a rundown bar by the St. Johns River. Dan Thorpe had a whore sitting on one knee, whispering in his ear, trying to entice him upstairs to make her two dollars. She would settle for a dollar if she could just get him upstairs.

"Take that nasty whore somewhere away from here," Red said, kicking Dan's chair under the table. Red Mangle and his band of murderers were some of the most sought-after outlaws in the South. They had been hunted from Kentucky, through Tennessee where they had lost two men in a bank robbery. They were ambushed in Georgia after they had killed a farmer and his wife. The men burned the house down on top of the old people after they had spent two days resting. But they were spotted riding away from the burning home.

The next morning as one of the men took a walk away from the camp to relieve himself, he was squatting in the bushes with his pants down, when one of the scouts from the town's posse came sneaking through the woods and walked within three feet. Pulling his pistol, he shot the scout and then pulled his pants up, holding them with one hand as he ran for the others. He heard gunfire behind him, but he knew they were too far away, and there were too many trees between them to hit anyone. An hour later they slowed down when Red saw one of his men leaning over his saddle hanging on. Riding back to where the man sat his horse, Red saw blood covering his saddle.

"How in the hell could you get hit from where we were? There were too many trees between us for a bullet to get through."

"It was the boy holding the horses; he shot me as we rode by, and hell, he couldn't be more than twelve or fourteen."

"Well, I guess he was old enough to shoot. We are not slowing down, you know the rules, keep up, or we leave you." An hour later, he fell from his horse dead.

"We are going to have to find another place to go and make some money," Red spoke to the men at the table. "Too many people know us around here now. Every sheriff in this territory is looking for us, and I don't want to get ambushed, like what happened when the union soldiers caught up with us and killed Quantrill in Kentucky. Since we can't go back to Georgia, we are going south."

Red Mangle and his band of outlaws were on the move again, following the St. Johns River, working their way south and avoiding St. Augustine where there were too many soldiers looking at wanted posters. They reached a small settlement on the river called Palatka and found a rundown saloon with rooms above it. Red and his men stayed for two days drinking pretty much alone because as soon as the people saw the red hair, they knew who he was from posters nailed to the wall at the small jail, and they did their best to avoid him.

Even though they didn't have a real sheriff, the town's folks had locked up a drunk or two until they sobered up and agreed to work off any damage they had caused. Just to show their appreciation before they left, Red and his gang robbed the small bank and killed the teller for not giving them the money fast enough. Red Mangle and his men were a plague moving across Florida, from small settlements to larger towns like Deland.

The sheriff found out they were at the hotel on the edge of town, where all the drunks and thieves hung out. He formed a posse of townspeople and set fire to the building to shoot them when they came out, but they shot their way out the back. There were fewer men in the back, and they were cautious about exposing themselves to the hardened veteran killers.

Red's men came out firing as they ran for their horses in a stable down the street. Mangle and two men kept the posse at bay, while the others saddled the horses. Red took aim at one young man, who had more courage than brains as he made a run to reach the stable with a lit torch. Red shot him through the chest. The man lay in the street while Red and the others rode off killing one man running for shelter. He was too late; they all took shots at him as they rode by and disappeared in the dark.

Red decided to leave the river where the word was spreading by fishermen from town to town, and he didn't want to ride into another ambush. He headed south and west where he had heard of a cow town called Kissimmee, where they didn't ask strangers any questions.

Red and his gang waited until after sundown to ride into the little settlement called Orlando, slipping around back of a small store and dismounting. Red saw the light from a lamp shining through a window. He figured it was the room where the owners lived in the back and knew they were still up.

Randle Harper was over six feet tall and weighed two hundred and twenty pounds. Red stepped aside as Randle kicked once and the door flew open. Daniel and Bette Morrison were in their fifty's and happily married for over thirty years. They loved running their store in a small town, but now they stood frozen in fear, watching the man with red hair step from behind Randle and smile at them.

"Don't be afraid," he told them in a patronizing voice, "we won't hurt you; we just need food and some supplies, then we will just ride on." The others laughed. One of the men took the old man by the arm as another of the outlaws reached for the old lady and led them through the curtain separating the store from where they lived.

Ted Kiser stopped by the store to order a loaf of bread from Bette since he was a bachelor and didn't do much cooking. He banged on the door louder and louder until he realized something was wrong; the store was always open this time of day. John Daly walked up and asked if anything was wrong. Looking through the store window, they saw nothing, and that worried them even more. Walking around to the back, they saw the door open with busted hinges.

Hesitating for a moment as they looked at one another, Ted stepped through the door and stumbled back immediately, his face ashen. John stepped around him and froze when he saw the couple lying on the floor. Their throats had been cut from ear to ear.

Red Mangle and his gang rode down through Kissimmee until they heard a loud and poorly played piano and figured this sounded like as good a place as any to wet their throats after the three-day ride from Orlando. The men were in a bad mood when they walked through the saloon doors. Red spotted a table in one corner where three men were enjoying a bottle between them.

They looked up when they saw the men headed toward their table, and as they got close, one of the seated men said, "Fellows, there's not enough room at this table for everyone."

"You're right," Red said as he leaned close enough for the man to smell his bad breath. "You and your pals there have three seconds to leave before these men behind me shoot all of you." He stepped back and smiled the evilest smile they had ever seen.

It gave the man who had spoken chills as he and his friends scrambled from the table. As one of them reached for the bottle they were drinking from, he heard Red say, "Leave it."

After watching the kind of people that came and went from the saloon, Red had a good understanding of where most of these men were getting their money, and it wasn't from sweeping stores. He knew this would be an agreeable place to come and go from, so he told the boys to keep it down some; he didn't want to give anybody reason to go and alert the Feds that they were there.

Red had been in Kissimmee for only a week and learned there were a lot of scrub cows being rounded up and pushed to Tampa to sell. He decided there was an opportunity to make some easy money. After warning the hotel manager that there had better not be anything missing from their rooms or he would take it out of his hide, they rode out looking for some cows to steal.

They rode south and west for two days before they saw a small herd of about thirty or more head in the distance with only two riders. Keeping out of sight, they rode ahead of the cattle and waited in a pine thicket. When the cows were close, they shot both riders and hurried to keep the small herd from scattering. Red and his men kept the cows moving in the same direction until they saw the river and followed it trying to find a shallow place to cross. Then they saw the ragged looking wagon, and as they got closer, Red saw a man with a shotgun and young boy standing in front of the wagon.

Leaving the cows by the river to graze, Red and his men rode forward. Pulling their horses to a halt, twenty feet from the man and boy, Red pulled his gun and shot the man in the head. When the boy reached for the gun, the others shot him, then shot the man on the ground again just for the hell of it. Red dismounted and walked around the wagon, looked in the back and seeing the three females huddled together, smiled that evil grin.

"Get down boys and come see what I found; we are going to have some fun." Still grinning, he grabbed the youngest by the ankle pulling her out of the wagon as they all began screaming. "Scream all you want, doll, nobody is going to hear you out here." As Red pulled her away from the wagon, the other two jumped down and tried to run, but the mother only got five feet, when one of the other men caught up to her and kicked her feet from under her. She heard her oldest daughter scream, as one of the men pulled her down by the hair.

Waiting their turn, the other three started ransacking the wagon. Randal Harper jumped up inside and began throwing sacks of flour and buckets of lard, almost hitting one of them in the head with an iron skillet. Unwrapping an oily cloth, he found half a smoked ham and a slab of smoked bacon.

"Put these in your saddlebag," he told one of the men as he finished going through the wagon, throwing away anything they couldn't use, which was most everything. It was two hours before Red and the others left the slaughtered family and crossed the river, then started south to the Hillsborough River with their cows to sell.

Jessie and Justin were almost to the mill before John saw them, shut down the steam engine, and walked under the shade to wait. They were dismounting when Frank joined them.

"Did you get to see the governor, and did he give you any answers about getting some real law down here?" John asked as he shook hands with the two men.

"I didn't get what I asked for, but I do have some news that I would like to discuss with you, including Dave and Bill."

"It sounds important; I will be at your place after coffee in the morning, and I will bring Dave and Bill with me."

Justin and Jessie stopped when they reached the quarters and saw Ed's horse tied in front of the blacksmith shop.

"I want to thank you for letting Belle talk you into coming with me. I enjoyed your company, and I would never have gone to that men's shop if it hadn't been for you or have these packages behind me." Jessie smiled and held out his hand.

Reaching for his hand, Justin said, "I'll have to thank Belle myself for talking me into going, or I wouldn't have a new set of clothes or new boots for a wedding or funeral one day because that will probably be the only time I will wear them. But I think they impressed the governor," he said, laughing.

Jessie chuckled. "You could always wear them to church on Sundays like Belle's going to make me do."

"Maybe I will see you in church one day," Justin said, kicking his horse lightly in the ribs, anticipating what was waiting for him at the village.

Jessie found Ed and Troy looking over a piece of equipment, trying to decide if it was still worth fixing. Ed saw movement and looked up to see his pa standing there smiling. Turning around, he almost hugged him, but stopped short and stuck out his hand. His voice became a little deeper as his pa shook his hand.

"It's good to see you Pa, have you been home yet?'

"No, I saw your horse and stopped by first." Turning to Troy standing there still holding the piece of equipment, he asked. "How is everything going?"

"Fine, Mister Tucker," he answered in his rumbling voice that commanded everyone's attention when he spoke. Showing him the piece of metal harness, he said, "Sooner or later we going to have to start replacing this old equipment we brought from Georgia."

"Pa and I will talk about that, now that he's back," Ed said and started outside to talk with his pa. "What did you find out Pa?" Ed asked, anxious to know what happened with the governor. "Did you and Justin stay at the stateroom?"

"Yes," Jessie answered.

"What about the man in the funny little hat?"

Jessie laughed. "He was still there. I'll tell you more on the way home. I'm kind of looking forward to your ma's smile and a home cooked meal."

Jessie and Ed rode together from the quarters. When they reached his pa's house, Ed headed to the barn to talk to Franklin and let his ma and pa have their time.

Belle watched as Jessie approached the house to see what mood he was in. Seeing the smile on his face, she hurried and removed her apron then fluffed up her hair just as he opened the door. Jessie grabbed her, swung her around, and kissed her hard on her lips.

Pulling back, he said, "This is the reason I go away just so I can walk through that door and hold you in my arms." He kissed her again, long and hard. They had a lot to make up for. Jessie felt her tears on his neck as she held on tight. Whatever happened on this trip, she would go to church and thank God.

⁖

Justin was sitting outside his lodge with his wife White Dove, enjoying the coolness of this time of year when he saw John, Bill and Dave start down into the valley. Giving his wife a kiss, he rose and started for Jessie's barn and one of the most critical meetings they would ever have as a community. Jessie stood in the door of the barn watching Justin and the others as they arrived. After greeting John and Justin, he shook hands with Bill and Dave.

"I did not ask the braves from the village for obvious reasons. What has to be done here has to be done by us. I will explain what the governor and the attorney general told Justin and me."

When he and Justin finished, Jessie opened a leather bag and shook out the handful of badges the governor had given him. He picked out the marshal's badge and pinned it to his shirt. Justin reached down and took one of the deputy badges and pinned it on his chest.

"This is something you will have to think about; each of you has family and work." His passion rose as he kept speaking, "If these outlaws are allowed to roam our country because there is no law for them to fear, none of our families will be safe. I'm not talking about local outlaws; the town sheriffs can take care of that. We go after killers who have no fear of stealing from or killing everyone they come across. I've had enough worrying about my family every time we leave the lake to hunt cows or push them to market. I don't know where the next killing will take place in our territory, but when it does, I intend to hunt them down and hang or shoot them dead." Looking at each one in the eyes, he said, "This is something each of you will have to make your own decision on because once we start, there will be no turning back."

"Hell," John said, as he picked up a badge and pinned it on his chest. "I been looking for a good fight ever since we left the Everglades."

"I get damn tired of carrying a shotgun across my plow handles all day, looking over my shoulders," Dave said, picking up one of the badges and rubbing it on his shirttail before pinning it on.

They all looked at Bill as he picked up a badge. "Hell, you ain't going without me. I've got two daughters, and I'd like to see them grow up and have me some grandkids." He pinned his badge to his overall strap.

The men had been in the barn for over an hour when Belle stopped hanging clothes. She saw them mounting their horses and caught her breath when she saw the sun flashing off the badges.

My God what have they done... Belle thought. Leaving the rest of the clothes in the basket, she headed for Jessie as Justin was walking away.

"Maybe you should tell me what's going on," Belle said, shaking as she stared at the badge on Jessie's shirt.

Jessie reached for her shoulders to calm her fears, but she pulled back. "Tell me the meaning of this," she demanded with anger.

"Come in the house, and I will explain everything to you."

"No! Tell me now."

Jessie walked past her and said, "I'm going to have a cup of coffee, and if you can calm yourself down long enough, I'll explain what happened in Tallahassee."

Jessie and Belle sat at the table for more than an hour while Jessie answered questions after he explained that this was the best he could get from the governor.

"But why you and the others?" Belle asked, more calmly now.

"Because we know how," Jessie answered.

"What about Ed and Frank?"

"No, they are too inexperienced, and they will be needed here when we are gone."

"Oh Jessie, I understand you have to do this, but promise me you won't take chances; there are bad people out there."

"Yes," Jessie said, rising from his chair to go talk to Two Worlds.

Jessie had been back home less than a week and was enjoying the cool as he rode alone, except for Rebel and Zack. They ran, one on each side of him, exploring the many smells from passing animals. They headed for the thousand acres or more of wetland pasture two hours away, where they were keeping over seven hundred Andalusian cows and bulls. These were brought from the hammock for breeding. Now they could sell the smaller scrub cows they had been raising to the fort. He wanted to add at least another five to six hundred head he could breed, and eventually, when it was too far to find cows, they would have enough every year to send to market.

Jessie made his way around the palmetto patches as he rode through the pine forest that joined the lush wetland. He came to the edge of the pines and pulled his horse up short—the sun was glistening off the blue-black hair of a legend he had hoped he would never see again. His breath caught, and he could feel his heart beating faster as he gave a short whistle bringing the dogs to him. Jessie pulled the rifle from the scabbard and pumped a shell into the chamber then braced the stock against his shoulder.

He sighted down the barrel but could not pull the trigger. The enormous creature mounted a cow, watching Jessie all the while. Jessie kept the sights on him as the bull backed away from the cow he had just bred, never taking his eyes off Jessie as he made his way through the herd to breed another cow.

"Come," Jessie called to the dogs as he backed his horse into the pines until he was out of sight, then turned back the way he came. His heart raced as he fought the urge to kick his horse in the ribs and get as far away as possible. What is the bull doing here? Jessie wondered. Two Worlds said they lived in the hammocks.

Jessie rode through the village and found Two Worlds sitting on his fur covered backrest under the oak limb. The two dogs lay five feet from Jessie as he squatted on his heels and greeted Two Worlds. Then he waited to speak. Two Worlds spoke first.

"You have changed what until now had been a legend, and you will now become part of the legend. The cows you now keep breeding for the future are his. He has bred and kept them safe in the hammocks until your search for cows to sell. If you leave him to do as he has always done, he will come and go, and you will have plenty of his offspring to sell in the future." Lighting his long stem pipe, he waited.

"I am not sure if I can ever overcome my fear of him, but I have no desire to kill him either. What you say will change the way we raise cattle in the future—it is a good thing what you say. But, the others will have to deal with him sooner or later, and I don't want anyone killed by this creature."

"Make the others aware. You have a spirit connection now with this legend of yours. He will harm no one if you do not try to take his freedom."

It had been a week since Jessie talked to Two Worlds about the Andalusian bull, and all the men were at the mud bog a half mile away, breaking in some new two-year-old foals to be trained as cow ponies in the future.

They watched as Spirit Snake sat on his horse holding the halter of a Marsh Tackie, and Warrior Spirit held the other side as they led him out knee deep in the mud. Spirit Snake jumped from his horse onto the back of the Marsh Tackie, and Warrior Spirit turned loose the halter. The Marsh Tackie tried everything except laying down but just could not get his feet out of the mud to buck, and after five minutes the little horse stopped and stood there.

Warrior Spirit rode next to him and grabbed the halter, leading the horse around the mud bog several times then out where he stood still while he and Spirit Snake put a saddle and bridle on him. It only took five minutes before they knew he was ready to be trained to work cattle. They were almost at the lake and ready to turn the newly broken horses loose with the others when they saw three men coming from Fort Dade.

Jessie saw that two of them were soldiers, one on each side of a badly dressed, poorly fed man on a skinny horse. That peaked his curiosity. He glanced at Justin, and they broke away from the others and rode toward the soldiers. Twenty feet away, Jessie recognized one of the soldiers who had been to the ranch on other occasions and pulling his horse to a halt, he waited. The three men stopped five feet in front of Jessie and Justin.

Sergeant Whitman spoke first. "Mr. Tucker, the colonel sent us. This is Floyd Banner; he came to the fort yesterday and was talking about some outlaws in Kissimmee getting drunk and laughing about the killing of a family of homesteaders in a wagon. The colonel thought you might want to hear what this man has to say."

"You are right! I do want to hear what this man has to say, so come with me, and I'll have some food brought to you while we talk." On the way to the barn, Jessie rode by Sara Mae's house where she was hanging clothes. As they approached, she stopped and waited.

"Sara Mae, could you bring some food to the barn for these men?"

"It will only take me a few minutes, Mister Tucker," she answered and headed for her house.

Jessie and the others dismounted and tied the reins to the fence rail, then Jessie took them into the barn where they could talk. Squatting on their heels, they all listened to Floyd as they waited for Sara Mae to bring the food.

"I was drinking in a saloon in Kissimmee, and a really bad group of men led by one of the most evil looking outlaws I ever seen took over the saloon. They are always getting drunk and loud with their bragging of stealing cows from other cow hunters, and I overheard them laughing about killing an old couple in the settlement of Orlando."

"What are you doing here?" Jessie asked.

"I'm on my way back to the Carolinas. I thought things were bad back there, but ain't nobody safe down here. I just stopped to see if I could earn me a meal working for somebody when I was talking to a soldier telling him about them outlaws. Then he had me tell the colonel, and the next thing I knowd, we was headed here. I want to thank you for the food."

Justin watched Jessie as he listened to Floyd's story and saw the scar across his forehead turn red and the clenched fist by his side as he controlled his feelings.

"I'll make sure you have food to take with you," Jessie told Floyd. "How long has it been since you saw these men?"

"I was there five days ago, and they were still there. I think they feel pretty safe there."

Jessie and Justin stood and watched the riders disappear in the distance, and then Jessie turned to Justin and said, "I'm going to see Bill and the others; it's time to let the outlaws know we are here."

The days were getting shorter, and the wind was starting to get a chill this time of year. As the light was fading into the western sky, Jessie rode his horse to the barn and turned him over to Franklin, then headed to the house where he knew an upset wife was waiting for an explanation.

The sun was just starting to show itself in the eastern sky when Bill, Dave, and John rode up to the commissary and met Jessie, Justin, and Race who were bringing supplies and laying them out on the porch. There were extra blankets, rope, and dried and smoked food. Each one took what they thought they would need. Jessie offered them .44 rifles, but they wanted to stick with their shotguns, so Jessie had Race bring an extra box of double ought buckshot for each man. Jessie and Justin kept their rifles.

The five men were silent, riding past the village as they started on their trip, not knowing how many would ride back, but they had done this every time they entered the Everglades during the war. As they passed the lake, Jessie saw Two Worlds sitting, holding his pipe in one hand and looking up, chanting to his ancestors. He had a strong urge to go sit with him and listen to some words of wisdom that would guide him through this ordeal, but the sound of chanting faded. Somewhere in his mind, he knew Two Worlds would be with him, so he settled in for the long ride feeling surer of himself.

Jessie and the others rode east and south passing Fort Dade to the west and crossed the Withlacoochee River. They headed east skirting around the hammocks where they had been hunting cows for the past two years, then turned more east getting directions from travelers they met, who were moving from settlement to settlement trying to find a permanent place for their families.

It was a somber group that reached a vast lake and followed the banks east until they found the outskirts of Kissimmee. They were still half a mile from town when Jessie stopped and dismounted. The others did the same and gathered under a large live oak next to the lake's edge.

Justin spoke first. "I should ride in and find out where they are staying and if they are even here."

"I agree," John said, "before we can make a plan, we need to know what we are facing. These men are hardened soldiers and will not be easy to stop and will die before giving themselves up."

By the time Justin was out of sight, Bill had a pot of coffee hanging over a fire, waiting for it to boil. The men sat around the fire quietly, waiting for coffee and news from Justin.

Justin returned, guided by the light of the fire, and a hundred feet before he reached the camp, he hollered out, "Coming in boys, don't shoot." Then he rode into the light and dismounted, unsaddled his horse, and hobbled him, leaving him to feed with the others. Walking to where he had left his saddle, he took a tin coffee cup and poured himself a cup of coffee. Looking at the seriousness of the men waiting for him to speak, he squatted in front of the fire and blew into the cup of hot coffee before he took a sip. Then he spoke.

"You're not going to like the news." Looking at each man before he continued, he took another sip of hot coffee. "They rode out two days ago, and according to the hotel clerk, they took all their belongings with them without paying their bill."

"So, they are on the move again, and we don't know which way they are headed?" Jessie asked.

"According to the clerk, he overheard them talking about Alabama being a long way away. Their leader with the red hair said they would head to the west coast, after they stopped in Brooksville, and see what they could find there and stay a while if it was friendly."

"We are not that far behind, and if we ride hard, we can cut them off before they reach Brooksville," Jessie said.

"There isn't enough moonlight to ride tonight," John spoke up.

"We'll start out at first light, so let's get what sleep we can. It's going to be a hard ride to catch those bastards," Jessie said with controlled anger.

Red Mangle and his men rode west around the lake until they came to a wagon trail and headed north, then kept to the road until they came to Fort Drum. They skirted west to avoid any soldiers, then rode two more hours before stopping for the night. It was still an hour before dark, but they were hung over from a drunk last night and needed rest.

Red watched Randle worry about something in his head, mumbling to himself now and then. They were all watching Randle when Red asked, "What in the hell are you mumbling to yourself about?"

Randle looked up to see a threat in Red's eyes. "I was thinking about that half-drunk man we were talking to at the bar, the one that convinced us to leave. Well, that half-drunk just came from Fort Dade, and they are talking about a state marshal appointed by the governor with a posse of ex-soldiers on the way to Kissimmee to capture us," Randle warned.

"Well damn! There is always a posse after us; why are you afraid of this one?" one of the other men spoke up.

"I ain't afraid of any man, but from what the man told me, these aren't just any men. He was there when they walked into a bar in Brooksville and killed several bad men. 'They threatened to kill anyone of us if they saw us again then walked out,' is what the man said. That's why they're here now."

"Why are we headed to Brooksville, if it is that dangerous?" Another man spoke-up.

"Well," Red answered, with his evil grin, "I don't know about the rest of you men, but I'm getting bored just riding from one small town after another, waiting for a posse, or an ambush. I think it's time to strike back like we did during the war. We should still be fighting to the last man. Quantrill didn't quit just because that coward Lee surrendered. He fought to the end. If they have sent a posse after us, then we will become our own posse, and I'm sure we can find a way to let them know we are in Brooksville if they want us," he said and laughed.

As soon as daylight broke, Jessie and the others finished their coffee and saddled the horses.

"We will head to Fort Drum and see if anyone has seen Red Mangle and his gang of men, then head west and cut them off before they can get to Brooksville and do any more damage," Jessie said.

Jessie and the others reached Fort Drum just after noon and went straight to the commander's office. Jessie knocked on the door, opened it and walked in. Major Hansen came out of his seat when he saw the badges on the men and walked around his desk to meet them. From the hard look on their faces, he knew this was a serious matter.

"What can I do for you men?" Major Hansen asked as he held his hand out.

"My name is Jessie Tucker, state marshal appointed by Governor Perry," he said, taking the major's hand. "We need any information you can give us about a gang of outlaws headed this way."

"I know who you are. I received a letter by courier from the governor himself. I don't have the information you are looking for, but I can give you a few soldiers to go with you."

Captain Rogers came through the door with four men behind him with pistols drawn. "Stand where you are!" he said to the surprised men.

"Captain, put your guns away and send the men back to their duties, but you stay," the major said. "These men are here on business, and we are going to give them all the help we can."

Jessie thanked the major and captain, and since they had not seen or heard of the men they were looking for, he turned down the offer of soldiers from the major. They headed west to travel as many miles as they could before the sun went down. The sun had disappeared behind the trees, and the light was fading fast as Jessie stopped next to a small creek, and the men built a fire and put on coffee.

There was a sense of urgency the next morning as the men mounted their horses before good light and started west, pushing their horses hard. They came to an old cow trail heading into the hammock where Jessie and the braves had hunted the past spring. They were almost past the trail when they heard Justin's raised voice.

"Hold on men, I want to take a closer look at that old trail." Dismounting, Justin walked a ways down the trail as the others waited on their horses. "Jessie," he called, "come take a look at this."

They all dismounted and tied the reins to a limb and walked to where Justin was down on one knee. "If I'm counting right, there are seven sets of tracks here, and they were made a few hours ago. They are cutting through the hammock instead of taking the time to ride several hours out of their way."

"You two have been in this area before, but we haven't. Can we find them in here?" John asked.

"Can you track these men, or do we need to ride fast as we can and bring Silent Stalker?" Jessie asked Justin.

"It's not real difficult to follow tracks in this wetland. The problem is if we keep following them and they hear or see us first, we will be the ones getting ambushed."

"How far ahead of us do you think they are?" Dave asked.

"I can't say for sure," Justin said, "but I would guess no more than three or four hours."

"What now?" Bill asked Jessie.

"Let's track them further in and see if we can tell where they are headed, and maybe we can get a jump on them," Jessie answered.

Justin led the way, and every so often he would dismount and study the tracks. "They are starting to wander off the trail where it gets boggy, and they're losing a lot of time in this hammock. If we go west from here, it's only a short distance to an opening, and we can travel faster than they are."

They followed Justin for half a mile and came out of the wetland into a sparse pine forest full of wild cows that spooked as soon as they saw the riders. Jessie barely noticed the cows as he kicked his horse in the ribs to keep up with the others. They all felt that adrenalin rush they had experienced just before a raid in the Everglades. Instinct kicked in as they slowed their horses to a walk searching for hoof prints of seven horses.

Jessie recognized the palmettos where he had looked death in the face, and a chill ran down his spine as he felt he was being watched. But, he rode on, keeping up with the others until he recognized the area where he and Red Sun had found cows.

"Hold up," Jessie said. Sitting his horse, he listened, and above the sound of the wind through the tree limbs, he heard it again and looked up. The osprey was barely visible, circling above the cypress strand, getting closer and closer.

"They're coming," Jessie said, stepping down from his horse. He saw the others dismount, pull their weapons from their scabbards and check the load. Putting several shells in each pocket, they turned to Jessie. They had fought with him long enough not to question his instinct.

"They are coming out below where you see that osprey circling. We have maybe twenty minutes to be ready for them. I think we should leave the horses here and set up an ambush where they are going to come out of the swamp into this pine forest. If anyone has a better plan, now is the time to say so." They all nodded their heads and followed Jessie. They had trusted him to set up ambushes in the Everglades too many times to question him now. Then, they heard rifle shots back in the swamps.

Red Mangle cursed the soft muck they had been trying to get around for the past hour when they finally reached the hard ground, where they could make some time. They rode for another hour when Red heard the osprey circling above them with its constant screeching. Red took aim with his rifle and fired and then fired again as the others just shook their heads, knowing the bird was too far away for anyone to hit.

Red and the men had just come out of the thick brush and were glad to see open pine and dry land when the first shots knocked three men from their saddles with one horse down. Red dove from his horse into a thicket and began to crawl toward the swamp as he heard the fight going on behind him. Justin and the others kept firing and reloading and then shot again until only one man was firing back. John saw Jessie bent low running toward the swamp, circling the man who was still shooting, but realized that was not where he was headed.

When they realized the last man in the thicket had stopped firing and was down, Dave and the others ran, holding their guns ready when they came upon the dead men.

"Where is the one with the red hair?" Justin asked, looking at six men on the ground.

"I know," John said as he started running in the direction he had seen Jessie go, hearing the others following him. Now he knew why as the limbs broke across his huge arms.

Red crawled from under the thick brush and wiped the blood from his eyes that came from the bushes scratching his face. He saw Jessie standing twenty feet in front of him, holding his pistol by his side. Clearing more blood from his eyes again with his shirt sleeve and seeing the badge pinned to Jessie's chest, he grinned the evil grin that Jessie would see for months to come and started to raise his pistol. Before he could bring it up and pull the trigger, 1600 pounds of blue-black anger came charging through the thicket, and Red only had a moments glance before a horn went all the way through his chest. The animal never slowed down and left Jessie standing, stunned as the sound of breaking brush faded to nothing. Then he heard the men.

Whirling around to face the next outlaw, he saw John break through the brush, looking confused when he saw Jessie standing in the clearing alone. "Where's the other one?" John asked.

"He must have gotten away," Jessie said, not knowing how to answer him now. He wondered if he could ever explain what happened.

Bill walked past John to a bush covered with blood. "He won't get far losing this much blood," he said, pointing to the bushes.

"Maybe we should go after him just to make sure," Dave spoke up.

"No!" Jessie said as he started for his horse. "He'll be dead before we can find him. It's time to go home."

The others followed, confused at Jessie's answers. Going around the dead men left behind, they found their horses and mounted. Following Jessie, they started out of the hammock, leaving the dead men where they lay. They rode quietly as the adrenalin wore off, and they thought about what they had done, wanting it to be over with before they got back. No one wanted to take this home to their family.

Five

THE GROVES

At the first hint of daylight, Leo McCracken called his three sons together to discuss their future. Things were going badly ever since the carpetbaggers taxed Thomas Cannon out of his orange grove plantation, and that started the downfall. The day the new owner took charge, he called the workers together. The owner stood on the front porch and introduced the new company's foreman of the plantation, Charles Aikman.

"He will have total control. He is going to tell you the new work rules around here, so listen carefully."

Stepping forward, Aikman stood next to the new owner with his hands on his hips, swelling out his chest as far as he could. "My name is Mister Aikman! That is what you will call me. As of today, you will start work as soon as you can see in the mornings and work until you can see only enough to put the equipment away before dark. Your wages will be cut by twenty-five percent until orange production is up. Any man that don't like these conditions can pack your belongings and leave this plantation today. If you stay, I don't want to hear any complaints. If anyone slacks off, you are fired. McCracken, you are no longer in charge of the men and groves. I will do that myself. Now everyone that is staying get to work."

The eight blacks and Leo with his three sons turned and headed for the shed to get saws and axes to prune the trees. They needed to be pruned before they would begin to bloom and fill with oranges.

That was three months ago—things only got worse from there. The wives or kids had to bring them dinner when they were working in the grove, so they could eat faster and get back to work. No more going home for the noon meal. Sundays were cut to a half day, and which half it would be was decided every Sunday by Aikman.

"Boys," Leo began, "I have had enough watching my family do without enough money to buy food to feed our wives and children or cloth to make or even patching clothes. Look at ourselves, our clothes barely cover us, and we all have holes in our work boots. I started work here when I was a young man after marrying your ma. You were all born in the same house your ma and I live in today, but it is no longer a happy house. The roof leaks and we are given no time even to fix things. Most of the blacks have run off and made everything even harder on the rest of us, and I've had enough."

Leo's oldest son JR spoke first. "Pa, we have all had enough, but where else can we go? All we know is grove keeping. We have all watched our wives do without food, to feed the rest of us."

"I'll go and do whatever it takes to get my family away from here. How much worse can it be?" Todd, his youngest son, spoke up.

Leo's middle son David spoke last as usual, and he always chose his words carefully before speaking. "Pa, I'm sure you have thought things over before today, so what are your plans for all of us to stay together?"

"Leave this place and head south. I've been told from others that oranges grow even better south of here. I don't know how far south, but we will know when we find it." Leo saw JR start to ask more questions and held his palm up for him to wait. "We have given too much of our lives and the lives of our families to leave here without even good clothes on our back. We have over two hundred small trees in the nursery grafted and ready to plant, but they will never get planted here. The new owner will lose what he has before this is over. We will leave two of the work wagons by the nursery and load them at night. Aikman pays no attention to any of that area.

The wives will quietly go about putting all the things we can take with us together. Sunday after Aikman turns us loose, he will go home and get drunk with his whore he keeps and won't come back out, and he can't see us from the main house. That's when we will load the other wagons with family and what goods we can carry. We have enough mules to pull all the wagons. David, you and JR will drive the wagons with the trees. Todd and I will drive the other wagons." Leo stopped talking and waited.

It was David first this time. "Pa, what happens when Aikman finds us gone with most of the grafted trees? What about the law?" They all waited for an answer.

"What law? Jacksonville? St. Augustine? Where is the law that protects people like us from the carpetbaggers? Ever since the war ended, this country is full of people trying to find a place to resettle their families—we will just be one more."

JR handed his oldest son Jason the reins to the two mules pulling his wagon. "Keep-up with the other wagons, and I will catch up with you later." He pulled his shotgun from under the seat along with the few shells from the small wooden box. "Pa won't know I'm not with you until in the morning; by then I should be caught up with you. If I am not, tell him I said keep moving."

"Pa, what are you going to do?"

"Make sure he doesn't follow after us," JR answered. "Now keep up with the others."

Leo and his family reached the St. Johns River by daylight the next morning and stopped under a small stand of oaks. That was when he realized JR was missing. Julie, JR's wife, who had been riding with Todd and his wife Virginia, panicked when she saw Jason driving the wagon by himself. Julie had checked during the night from the back of the wagon she rode in but could barely see a driver past David and his wagon. She ran past David and grabbed Jason standing by the wagon. Watching his mother coming at him, he wondered where his pa was; he had been looking behind him all night—waiting—hoping to see his pa catch up.

Grabbing her son by the shoulders and shaking him, she demanded, "Where is your pa?"

"Ma, I just did as Pa told me to do."

"Where is he?" she demanded again as she felt strong hands take her by the shoulders.

"Calm down," she heard Leo saying, then heard him ask the same question. "Tell me what your pa told you, son," he said in as calm a voice as he could, seeing how upset his grandson was.

"I only did what pa told me to do, Grandpa."

"I understand," Leo replied. "Just tell me what he told you."

"He told me to keep up, and he would catch up with us by this morning, and if he didn't, to tell you to keep going."

"We're going nowhere until JR gets here," Leo said loud enough for all of them to hear. Everyone had followed him and were all in a panic listening to Jason explain what happened.

"Did he say why he stayed?" David asked.

"To make sure that Mister Aikman didn't find out we were gone and come after us," Jason answered.

"I'll take one of the mules and go find him," David said, in too calm a voice, which worried his pa.

"No, we will wait. If JR is not here soon, I will go look for him, so everyone calm down now. We could all use some breakfast." Leo sounded calm, but his wife Bonnie knew it was taking everything he had not to start out now. He knew his family was watching him, and he couldn't let this get out of hand.

They were still pulling the wagons together, and the younger kids were gathering firewood for their mothers, anticipating food for their hungry belly's, when one of the boys hunting firewood yelled, "Here comes Uncle JR!"

JR went straight to Julie, and he saw the scorn and anger on her face before he got to her.

"JR McCracken, don't you ever do this to me again," she cried, burying her face in his chest.

"I'm sorry Julie, but I didn't want everyone worrying all night. I thought I would catch you before now."

"You have scared us all nearly to death this morning when we found Jason by himself. Don't ever pull that stunt again, or we will all take turns flogging you," she laughed between tears. "I know your pa and brothers will want to talk to you, so go on, and I'll fix you something to eat," she said, releasing her grip on him.

Leo and the brothers were waiting on him. They stood next to one of the wagons loaded with small trees pretending to be checking ropes, but they kept looking from under their hats waiting for Julie to get through chewing on his butt. They all knew what he had done, and their pride in him came through in a small smile on their lips as he joined them. Todd jokingly stepped next to him looking behind him at his backside.

"What are you doing?" JR asked, looking puzzled.

"I was just looking to see if Julie left anything back there. Not much!" He said as they all laughed, breaking the mounting tension. While the wives were making hoecake and brown gravy, made in a large iron skillet from the grease of thick cut fatback, they talked until all the kids were fed.

"What do you think you were going to do if he had found out?" Leo asked his oldest son.

JR looked his pa in the eyes when he spoke. "Stop him," he spoke softly. It was the deadliest sound Leo had ever heard. There would be no more questions.

"Let's talk about where we go from here. Unless someone has a better idea, I'm thinking we follow the St. Johns River as far south as we can and decide from there. We need to find the right place to plant these trees if we are to start our own groves, and I have no idea where that is right now," Leo admitted.

Leo could see the questions on David's face before he ever spoke. "Pa, we took all the food we could find, but it won't last that long feeding all our families. I know we can kill enough wild meat, but we only have enough vegetables for maybe two weeks, if we stretch it out."

"We have close to two hundred trees that are worth money, and somewhere between here and where we wind up, there will be other groves where we can sell some of what we have but still keep enough to make a new start." Looking at each of his sons, he asked, "Anyone thinks we should go back?" Looking at the puzzled look on their faces, he knew their answer. "Then let's go eat; we have a long way to go. After the children and menfolk had eaten, the women ate and cleaned up—it was their way!

They had been traveling, following the river south when they came to the edge of an orange grove that went for a quarter mile along the river. Leo turned his wagon down a row running through the middle of the grove until he came to a well-used road. He turned and followed it until they came to a clearing with a small creek, seeing what he knew was the worker's quarters.

As they drove the wagons past, they saw several black women and kids hoeing in a garden that covered more than two acres. Two hundred yards further stood a two-story house with the veranda built all the way around. He saw rocking chairs and small tables between them. Leo knew this was not owned by carpetbaggers, and his hopes of selling some of the trees rose as he stopped the wagons that carried the small trees in front of the house.

Francis McCain had hair as white as snow that fell to his shoulders. He walked to the edge of the veranda and stood looking at one of the strangest sites he had ever laid eyes on. What in the world, he wondered. As he came down the steps, he spied the two loaded wagons of small orange trees.

Leo was already walking toward the veranda when McCain reached the bottom step and waited for answers.

"I'm Leo McCracken, and these folks are my family," he said holding out his hand.

"I'm Francis McCain, and this is my place as long as I can hold onto it," he added, taking Leo's hand. Then he turned to meet Leo's sons.

"If you are looking for work, I can't help you. I have local people here every week asking." His curiosity got the best of him as he walked toward the wagon of trees wrapped in burlap. "Those are some fine-looking trees you have there, are you selling them?" Pulling back the burlap wrapping on one of the trees, he looked at the roots, still damp from their last watering before they left camp by the river that morning. Turning to Leo, he offered, "If they are for sale, I'll give you a dollar apiece for them."

"Well, Mister McCain, I can't say we wouldn't take a job on a grove like you have here, but we are headed south to find land to start our own grove. I was hoping I could sell enough trees to buy food and supplies to get where we are going," MacCracken explained.

"How many trees do you have there, and what type trees did the stock come from?" McCain asked.

"We have close to two hundred, and they are Valencia, the sweetest juiciest oranges you will ever taste. I would be willing to sell maybe forty, and your offer is reasonable.

McCain laughed at Leo's answer. "I have heard of this type orange but never tasted one, so I guess I will have to raise my own to see if you are right. Forty trees will give me plenty of stock in the future. If you will pull the wagon next to the shed yonder, I will get some men to unload all you will sell me."

"I've got plenty help, so just pick out the ones you want, and the boys will unload them," said Leo.

Jason, hearing the conversation, jumped up on the wagon and picked up the reins. He turned the mules to move the wagon to the shed McCain had pointed out.

"I've heard that there is fine land in the central part of Florida for growing oranges, and it is not very populated. A man can still homestead land in those parts," McCain offered.

"That's a mighty big river we will have to cross; is there a ferry close by?" Leo asked.

"Just follow the river for another mile or so, and you will find a ferry to take you across to Palatka, a small settlement, where you can get some supplies. Then you might want to turn more to the southwest. But from what I keep hearing, it is still pretty wild in those parts."

Leo and Todd started toward the shed where they were finishing unloading the forty trees Leo had agreed on. Walking over and pulling back the burlap on another small tree, McCain asked again, "You sure you don't want to sell more?"

After crossing the river on the ferry, Leo and the others slowly disembarked and headed toward Palatka. He could see the buildings of Palatka in the distance, and they all felt relieved now that they had money for supplies. They came to a stop in front of a rather large building with a sign tacked to the front of the porch, "Saint Johns Foods & Supply."

Sam Robison looked surprised when he saw all these strangers invading his store. He came from around the counter looking at the patches on their clothes and said, "Unless you can prove you have a job, I don't give credit."

Leo grabbed JR's arm just as he started forward, stopping him before he could start. Stepping forward, he said in a voice that left no doubt. "I have cash, and we need supplies, so why don't you take the women and show them what you have."

Leo and his family had been traveling for over three weeks and for the past several days had been searching for a place to stop where they could homestead a piece of land and plant the trees. At last, they reached a land of hills and valleys with overflowing springs and creeks you could drink from.

They pulled the wagons under the shade of a small stand of giant water oaks and decided to stop and explore the area. By nightfall, Leo and the boys knew they had found their new home and started setting up shelters to live under until they could cut enough logs to build their house. They all knew it would take time, but no one doubted they had found their new home.

Red Sun and Justin rode out front of over three hundred head of Andalusian cattle. After spending three weeks hunting the swamps, they left the smaller mixed breeds only keeping the larger Andalusians. Warrior Spirit, Big Cypress, and the others were spread out along the herd, keeping them together with the sound of whips cracking up and down the line, moving the ones wandering away from the herd back with the others. Jessie rode in the rear on the same Marsh Tackie and with the dogs he had used since they escaped death from the legend that was breeding his cows.

Sara Mae kept pace with the wagon a hundred yards behind Jessie. They were headed for the salt marshes, where they would keep the new cattle until they fattened them up. Jessie hoped the enormous bull that had tried to kill him and then saved his life would breed with the new cows as he had done in the past. Once fattened up, they would join the main herd where there were several large bulls he had kept from market to breed with over a thousand head of the Andalusian cows. Jessie now raised these cows on over thirty-two thousand acres of land bought with cattle money. They would move the herd every couple of years from one valley to another to keep them in fresh grass.

They were no more than a day and a half from the salt marshes when Jessie sat still on his horse, confused by the faint sound he heard off in the distance. Suddenly, he was sure he was hearing the sound of axes. It was coming from a small stand of oaks and tall red gum trees growing along a spring fed creek no more than a quarter mile away. Jessie started forward when he saw Justin riding toward him.

Pulling to a halt next to Jessie, Justin spoke. "You might want to come and see this," he indicated, turning his head toward the oaks. "Red Sun will keep the cows moving," he said, turning his horse to catch Jessie already on the run.

As Jessie got closer to the trees, he saw several wagons spaced out along the creek with canvas shelters stretched from the wagons to trees. Women bent over cooking fires, and kids were everywhere, carrying arms full of limbs for fires. Then he saw several men: some cutting trees, others trimming limbs. Jessie saw all the signs of homesteaders starting to build their log cabins.

Jessie and Justin entered the woods where the men were cutting timber. He heard Justin unsnap his holster, and he unsnapped his, hoping this would not turn into an angry confrontation. He saw the old man stop cutting and raise his hand to the others to stop. They all came close around the old man, still holding their axes ready to defend themselves if needed and waited for the riders to approach.

Jessie counted four adult men and six young boys ranging from about thirteen, he guessed, to maybe seventeen. He knew they were from one family when he saw they all stood over six feet tall and looked like the older man with long red hair that hung to his shoulders. The older man had a full beard peppered white with age and was lean and still muscled with no fat. He knew these were hard-working people, but they were still on his land.

Jessie dismounted when the old man leaned his ax against the tree he was cutting and started toward him. "I'm Jessie Tucker," he said as he shook the man's hand.

"I'm Leo McCracken, and these here are my boys," pointing behind him, "and that's their families by the wagons. Jessie saw the three men nod their heads and noticed the women and kids had stopped what they were doing. The women were bunched together with the children peeking from behind them.

"What are you doing here?" Jessie asked.

"We are building a new homestead and plan to start an orange grove in this valley. We were the grove keepers for over a thousand-acre orange plantation before the war. The carpetbaggers taxed him off his place and took over. Our wages were cut, and they demanded we work from daylight until we couldn't see any more. The blacks that stayed after the war and worked began to leave until there wasn't enough help to keep the groves cleaned of brush. So we figured it was time to find a place of our own, and we heard of land in central Florida, where a man and his family could find some good land and start over again. We brought close to two hundred young healthy orange trees to start, but we sold some to another grove next to a settlement called Palatka, on the St. Johns River, to buy some supplies. We still have plenty to get started, and when we get these planted, I'll go back and get more."

Justin dismounted, walked over, and introduced himself to everyone. Now he stood next to Jessie because he wasn't sure how Jessie was going to react.

"I understand," Jessie said. "I had to do the same thing with my family during the war, for what little good it did," he added. But you are on my land," Jessie stated. "This is where I graze my cattle every couple of years."

Jessie saw the shift in the older man's posture as his shoulders dropped. "How far would I have to go before I'm not on your land?" he asked.

"At least two to three days drive from here with those wagons. If you go south and west, you will cross the Withlacoochee River, and after another day's travel, you will find good land. But, other cow hunters are pushing their cows to Tampa while the Cubans are still buying, and you will have to deal with them, although they don't own the land yet. It is being bought up fast now that the carpetbaggers are moving in and buying up the land while it is still cheap."

"Well, mister, this is too bad. This valley is perfect with its lakes and this soil; you could plant a thousand acres on this land. I wish I had known this before we wasted three weeks cutting timber."

"It could have been worse if we had not been bringing those cows this way out of the swamps it may have been two or three months before we found you."

"Give us a couple of days to get our things together, and we'll be on our way. We're not here to cause anyone trouble. We've had enough of that these past several years. We're just trying to find a place to be left alone."

"Take your time," Jessie said as he turned to mount his horse.

Justin mounted his horse and faced the men. "If you have guns, you might want to keep them closer. Bad men are passing through this territory, and those axes won't get you far against guns." Turning, Jessie and Justin put their horses in a run to catch up with the herd in the far distance.

Red Sun and the others still had another day and a half before getting the cows to the salt marshes. Jessie brought them up to date on the settlers and turned toward the lake. It would still take him another two hours before reaching home.

Jessie smiled when he saw the two boys riding toward him on their own Marsh Tackies they had been riding for the past three years. He laughed, watching the two twelve-year-old boys urging their horses on, racing to get there first. Everything they did was a contest, whether it was eating, working, running, or swimming. Half of their playtime was spent in the lake racing each other. They had been swimming ever since their mothers had taught them before they could walk.

Pulling back on the reins, they brought the horses to a sliding halt. "Hey Paw Paw," they both said at the same time.

"Where are the others?" Hawk asked.

"They will be a couple more days getting the cows to the feeding grounds," Jessie answered.

"Can we go help?" Jake asked.

"We are twelve years old now. We are almost grown," Hawk spoke up, hope all over his face.

"We can crack a whip too," Jake said as he whirled the six-foot whip over his head snapping it back as it reached the end making a sound like a rifle, looking at Jessie with a big grin on his face.

"If you stay out of the way and do as you are told," Jessie said, trying to sound serious, but he couldn't keep the grin off his face.

"Can we go now?" Hawk asked.

"Go on," Jessie said. "Let Sara Mae know when you get there; she'll feed you." They were gone before he had finished. He was grinning, and his heart was about to burst out of his chest as he watched them race each other until they were out of sight. Then he turned for home.

"Are you sure the boys will be alright?" Belle asked Jessie, as she put the last bowl of food on the table. She sat down next to Race across from Little Otter and Jenny, looking nervously at Jessie.

"I'm sure," Jessie said, grinning. After the blessing, Jessie told them about the families he had met today. Halfway through his story, he noticed Belle had stopped eating and was concentrating on what Jessie was saying. When he finished, Belle was first to speak.

"Why are you making them leave? Don't we have enough land that you could feed your cows somewhere else? Where are they going to get help? Where you are sending them?"

Jessie was set back by her passionate concern for these people she had never met. He sat stunned as Ed broke in.

"Pa, you said they were grove keepers where they came from and had orange trees to plant. We have talked about planting oranges one day. Everyone else is settled into their jobs in the quarters, and with a family like them, I think it may be the best opportunity we will get."

Everyone had stopped eating now and were watching Jessie.

"Well! There is certainly something going on here beyond my understanding."

Looking carefully at his mother, Ed then said, "I guess we better go tomorrow and talk with them and see what we can offer."

"Well then, unless you are in a hurry to run them off, then I think you should," Belle stated with a resolve that Jessie knew well. "In fact, Ed, have Franklin get the buggy ready. I'm going with you. Race, I want you to load the carriage with a twenty-five-pound sack of flour, ten lbs. sugar, a sack of salt and two pails of lard. If they have been traveling that long, they are going to need food. Jenny, put together some needles and spools of thread."

"Do you want me to come with you, Ma?" Jenny asked.

"No," Belle answered with determination.

Jessie stood-up slowly, confused at the reaction from the news he had brought to the table. "Belle, you are welcome to come with us tomorrow. Race will get the things together for you, so let's everyone calm down."

Race and Jenny looked at each other and began to eat. This was beyond their understanding. Usually, their mother wasn't so headstrong.

It was just breaking daylight when Belle, Jenny, and Little Otter finished cleaning up after breakfast. Franklin and his adopted son Jeremy drove the carriage to the commissary and helped Race load Belle's supplies. Jessie and Ed rode up to the front yard just as Franklin stopped the loaded carriage in front of the house and was helping Belle onto the seat and handing her the reins. Looking at Jessie, she waited until he headed out with Ed riding beside him. She couldn't help the extra beat of her heart looking at father and son. You could hardly tell them apart from the back. Ed was as tall and almost as heavy as his father now.

Leo watched the two riders as they rode to catch up with the others until he heard JR ask, "What are we going to do, Pa?"

He turned to face the boys and saw the women and children standing by the wagons waiting for his answer. Leo stood up straight, and his answer came. "We will pack our things and find another place; there will be other land just as good."

They sat around the fire watching the older girls wash the supper dishes in the creek. The wives waited to hear what their husbands were going to do. They all dreaded the thought of leaving what they had started and going God knows where, maybe being run off again by another landowner. Leo knew they had only a few dollars left for supplies as he reached for his wife Bonnie's hand and spoke to the group.

"This is not the worst thing that could happen to us. We made it this far, and I know everyone is getting weary of always looking for that place of our own, but I really feel we are close now. I haven't seen land like this since we left, and if Mister Tucker is right, we will find good land ahead of us."

"But what about the cow hunters he talked about?" His youngest son Todd asked.

"We'll find the piece of land we want that is not owned by someone else. We'll build a pole fence around the orange trees to keep the cattle away from them until they are big enough the cows can't bother them," Leo answered, in as a matter of fact voice as he could muster. They all heard the strain in his words.

Bonnie lay for over an hour in their wagon where they slept and felt her husband toss and turn until she reached over and placed her hand on his shoulder. She said in a whisper, that carried throughout his body, "You are not alone in this." She felt him relax under her hand. He never saw the tears that wet her small pillow as she thought about how magical it felt here. This was to be the place to keep her family together. She smiled sadly as she thought about how happy they had been before the terrible war that had split so many families apart.

Bonnie had all the wives and older girls taking up the bedding and rearranging the wagons to be reloaded. The men poured buckets of water from the creek over the young orange tree roots wrapped in burlap to keep them alive until they could find a place to plant them. If they wilted and died all their money and efforts to create their own grove would go to waste. They all knew the trees had to be planted soon if they were going to save them.

Leo felt someone tugging on his pants leg and looked down to see his grandson Pete pointing to someone coming toward them in the distance. Shading his eyes with his hand, he could make out a buggy with a horse and rider on each side. "Boys!" he called out without taking his eyes off the buggy and riders. "Go get your shotguns and bring mine."

Jessie saw the four men walking out front ahead of the women and children to meet whatever danger was coming at them. He watched as two younger boys in their teens, each with an ax in their hand, walked up behind the men and waited.

They all lowered the gun barrels toward the ground when they saw the woman driving the buggy. One of the men was the man they spoke to yesterday. From the looks of him, the man on the other horse was his son.

Bonnie's heart beat faster as she walked to meet the wagon the woman rode in, watching as she came toward them. Belle drove the wagon past the waiting men and stopped. Belle didn't wait for help as she jumped from the seat and started for Bonnie. They approached each other, stopping no more than a foot apart. Belle reached and took Bonnie's hand, immediately feeling the connection, seeing in her mind the image of two small girls playing and laughing together. Everyone stood stunned, not knowing what they were seeing.

"You are Bonnie."

"You are Belle," she answered back.

They let the tears flow freely as they hugged, kissed each other's cheek, and hugged some more before turning to the stunned crowd and smiling. Belle spoke first to Jessie and Ed still sitting on their horses.

"I can hardly believe it! I want you to meet my mother's sister's, daughter—my cousin. We grew up together until we were both ten years old, and their family moved away. We never saw them again."

Jessie was smiling to himself as he stepped down from his horse. He would have been as surprised and awed as the others if he had not known Two Worlds. Two Worlds would be smoking his pipe and smiling as they sat waist deep in the lake, telling him of this happening. He smiled again as he now understood Belle last night at supper and wondered if she could explain what happened.

Women's intuition was almost as magical as the ancient shaman's power.

Jessie walked with Leo as he led the way. Leo pointed out to Jessie where he wanted to plant the first trees. They would be protected on the south side by a long stretch of pines that would block most of the cold northwestern winds in the winter. They needed a few years to grow and be strong enough that the winter winds wouldn't bother them. Ed and JR rode together with a younger brother on each side talking about plans each had and where each family had picked out their place where they wanted to build a home.

It was afternoon when the men rode back, stopping at Leo's homesite, where he had already started the first layer of log walls. Bonnie and Belle were still sitting under the shade cloth stretched from Bonnie's wagon. Catching up on the years past, they watched now as some of the men squatted on their heels. Others stood, but all listened as Jessie and Ed discussed with Leo how to get enough lumber to build all their homes instead of the backing breaking job of cutting and hauling logs to build four houses. Jessie told Leo that the Double T Ranch would pay them to keep planting trees. Jessie would pay for new trees they would travel to find, picking out the best ones and hauling them back.

"Once we get settled and plant the trees we have now, we can buy more around Jacksonville and St Augustine. We can bring over two hundred at a time with the wagons I have now," Leo stated.

Ed spoke up. "My younger brother Race and sister Jenny will set you up a credit at the commissary. If there is anything special you need, I can order it for you the next time we pick up supplies. We can get most things like food and cloth in Brooksville, but if it's unusual, I can order it from Tampa, and that could take up to six weeks.

Belle saw the men start toward them and quickly said, "We can make room for you and the other wives and children to stay at the lake until the men get the houses built.

Bonnie smiled and said, "I can't wait to see your place, but we will stay to feed and care for the men here. I will come with Leo when he comes for supplies in the next few days." The cousins leaned forward and hugged.

They were halfway back to the lake with Jessie driving the buggy when Belle slipped her arm through his. She leaned against him and asked, "Do you understand what has happened?"

Jessie tried to think of a way to tell her but knew he would have to talk to Two Worlds. "No," he answered. They rode the rest of the way home in silence, both deep into their own thoughts about today.

Leo started down the slope toward the lake when suddenly he pulled back on the reins bringing the two mules to a halt. He and Bonnie sat staring at the strangest sight they had ever seen. They looked at one another, and Bonnie asked, "Are you sure we are in the right place?"

"I don't know," Leo answered, amazed at what he was seeing. He looked at the lodges with Indians walking around as if they belonged there. How can that be? he thought. They studied the wooden houses and a building that had to be the commissary Jessie had mentioned. At the other end of the lake, he saw the quarters along both sides of the creek flowing from the lake. He saw rows of blacks behind mules and plows.

Belle saw the wagon start down into the valley and walked out into the yard. She waved and waited until Leo stopped in front of the house.

"Jessie is at the barn with Franklin and Jeremy," Belle said, pointing. "Bonnie and I will walk to the commissary, and we'll meet you there later." Taking Bonnie by the arm, Belle led her inside. They would spend the next several hours continuing to catch up on the years past.

Bonnie told Belle how the army came by the grove and recruited JR and David to fight in a battle with close to five thousand men under General Finegan at the Olustee River bridge. "General Seymour of the Union army had five thousand soldiers when he reached the bridge where JR, David, and the others were dug in and waiting. When General Seymour and his army retreated at the end of the day, eighteen hundred Union soldiers were killed, wounded or missing and more than nine hundred Confederate soldiers also dead, wounded or missing. After the battle, JR and David were sent back to the groves to help produce food for the army."

Then Bonnie sat and listened as Belle described how the Confederate Army came and threatened Jessie and the others if they didn't go and fight. Tears welled up in Belle's eyes, telling Bonnie the horror of being told that Jessie had been killed somewhere in the Everglades while scouting for the small raiding party. They had hunted for him for over a week before they gave up. Bonnie hugged Belle as she pulled herself together, telling her that she knew from Jessie what happened. He brought the Indians to the lake, and they taught him about rounding up the Spanish cows. Together, they took the cows to market where they were sold for Spanish gold that they used to buy land.

Jessie and Franklin looked up when they saw the shadow of Leo cross them from the doorway. Leo moved slowly into the barn, taking in everything around him. He had not been sure what to expect today when he and Bonnie started out this morning, but it was beyond what they could have imagined when they entered a different world going on in this valley.

Jessie was the first to speak. "Welcome to the "Double T Ranch." I'm guessing Bonnie is with Belle," he said, grinning.

"She is, and I'm sure they won't stop talking for at least two hours, if not longer," Leo said and laughed. "She had me up before daylight this morning. In all the years we've been married, I have never seen her this happy. I guess they were very close growing up together, and it was awfully painful for a long time after her father took them away."

"I am happy for them; it has been a long time since I have seen Belle this excited. So, while they talk and shop for supplies at the commissary, we can ride over and talk to John and his boys about getting you some lumber." Turning, he said to Leo, "This is Franklin. His wife Sara Mae and son Jeremy are part of our family here."

"Glad to meet you, Mister Leo," Franklin said, nodding his head. "Mister Tucker, you need me to saddle your horse?"

"Yes, Franklin, and saddle one for Leo." He turned to Leo and said, "Unless you would rather drive the wagon. If not, we will leave it at the commissary and let Race have it loaded."

"We will leave it," Leo said and turned for the door to move the wagon.

"Don't bother, Franklin can have Jeremy take it."

Jessie rode wide of Dave's and Bill's homes, thinking he would introduce them on the way back. Crossing the creek and riding toward the mill, he noticed the new houses of John's sons, Frank and Todd. The oldest son Frank and Dancing Sun had two little girls, who led Grandpa around by his little finger. Myra almost had to stop him from taking them away and keeping them with him. Myra sometimes thought John would give up the mill if he could, so he could play with those granddaughters. Todd, their second oldest son, was married to Sharon Walsh, Bill and Martha's oldest daughter, who was expecting her first child.

Jessie noticed two newer houses built a ways down the creek from the mill and assumed they were white families since John had added four new families that lived in the quarters. They cut and hauled logs with the mules. As they rode closer, he noticed that John was not running the saw, rather one of the new men. Seeing Frank helping load a wagon with the cut lumber, they rode around the saw until Frank saw him and came to meet them.

"Howdy, Mister Tucker. Pa's gone right now; he's west of here checking out a large forest of pine. You can wait at the house if you want to," he said, looking at Leo. He thought the man looked a lot like Mister Tucker with that red hair.

"Frank, this is Leo McCracken. You will be seeing a lot of him and his family in the future. They are going to build homes and plant orange trees in the valley southeast of here." Jessie waited until Frank shook hands with Leo before he said, "We're going to ride and maybe find your pa. I've got a good idea what area he's looking at. I believe it's on the way to Brooksville."

"Yes sir," Frank said, "I'm pretty sure that's where he went."

It was an hour before Jessie and Leo entered the forest of huge pine and another twenty minutes before they saw John. He was trying to reach his arms around one of the trees. They were immense, and as long as his arms were, he couldn't reach all the way around the trunk.

Twenty feet away Jessie called out, "Does Myra know you sneak off and hug trees?" Jessie laughed when John jumped back, startled.

"You could get shot sneaking up on a man like that."

"You were too busy hugging trees to hear anybody coming," Jessie joked.

"Get down off that horse and tell me why you're out here hunting me," John said, walking toward the stranger sitting on his horse next to Jessie's. He held out his huge paw. "I'm John Campbell. I run a mill back a ways."

"I'm Leo McCracken. I met your son back at the mill."

"Leo is the reason we came to find you," Jessie said, slipping his leg over the saddle and stepping to the ground. Leo did the same.

"Well, tell me about it. I'm not surprised by anything you do anymore," John said and smiled. "Walk with me while you tell me what you have in mind. This is where I will timber this winter when the sap drops." For the next hour, he listened to Jessie and Leo and measured in his mind how much lumber he could cut from each tree.

Jessie saw Belle and Bonnie sitting arm in arm on the bench Franklin had built under one of the large live oaks by the water's edge. As he and Leo rode to the commissary, they saw the wagon had been loaded with supplies, and the mules were feeding on the lush grass by the lake. Riding on by the loaded wagon, they reached the barn where Franklin and Jeremy took their horses.

"Send Jeremy for the mules and get them hooked to the wagon," he said to Franklin.

"Yas sir, Mister Tucker." Franklin turned and saw Jeremy going out the door heading for the lake.

Belle stood in the yard holding onto Jessie's arm until their new friends reached the top of the valley and disappeared. Turning to Jessie, she asked, "Can't they plant the oranges closer to the lake?"

Jessie looked down and saw the sadness replacing the smile he saw only a few minutes ago on Belle's face. "They picked the place, not me," Jessie responded.

"I know," Belle said sadly, "but they are almost two hours away, and I don't want to lose her again."

Looking at that sad face, Jessie said, "Anytime you want to go for a visit, me or one of the boys will take you. That's the best I can do."

"I know," she said as she turned them toward the house, looking back toward the ridge once more.

Sara Mae stood on the porch watching as Franklin and Jeremy finished checking the ropes and then stepped back to study their work. Smiling, Franklin started toward the house, and as he put his arm around Jeremy's shoulders, her heart jumped in her chest. She thought about the first time she saw Franklin with his arm around the young boy's shoulder, bringing him home.

Franklin had gone to the barn to feed the animals and start his day. That day, he was working on a dining table for Ed and his new wife. Lighting a lantern, he started to the back of the barn when he saw movement in a stall. Holding the lantern above his head so he could see better, he was taken aback when he saw a young black boy curled up in the corner. "What are you doing in there, boy?" He asked. "Come over here where I can see you."

The boy was shaking as he slowly limped forward. Franklin's heart broke when he saw the clubfoot as the boy came across the stall into the light.

Franklin's voice was gentler as he asked, "Son do you know where you at? You suppose to be sleeping at home in the quarters with your family." Franklin barely understood him as he lowered his head and mumbled.

"I'se don't want to live there anymore, I'se want to live here."

"Why don't you want to live at your house anymore?"

"The bigger boys makes fun of me, cause I'se can't keep up with them with my foot twisted and all. Sometimes they push me just to see me fall down."

"What about your ma and pa?"

"I don't have no pa. Ma was bred by the master. He blamed Ma for my bad foot and wouldn't have no more babies by her. Ma said he was going to have me put down, but she convinced him to let her keep me. He told her she better finds something for me to do when I'se got bigger, cause he weren't feeding no worthless nigger."

"Well, your ma will want to know where you are."

"No sir, she done got her a man, and they don't want me around anymore either."

"How old are you, son?"

"I'se don't rightly know; nobody's ever told me."

"Well, you can't be more than twelve or thirteen. You said your ma had to teach you something you could do to stay. What did she teach you?"

"When I gots big enough to work for my keep, Ma took me to the wood shop and talked the shop boss to teach woodworking, or the master was going to do away with me."

"Did you learn anything?"

"Yas sir, I'se the best wood worker on the plantation. They says I'se a natural, whatever that means."

"It means you are good."

"Yas sir, I'se knows that," he said and grinned.

"I could use some help here the way this family is growing. I can't keep up with tables and chairs, but first, you can't live out here in the barn. Mister Tucker wouldn't allow it, and we will have to talk to Sara Mae about you staying with us." Franklin's heart started to beat faster as he watched the young boy begin to stand up straight and saw hope come into his eyes.

"I's work hard, Mister Franklin. You won't never regret it, you got my word. I's work all day every day; I's won't be no bother, promise."

"Well, come out of there and let's go see Sara Mae. She'll have breakfast ready, and we can talk to her."

It was breaking daylight as Sara Mae looked through the kitchen window and saw Franklin leave the barn with a young boy limping along by his side. She wondered, what in the world? Tears came to her eyes when she saw Franklin looking at the boy's clubfoot as he tried to keep up. Slowing down, he put his arm around the boy's shoulder. Hurriedly, she turned and took another plate from the shelf and placed it on the table. Then she tried to look busy when she heard the two of them walk across the porch. She attempted to look surprised when they walked through the door but saw Franklin smile at her when he noticed the extra plate on the table.

"We have company," he said. "I found a surprise in the barn this morning, and I'm not sure I can get rid of him. He looks like he could use some good food."

"Well, are you going to introduce him to me?" she asked, walking toward the young boy, who was standing by the stove, looking confused. "I am Sara Mae," she said and waited.

"Yes, Mam. Everybody knows who you are; you the one who feeds Mister Tucker and the Indians when they take the cows to market for money, so's we can be here. I'se come to help Mister Franklin in the wood shop," he added.

"You have?"

"Yes, Ma'am, and I can sleep in the barn and won't be no bother to nobody."

"Well, first I think we should have some breakfast and talk about this and see what Franklin wants to do."

Sara Mae and Franklin watched the boy eat without hardly taking a breath. Looking at Franklin not able to take his eyes off the boy, she knew there would be an extra plate at their table from now on.

"I could sure use the help," Franklin spoke up. "I'm so busy now that I'm way behind and if..." He looked at the boy trying to remember his name.

"Jeremy," the kid spoke up.

"Well, I'm glad he has a name," Sara Mae said, smiling.

"If Jeremy can do what he says, he could sure be a big help, and when you are gone on the cattle drives, he would be company," he added as if she needed convincing.

"After we eat, I'll go to the quarters and talk to your ma, and we will go from there."

"I don't think she wants him anymore," Franklin said.

"I'll go see," Sara Mae said as she left the table to get more grits and bacon for the boy. He looked like he hadn't eaten for weeks. Whoever this boy is, she thought, he has already made a change in my husband. She had never seen him this worked up about anything since the fall crippled him.

It was still early as Sara Mae walked around the lake and followed the wagon tracks toward the church. She was going to need Reverend Ellis' help in this matter. She found him and Mrs. Ellis behind the church next to their house, hoeing in their small garden and saw the concern on their faces when they recognized her. Reverend Ellis handed the hoe to his wife and started forward, "Good morning, Sara Mae."

"Good morning, Reverend, could I have a minute of your time?"

"Of course. Come on in the church; it's still cool in there." They were both silent as they entered the church and sat on the front row seat.

"Tell me, Sara Mae, is there something wrong with Franklin?"

"No, Reverend." She spent the next half hour explaining about Franklin and the boy.

"Well, what do you need from me?"

"Franklin and myself," she added, "wants to raise the boy as our own, but it has to be right with his ma."

The reverend took a few seconds to think on this, then taking her hand, he spoke softly, "I know the situation with the crippled boy and how he is teased and picked on because of his weakness. I also know his ma's new man don't want him, but I also know she has always protected him as best she could. If you can wait a while, I will send for his ma, and we'll see if we can work this out."

"I'll wait as long as I needs, this is one of the most important things in our lives right now," Sara Mae replied. She watched the reverend go to the back door and call his wife to him.

"I need you to go get Miss Lavern and bring her to the church."

Sara Mae walked slowly back around the lake, still shaken from the emotion. Her eyes were still puffy from the tears she and Lavern had shed as they talked and hugged. Lavern explained that she could only do so much to protect him, and Sara Mae promised she and Franklin would not let anyone ever pick on or harm him again.

"He will always be yours, and we will always make sure he knows that. We just wants to share him for a while before he becomes a man."

The reverend prayed over them as they knelt together at the altar.

Sara Mae got to the wagons and reaching Dolly first, she stroked the side of her face. "Are you ready for a trip, you should be able to get there on your own by now." She smiled and walked around to the other side. Stroking Preachers nose, she said, "You behave yourself now and just help Molly get us all there safely.

Jeremy was the first to hug her goodbye, then Franklin stepped forward to hug her. He whispered in her ear making her smile. "Don't ya'll take too long to drive them ole cows to market."

She smiled when she felt his hand slip down her back and give a pat on her behind.

Justin fell back to help Sara Mae bring her wagon across what they called Cow Creek, a spring-fed creek no more than ten feet wide, winding its way through a pine forest dotted throughout with cabbage palms. It then flowed for more than a mile across grassland, finally working its way to the Withlacoochee River. No one was sure who was first to call it Cow Creek, but it made sense because you could always find cows grazing along its rich grass edge.

The Crackers Tuckertown

Justin started toward the herd, a half mile away by now, but watching the black clouds rolling across the sky a couple of miles away, he felt a knot start in the pit of his stomach. He knew from the past that these thunderstorms were unpredictable, and this one was moving fast. He saw the lightning bolt strike the ground and send streaks of fire in every direction, starting a flame in the already dried knee-high grass.

Everyone's fear became a reality. Grass fire! It took seconds for the twenty mile an hour winds to start spreading flames across the open flats. Uncoiling his whip Justin cracked it as loud as possible, to make Jessie and the others hear it above the bellowing cows. Seeing no response, he pulled his pistol and fired three shots in the air. Turning, he rode back to the wagon.

"Miss Sara Mae, you need to get this wagon back across the creek and keep going until this fire has passed." Justin saw the fear in her face as she sat and stared at the flames rushing across the land and coming her way.

"Miss Sara Mae," Justin yelled, "get the wagon moving now!" Reaching Preacher, he grabbed the halter and began to turn him and Dolly around, then felt the animals flinch as the reins came down across both horses' rumps. Sara Mae took control, yelling at Justin, "I gots them Mister Justin; you go help the others," as she slapped the reins across their rumps again.

All the men turned and looked back when they heard the three pistol shots, then they saw the dark grey smoke from the fire and realized it was heading their way. Jessie kicked the horse in the ribs, riding toward the front of the herd, yelling as loud as possible over the noise of the cows. "Turn them back to Cow Creek! Get them to the creek!" Jessie watched Red Sun and the others cracking their whips turning the herd.

Heading back, he reached the end of the cows and saw Snake Handler riding his horse in circles confused. Jessie yelled, "Get out of the cow's way before they run over you."

Confused, Snake Handler headed toward Jessie, kicking his Marsh Tackie in the ribs, urging him on. By the time he reached Jessie, the cows in the rear were running past them, Jessie and Snake Handler raced to reach the outside of the now stampeding cattle.

Jessie and Snake Handler were now at the front of the herd and saw Justin turn and head toward Sara Mae, coming along side Preacher and taking hold of the bridle, starting the wagon west, away from the charging herd. The wagon crossed the shallow creek, and Jessie lost sight of them as the hot smoke ahead of the fire covered the horses and wagon.

Red Sun never saw the creek until his horse plunged into the water, splashing him as he tried not to breathe the heavy smoke. Then he saw a sliver of light up ahead and felt his breath start to come easier, the cattle still running wildly ahead of him.

Justin, Warrior Spirit, and Silent Stalker raced to help Jessie, Snake Handler, and Spirit Snake who had raced the little Marsh Tackie to catch them. The men moving out front were slowing the cattle down.

Red Sun reached good air and pulled his horse to a stop, turning to see if the racing flames were going to jump the creek. With relief, he watched the fire burn past, destroying everything in its path.

An hour later, the thousand head of cattle had settled down and spread along the creek quietly feeding as if nothing had happened. Jessie sent Snake Handler to help Sara Mae bring the wagon and gather firewood while the others rode up and down the creek to keep the cows from wandering off.

They were still a week away from Tampa, giving the cattle time to feed on the alligator weed and ferns in the vast cypress hammock. Big Cypress rode up alongside Jessie and pointed behind him. Turning his horse in the direction Big Cypress was pointing, Jessie saw a small herd of maybe a hundred head of scrub cows, a half mile away, being pushed hard.

Justin rode up next to Jessie and asked, "Why would anyone be pushing cows that hard unless they wanted to get rid of them as fast as possible?"

"Good question," Jessie said when he saw three men turn the fast-moving cows away from the feeding herd ahead of them.

Red Sun joined them and said, "Those cows would need water by now. Why would they turn them away before they could drink?"

"I don't know," Jessie said, "but I have a sneaking suspicion." Turning to Justin, he asked, "Could you go and send Silent Stalker to me?" Jessie and Red Sun waited, watching the herd of scrub cows as the three men kept them moving away. Silent Stalker and Spirit Snake rode alongside of Jessie and stopped.

"I want you to backtrack that herd there," Jessie said, pointing to the small group of cows. "See if you can find where they started."

"How far back do you want me to track them?" Silent Stalker asked.

"The way they are pushing them, they could not have kept that pace long. I don't think you will have to go that far back," Jessie replied.

"Unless you need me here, I will go with Silent Stalker," Spirit Snake spoke up.

Everyone was sitting around the fire enjoying a cup of coffee after eating their fill of Sara Mae's beef stew when Silent Stalker and Spirit Snake rode in. Jessie, Red Sun and Justin met them as they dismounted.

"There are two dead men back where three men left with the cows," Silent Stalker said.

"They were shot several times," Spirit Snake added, a grim look on his face.

"Damn!" Jessie said.

They all saw the scar across his forehead turn red. Jessie turned to Red Sun.

"I can't ask you or your braves to get involved in this bad thing that's going to happen. Justin and I are going after these men and kill them," he said with anger building. "Those men that were killed had family somewhere, waiting on husband and father to bring back food, supplies, and money from the small herd. God only knows how long it took them to round those cows up."

"The braves have waited and watched too many times while you put yourself and the others in danger to protect all of us," Red Sun spoke. "This time, I will lead the braves myself."

The men had been traveling for two hours. It wasn't hard to follow the tracks of a hundred cows in the light of the new moon. They saw a rider coming toward them, brought the horses to a walk, and waited for Silent Stalker to reach them.

"There are three of them a mile back, and they are all sleeping; they don't care if a few cows wander off."

Red Sun rode on one side of Jessie and Justin on the other. They saw Silent Stalker raise his hand when they got within a hundred yards of the sleeping men. Jessie and the braves dismounted, tied the horses to tree limbs, and started forward. He felt Red Sun take him by the arm and stop him. Stepping in front of him, Red Sun motioned the other braves forward, then released Jessie's arm and began leading the braves silently forward until they reached the sleeping men. He turned to Jessie and waited.

"Alright, get up with your hands in the air!" Jessie yelled at the sleeping men.

Ron Foster was the first one to sit up grabbing at his rifle and the first one shot through the chest with three bullets. A hail of bullets killed the other two before they had a good grip on their weapons.

Jessie and Justin never fired their rifles. Red Sun turned to Jessie and asked, "What do you want to do with the dead men?"

"Leave them where they lay," Jessie responded. "Leave the cows be; maybe someone else who needs them will find them. Let's get back to the herd. Snake Handler and Sara Mae will be worried."

The sound of whips cracking in the distance always made Tom Marshal smile, and by now he knew who was coming by the sounds made by the crackers from different ranches. The sounds he heard now made him rise out of his chair to stand on his balcony, to watch the Indians with their dogs turn the cows into the pens. He had never seen a group work so smoothly together. He smiled even brighter as Jessie and Justin climbed the stairs to his office.

Six

COMING OF AGE

Three years ago, on their fourteenth birthday, Paw Paw took his grandsons to the barn and handed each of them a pistol. Both boys stood and stared in awe at what they had been given.

"There is no firing pin. You won't get that until that gun becomes part of you. You will carry that with you every waking minute, and when you are not carrying something else in your hand, I want to see that pistol in it. You will carry it in each hand until you don't realize which hand it's in. Fire it, throw it in the air and catch it until you can spin it and catch it by the grip—it is to become part of you. You will take it apart once a week at least, or when it needs cleaning. Understood?"

"Yes Sir!" they both answered.

It had been a year, or close to it, they guessed, when they were called to the barn again to find Paw Paw sitting on the horseshoeing stool. Holding out his hand, he said, "Give me your guns, boys."

"Did we do something wrong, Paw Paw? We are doing what you said," Hawk asked, confused.

"Watch this," Jake said and flipped the gun in the air, spinning it, and when it started down, he caught it by the grip. He then started flipping it from one hand to the other, faster than Jessie could keep up with.

"Settle down, boys," he said grinning. "I'm not here to take your guns. I am satisfied with the way you have been responsible and cared for them." Holding out his hand to Jake, he took his gun and began breaking it down. They both looked at one another and smiled as they watch their Paw Paw take a firing pin, place it in the pistol, reassemble it and hand it back. He repeated the sequence with Hawk's.

"What about some bullets?" Hawk asked.

"Don't get ahead of yourselves now; I will take you to the lake and let you shoot."

"Now?" asked Jake, becoming excited about being able to shoot the gun after what seemed like years, pretending to shoot at everything that moved.

Red Sun, Spirit Snake, Big Cypress, and the other braves started for the lake when they saw Jessie walking toward there with the boys. They were flipping their pistols back and forth from hand to hand then flipping them to each other with both hands.

When they reached the lake, he told the boys to find some pine cones and pile them by the shore. Red Sun and the others walked up to watch as the boys finished dumping cones from their folded-up shirts. Jessie opened a box of 44 cal. shells, then handed the boys six each, reminding them about pointing a loaded gun. Picking up one of the pine cones, Jessie threw it no more than twenty feet into the lake. He motioned Jake to him as the others stood back.

"Remember how I taught you about aiming. Now see if you can hit that cone." Then he took a step back.

Jake went from excited to absolute doubt as he pointed the barrel and tried to aim. His hands began to shake, and then he felt hands grip his arms from behind.

"Don't think about it," he heard Paw Paws voice, "just aim down the sight as I showed you and squeeze the trigger." Boom! The gun jumped in his hand as the bullet hit the water a foot behind the cone. "Not bad," Jessie smiled at the shocked look on Jake's face. "Do it again, and this time be a little slower with your aim and anticipate the kick of the gun." On the fifth try, the cone exploded in pieces, and he heard the shouts behind him. He fired once more and came close.

"I got it Paw Paw! I want to shoot some more."

"We will, but let Hawk take his turn. Now empty your gun and save the casings."

Hawk stepped forward as Jake stood with the other men and Jessie handed him the six bullets. He looked at Red Sun, who was nodding at him, then stepped back as Red Sun walked next to his grandson and placed his arm around his shoulders. As Red Sun watched him load the cartridges in the pistol, Hawk thought he knew the gun so well until he saw what happened when Jake fired his. Red Sun saw the doubt in Hawk's face as he hesitated to aim the gun.

"Use both hands and take your time like you were taught." Hawk suddenly raised the pistol, fired and stepped back, shocked as the bullet missed the cone by three feet.

"I can show you how," Jake laughed.

"You just shut up," Hawk said angerly. He turned, raised the pistol and began firing one shot after another. On the last shot, the cone exploded.

On the next cattle drive, Justin visited the hardware store where he bought their saddles, scabbards, and whips. Francis Shere was always glad to see Justin and young Ed who came with him sometimes. They were excellent customers that spent a lot of money supplying what he guessed was for a growing ranch.

"What can I do for you?" Francis asked with a smile when he saw Justin walk in. After he had given Francis the list Race always sent, he had another request. Francis finished telling his hired help to fill what they had on the list and get Jefferson to help load it on the wagon. "Now, Mister Justin, what is it you need?"

"Mr. Francis, you are the best man with a piece of leather I know. I've got a special request." Justin pulled a piece of paper from his pocket and laid it on the desk, then smoothed the folds out until you could see what he had drawn.

"That looks like a cartridge belt and holster," Francis said, looking at it closely. "Not typical," he stated, looking questionably at Justin.

"Yes, I know. I need two; can you make them?"

"I can, but it would be easier if I had a gun to make the pattern."

Justin unsnapped his holster, removed the pistol, emptied the chambers, then handed it to Francis. "I'll pick them up in a couple of weeks when I am back this way."

"That will be plenty of time, I'll start on them right away."

"Thanks, Mr. Francis."

"No, thank you and your business," he said and grinned.

It had been two years now since Paw Paw had taken them to the lake and given the boys their first bullets. Hawk and Jake rode their

Marsh Tackies into the edge of the pine forest. They found a spot of grass to hobble the horses and dismounted. Removing their saddlebags and taking the rifles from their scabbards, they walked back to the outside edge of the pines.

"This looks like a good place," Jake said. They set their saddlebags on the ground, and he removed a box of cartridges. Leaning their rifles against a tree while they gathered a pile of pine cones, Jake said, "I will throw for you first." He picked up a couple of pine cones.

Hawk held the rifle to his shoulder and said, "Throw it!"

Twenty feet in the air, the cone exploded. Jake kept throwing pine cones until Hawk's rifle was empty, and not one pine cone rose higher than twenty feet before it exploded. Grinning, Hawk leaned his rifle against a tree, picked up a cone in each hand, laughing and said, "Let's see you do better than that. He turned and threw a cone as hard as he could. He laughed again when the cone exploded fifteen feet in the air.

"Is that what you mean?" Jake laughed.

"Let's see you do that every time, Jake," Hawk said and threw another one.

After a half a box of shells, they sat their rifles against a tree and pulled their pistols from their holsters that Justin had brought them.

Justin explained why the holsters were made that way. "It is made to wear on your left side with the gun butt pointed forward. It is angled, so it is easier to reach, and you pull it with your right hand. The small strap and buckle are for your knife sheath still on your right side as you wear it now.

They both took a pine cone and stepping off twenty paces, found the closest tree, and each placed their cone in the fork of a branch, then walked back and stood three feet apart.

"You say when," Jake told Hawk.

"Now!" Both cones exploded at the same time. "I hit mine first!" Hawk laughed.

"You can't see very good, I hit mine first," Jake protested.

"Ok, let's do more than one shot," Hawk challenged. They walked to where they had placed the cones before, but this time they each set six cones a foot apart.

Standing three feet apart, they each took a deep breath and let it out slowly.

"Now!" Jake yelled, and twelve cones exploded, and you could not tell the difference when the last two shattered.

Jessie was in the barn talking with Franklin and Jeremy when he heard the whooping and yelling and knew down inside who was causing the ruckus. Standing in the barn opening, it took a few seconds to figure out what was going on, then he saw them and started for the house to get his gun. He saw Spirit Snake and Red Sun with their rifles running for the lake. Belle was standing on the porch trying to see what all the yelling was about, but her vision wasn't the same as it used to be.

"What's going on Jessie?"

"Guess," Jessie responded.

Belle said, "Whatever it is, I bet it would be a good guess if I said it had something to do with Jake and Hawk."

"You would be right," Jessie said as he reached and got his rifle from the gun rack, then started for the lake. He saw Ed and most of the people from the quarters heading for the lake, even the men plowing had laid their plows sideways and were coming to see what all the ruckus was about. Ed just shook his head smiling at Spirit Snake as they met, heading for the crowd around the lake shore.

Jessie stood with Justin and the others watching, their hearts beating hard as the two boys raced each other across the lake. He found out later that it had all started with a dare, who could beat the other across the lake. Suddenly four rifles came up and fired together. Jessie watched as an eight-foot gator rolled twice and sank thirty feet behind the two boys.

The boys had no idea what the gunfire was all about as Hawk grabbed Jake's shoulder pulling him back getting a small jump on him, then Jake grabbed his leg and pulled him back and under, laughing. Coming up spitting water, Hawk swam with everything he had to catch Jake. Jake saw him coming and sped up, giving it everything he had left.

They were getting tired now as they heard the shouting, some calling one name the others calling the other. Hawk rolled over on his back when he saw Jake do it, relaxing as they slowly did backstrokes until Hawk turned over and gave one last push with everything he had left to reach the shore first. Just as he thought he was going to be first, he felt Jake grab a foot again and pull, but this time he fought against going under, kicked free and got his momentum back. They swam head to head, as people waded out into the lake cheering them on.

They were both grinning as Ed and Spirit Snake reached them, taking them by the arm and standing them up. "Are you trying to scare your mother to death?" Ed asked Jake, trying to sound serious, knowing his mother was watching to see what his father was going to do about this foolish act.

"So, you two think you are braves and can take foolish chances now?" Spirit Snake said to his son. "You could have been eaten by a gator."

"Is that what the shooting was about? How close did it get? Did I win?" Hawk asked.

"Neither one of you won, but I am proud of your courage if not your foolishness."

"Now you two go and apologize to your mothers," Ed said, trying again to be serious but kept seeing the image of him and Spirit Snake hog hunting with a bow. As the two future young braves went to take their scolding from their mothers, Ed and Spirit Snake looked at each other knowingly as they started toward Red Sun. Two Worlds had made his way to the lake to watch the future of his tribe earn the right to be thought of as braves. The smiles on Big Cypress and the other brave's faces filled him with pride and hope for the future of his people.

The sun was climbing the trees bringing the day with it, and Jake and Hawk were excited, barely containing their enthusiasm, impatient for their fathers to get started on the trip. They had not been told where they were going, but the young braves knew from their fathers' seriousness when they were told that they were being taken on an important trip. When they asked where, their fathers told them they would have to wait and see.

"Are you ready?" Ed asked, smiling as he and Spirit Snake rode up next to the boys. Both boys were awed as they stared at their fathers, dressed in leather leggings and deer hide vests, that had been decorated by their wives. Their headbands had several feathers, which moved in the light breeze.

"Yes sir," Jake answered.

"Won't you tell us where we are going?" Hawk asked.

"Well, then it wouldn't be a surprise now, would it? Ed grinned and rode ahead to catch-up with Spirit Snake.

By the end of the day, neither Jake nor Hawk had ever been this far from the ranch, and their excitement mounted as they passed through the valley where more than a thousand head of

Andalusian cattle were feeding. They saw a few breeding bulls, but most were cows with calves, and they were all feeding on knee-high wiregrass, getting fat and ready for market.

Spirit Snake and Ed laughed out loud as they watched the two boys trying to herd three cows that had wandered away from the herd and get them to go where they wanted. After all three had gone in different directions, they lost interest. Spotting a small herd of does, they decided to see if they could catch one. Ed and Spirit Snake just looked at one another and shook their heads still laughing.

The sun was making its final descent when Ed recognized the small creek where they had made camp on the cattle drives to Tampa, and it made his heart race as he thought about where they were going the next day.

"Let's make camp here," he suggested and saw Spirit Snake smile with understanding. "Before you young braves get off your horses, see that tree line about a half mile away? If you slip in there real quiet, you can get a young turkey coming in to roost for the night. We will roast it while we are sitting by the fire so we can eat it tomorrow."

Spirit Snake and Ed had the campfire going and were leaning back on their saddles on the ground, resting after the long day's ride, and blowing on cups of coffee. They saw the boys coming across the open field with a turkey hanging from Hawk's saddle. Between breaths to cool his coffee, Spirit Snake asked, "Do you think they are ready for where we are taking them?"

"They just had their seventeenth birthday a couple of months ago, and it was Two Worlds' suggestion," Ed answered.

"I know, but they seem so young."

"They are just full of life; you should know how that feels," Ed said and laughed, thinking of all the things he and Spirit Snake had gotten themselves into.

"Were we really that young and foolish?" Spirit Snake asked.

"Yes!" Ed replied, "maybe more so."

The two boys were wading in the creek as the sun pushed the moon out of sight, eating the legs they had pulled off the turkey, having breakfast while their fathers finished coffee.

"Do you know where we are going?" Hawk asked Jake, in a solemn voice.

"No, but the way they act, it must be important."

"Yes, I feel it too, but I don't think it is about hunting for turkeys."

"No," Jake responded in a more serious tone, shaking his head. "I don't think it's about turkeys."

The young braves were in deep thought when they reached camp as their fathers finished saddling their horses. Both men noticed the difference in the boys as they mounted their horses and started out.

Ed felt anxious as they rode into the same woods he had entered a lifetime ago when he met the panther at the springs. That day lead to this trip with his son today.

They stopped at the spring and ate some food. Ed kept expecting the panther to appear as he had before. He was a little disappointed when they were on their way, and there was no sign of Two Worlds' companion. Ed had a good idea where the panther would be. Looking back at Jake in anticipation, he knew his son would never be the same.

They traveled another two hours, when Ed and Spirit Snake stopped, dismounted their horses, and tied the bridles to a tree limb. Jake and Hawk felt confused as they did the same and walked to where their fathers stood. Hawk and Jake froze, feeling fear and excitement as they stared into the giant hole in the earth.

"What is this place?" Hawk asked first.

"I don't understand." Jakes fear showed as he asked, "Are we going down there? I don't see a way!"

Ed understood their fear, all too well. He had the same fear the first time he followed the panther here.

"Be careful and follow closely," Spirit Snake told the frightened boys as he started down the almost invisible path. Ed followed behind the boys, watching their excitement as the squirrels chattered overhead, and blue jays screamed, letting everyone know they were there. Small rabbits were sitting still, watching unafraid as the boys and men passed by.

Reaching the bottom, Spirit Snake walked to the small spring. He knelt on one knee, reached and scooped a hand full of water and quickly drank it. Turning to the boys, he motioned to them to come drink from the spring. The boys moved forward. Ed saw them reach and put their palms together as they had often seen their fathers do when something good happened, and they too knelt to drink from the spring.

Ed led the way from the spring to the large oak branch and began working his way through. Spirit Snake followed the boys, urging them forward as their fear made them hesitate. Ed disappeared, then pulled back a smaller branch and waited as Jake and Hawk stepped through into the opening. They stopped, paralyzed, staring at Two Worlds and the huge panther lying by his side. Spirit Snake pushed the two forward, and they all followed the old man and companion when he rose and entered the vast, dimly lit cavern.

Waiting for their eyes to adjust to the soft glow from the small flames of the fire, they began to see openings around the cavern walls. For the next half hour, Two Worlds sat by the fire, feeding it small sticks as Ed and Spirit Snake took the boys from opening to opening, explaining what they were seeing. Leaving the last small cave, they brought them to the fire and had them sit across from the old man. Ed and Spirit Snake stood behind their sons.

Two Worlds sat quietly puffing on his long stem pipe watching the two boys change in front of him. The cocky smile disappeared, they sat up straighter, and their eyes became more focused on him.

Two Worlds put his pipe aside and looking both young braves in the eyes, he spoke. "There comes a time in a young brave's life when he puts aside foolish things and begins earning the right to become a brave, respected by his people as a provider and protector of their future. Rarely have I seen two spirits connected as one like the two of you. The future of our people will one day depend on the two of you as it has with your fathers."

"As you are joined by spirit, you will also be joined by the blood that flows between you," Two Worlds said. He rose and stood in one swift motion and waited as the boys scrambled to their feet, surprised by the old man's quickness.

Their hearts beat faster as they watched the old medicine man pull his knife from its sheath. He reached across the small flames and waited for Hawk to give him his hand. Somewhere inside, Hawk knew when he gave his hand, the world as he knew it was going to be different. Without hesitation, he offered his hand and future. Two Worlds took his wrist and ran the blade across his palm. Spirit Snake moved next to Hawk and held his son's hand still as Two Worlds released his wrist. Two Worlds took Jakes extended arm and cut a thin line across his palm. Ed held his son's arm as the knife was slipped back in the sheath, and Two Worlds took both hands bringing them together. Calling to his ancestors, he began a chant that ended when he released their hands. Two Worlds turned and with his panther companion, headed for the entrance.

It was another half hour before the fathers finished telling their sons what was expected of them. They were no longer boys, but braves who would earn their place in the circle of warriors. Before starting back, the fathers removed the decorated headbands the boys' mothers had made for this occasion. Each father stepped around the new brave and slipped the headband over his head. Then they removed a feather of the great eagle from their own headbands and added them to their sons' headbands with a thin leather strip.

The four braves made their way through the opening and walked into the light. Kneeling at the small spring, Hawk and Jake placed their hands in the cool water until there was no more blood flowing from their cuts. As they started up the slope, each kept touching their feathers. These headbands would become the most sacred things in their lives.

The village was filled with excitement as they watched the men on horses starting down the slope riding side by side as braves do. When the new braves rode closer, the people of the village saw the feathers hanging from their headbands. The women began trilling with their tongues, and the braves were raising their fists into the air and shouting war cries. When they arrived at the village, the young braves were humbled and awed. They saw Two Worlds sitting on his fur covered backrest under the oak where he always sat. They both dismounted to hugs and pats on the back, then everyone became quiet and stood to watch as the young braves turned and walked to where the medicine man waited. Two Worlds was smiling and puffing on his long stem pipe. Kneeling, they bowed their heads, deferring their lives to him. Together as one, they said, "Thank you, Great Grandfather."

Seven

THE RECKONING

Hawk and Jake were getting their chance to prove themselves as young braves. Jessie approached Justin and said, "I need you to take Hawk and Jake to cut out a hundred head of cows without calves and push them to Fort Dade."

"We can do that—can't we boys?" Justin chuckled. "You want to be cow hunters, now is your chance."

Jessie rode next to the nervous young braves and stopped his horse. "Follow Justin's advice, and you will be alright. Justin will have his two dogs, so let them do their work, and be easy with those whips; there is a time to use the whip and a time to keep it on your saddle. This is your first trip, so be careful and always remember, if something happens out there, like lightning or any of a dozen things that can make them spook and stampede, you get out of the way and don't take chances!"

"Yes, Paw Paw," they answered together.

"Well, let's get started." Justin headed for the herd, the two young braves riding to catch up with big grins of anticipation on their faces. Two hours later, Justin saw the frustration on their faces from chasing one cow after another, cracking their whips over their heads, and losing them in the scattering herd.

Red Sun joined Jessie just inside the tree line, out of sight, watching the show below. "They would make great warriors, but I don't know about being cow hunters," Red Sun laughed. "Justin has his hands full trying to teach those two, but if anyone can, he will. I think we should give Justin a hand, or they may never cut out enough cows to take to Fort Dade," Red Sun added as he started toward the herd.

Jessie followed thinking, Poor Justin… I probably shouldn't have turned those two loose on him.

It was getting dark when they pushed the cattle going to Fort Dade into the next valley to feed on the lush grass around the ten-acre lake. Jake and Hawk rode proudly as they stayed alongside the others. Between the three experienced men, they had finally settled the boys down and taught them how to let the horses and dogs work the cows. Jessie and Red Sun headed back to the ranch, knowing that Justin and the boys would be able to handle the delivery of the cows.

By the time they reached the fort on the third morning, the young braves had become quite good at keeping the herd together and moving. Justin saw the sergeant send two men to open the gate to the holding pen. Jake and Hawk looked at Justin and he nodded. Justin let the boys along with the two dogs turn the cows into the gates while he watched.

When the young braves were done, they pulled up next to Justin, and Jake asked, "What's next? Can we go to the store? Paw Paw gave us a ten-dollar gold piece to split so we can buy us something, and he said, 'Find a purty gift for your mothers.'"

"Sure but be careful. I'll meet you when I get settled with the major." Justin walked in and was surprised to find a Major Stoddard in command. As they settled their affairs, Justin asked the major how long he had been at Fort Dade.

"Not soon enough. Hell, the last commander didn't do his job."

Justin thought this was odd but didn't say anything and let the major continue.

"I'm here to fix what he didn't do! There should be no Indians in this territory whatsoever. He did a shoddy job and should have rounded them up like cattle. They're no better than the cattle and worth less. I'm gonna straighten this territory out and make it into a civilized place. Hell, the soldiers don't even salute my lieutenant when he walks by."

The hairs on the back of Justin's neck stood up, and he felt the pit of his stomach drop through the floor. Realizing that there was no point trying to talk to this man, he said thank you and got up and left. He knew he had to find the boys as quickly as possible.

It was a half mile to the Dade settlement, which had more than doubled in the last five years. It wasn't always peaceful since two saloons had opened up, and they drew some pretty shady characters traveling south.

The two young braves felt like they had been given their freedom as they raced their Marsh Tackies down the dusty street until they saw the store and came to a sliding halt. They jumped off and tied their reins to the railing, pushing each other trying to reach the door first. As they raced inside, the owner yelled out, "Calm down, boys or get out, before you tear up my store."

"Sorry, sir," they said together, then Hawk pulled out the ten-dollar gold piece. "We came here to spend this," he said, waving the gold piece.

"Well, it will cost you more than that if you start breaking things. Now, what can I get for you boys?"

"We are not boys, we are braves," Jake stood straight, correcting him.

Noticing for the first time the gun belts they wore, he realized he had missed something when they came pushing and shoving their way through the door, like rowdy boys.

"What can I get you braves?" he corrected himself, looking at the gold piece Hawk was still holding in his fingers.

"Where is your candy?" Jake asked first.

"On the counter, but I don't think even braves can eat that much candy," he chuckled, relaxing some now. Walking behind the counter, he showed them the different jars.

They both had a mouth full and a bag of hard candy as they wandered around the store. Looking at all the strange things, Jake spotted a set of drinking glasses and a pitcher with the same rose pattern. "I want them for my mother," Jake said to the owner. "Do I have enough money left?"

"You have enough for the glasses and a set of dishes to go with them if you want." He reached up to a higher shelf and slowly brought down a set of plates for eight people with the same rose pattern.

"I have enough money for all that?" Jake asked, surprised at his find.

"The whole set is five dollars, but you can take them home for the four and a half dollars you have left. I will wrap them in paper and put them in the box they came in, while your friend looks around."

Hawk spotted the stack of blankets. "This is what I want; they will be warm this winter." Then he saw the small boxes of colored beads of all sizes and became even more excited. "There are enough beads for all the mothers in the village."

Hawk and Jake were excited as they tied the boxes and blankets to the back of their saddles. They didn't see the three men dismounting their horses until they turned to go see what else they could find in town.

"Hey! What are you two young bucks doing off the reservation? There's not supposed to be Indians in this territory. We thought we had all you Indians pushed deep into the Everglades; now I find you two here and with guns. Who gave you those pistols? Get them off and hand them to me before I kick both of your butts and send you back wherever you came from. Nobody would care if I shot you both right here."

Jake stepped up next to Hawk, "Mister, you will have to shoot us because you're not taking our guns."

"Fine," he said, and as the other two men with him spread apart, both boys took a deep breath and let it out slowly.

"Hank, maybe we should just leave them be," one of the other men said. "Let the feds deal with them."

"I lost friends to these savages fighting in the swamps, and I'm not about to let these two grow up and kill more friends. Now if this bothers you, just start walking and don't turn back." Hank declared."

I'm not afraid."

"Then shut up." Turning to the braves, Hank said, "I won't ask again, give me those guns."

"No," they said together.

Hank never cleared his holster, and three men lay dead. The last man died with two holes in his chest.

"Hold it right there, you two!"

Slipping their guns back in their holsters, they turned slowly, looking at each other than at the four soldiers pointing rifles at them.

"Take those belts off real slow, or you're two dead Indians." The soldier turned to his men. "Corporal, take those gun belts."

"Lieutenant, don't you know who these boys belong to?" the corporal warned.

"I don't care who they are, tie their hands. They're going to the fort—they just killed three men."

"Lieutenant, we saw those men threaten to kill them."

"That's enough, Corporal. I don't want to hear another word from you; do as you're told."

Justin was halfway to the settlement riding hard when he saw the soldiers and recognized Jake and Hawk riding in the middle of them. He felt a knot start to grow in his stomach, then he saw them holding on to their saddles with their hands tied. Pulling up in the middle of the road he waited until they stopped.

"Whoever you are, clear the road," the lieutenant called out.

"What are you doing with those two boys," Justin demanded.

"They have been arrested for murdering three white men, and I am taking them to the fort. You have any more questions you can talk to the major after these two are locked up. Now clear the road before I lock you up with them."

Riding past the lieutenant, he stopped next to the boys. "What happened?"

Jake spoke first. "They said they were going to kill us because we are Indians and weren't supposed to be here."

"We're sorry, Uncle Justin, but we didn't start anything," Hawk spoke up.

"Just take it easy, I'll go talk to the major and straighten this out."

"You will have to wait until I have made my report first," the lieutenant said. "Now get out of the way," he added, kicking his horse in the ribs."

Justin sat on his horse watching the two boys looking back at him until they were out of sight. Then he followed the soldiers back to the fort. Waiting until the lieutenant came from the lock-up, he followed him to the major's office, stepping inside before he could close the door.

"I told you to wait until I'm finished!" the lieutenant said.

"I want to hear what happened," Justin said.

"You'll wait outside like the lieutenant said. He will let you know when I am ready to talk to you," the major snarled, pointing his finger at Justin.

It wasn't more than five minutes Justin had paced back and forth in front of the door when he saw the corporal motion to him and step back behind the building. Justin walked with caution to the edge of the building to find the corporal waiting and moved around the corner out of sight.

"Listen," the corporal whispered, "I tried to tell the lieutenant what happened. He saw it too. Those men were going to shoot both of those boys, except I've never seen anyone draw a pistol that fast, but those boys were defending themselves."

"Did you tell that to the lieutenant?"

Yes, but he came here with the major, and they think all Indians should be shot or ran out of the state. I would tell the major, but he's not going to want to hear anything different than what his lieutenant says."

Justin was pacing back and forth when the lieutenant opened the door. He didn't wait to be invited and walked to the major's desk. Justin started to explain there had been a mistake.

The major stood up behind his desk, his face red like he was going to explode.

"You were not there. In fact, you were in this very office collecting federal money while two of your Indians, you protect, killed three white men. They are going to be court-martialed, then put before a firing squad and shot! Do I make myself clear? When I take care of these two," he went on, "I'm coming to get that bunch of savages you keep on that ranch, and if you are with them, I will shoot you too! Now get out of my office! And the government will no longer buy cattle from the protector of savages!" he growled as Justin was leaving.

Justin had never felt so helpless before as he made his way to the lock-up where they were keeping the boys. Walking up to the guard, he said, "I need to speak to the boys for a minute."

"Not without the major's OK. Sorry," he said as he looked down at the ground. Sliding his eyes from under his cap, he said, "I can crack the door enough that you can yell to them. They can hear you from here. I know this ain't right, but that's the best I can do."

Justin moved to the door. "Jake! Hawk! Don't worry, your pa and I will straighten this out. Just stay calm—it might take a few days, but you will be alright. I'll be back with your pa."

"Hurry, Uncle Justin. I don't like this place," Jake called out.

"You will be alright," he yelled back. Walking back to get his horse in front of the major's office, he met the lieutenant coming out the door with a smirk on his face.

Justin stepped up in front of him, really close in his face. "If those boys are harmed in any way, there isn't an army big enough to keep you safe. You have no idea what you have caused, and you got my word you won't get away unscathed. I would kill you here and now, but that won't do the boys any good."

The smirk was gone from the lieutenant's face when Justin turned and mounted his horse. Looking down at the lieutenant, he said, "I'll be the one to pull the trigger that blows your head off."

It was dark when Justin reached Jessie's house and dismounted. Taking a few seconds to get control of his anger, he knocked on the door.

"Come in," he heard Belle call out. Taking a deep breath and letting it out slowly, he opened the door and saw Jessie sitting at the supper table. Justin nodded his head toward the door. Jessie rose slowly from the table with a hard ball in his stomach, seeing the control Justin was fighting to keep.

"Come in and have a cup of coffee," Belle offered.

"Thank you, Belle, but I just need to speak to Jessie for a minute," Justin said and backed out the door.

Jessie closed the door and turned to Justin. "I can tell by the look on your face something's wrong. Did you and the boys get the cows to the fort OK?"

"Let's take a walk, and I want you to stay calm when I tell you what's happened."

"What?!"

Justin saw Jessie's scar turning red. "You can't do anything foolish," Justin said again.

"Just tell me now," Jessie demanded, looking around. "Where are Jake and Hawk? Why aren't they with you?"

Justin explained to Jessie what had happened and what the major had said, about coming here next. "Jessie, this is my fault. I should never let them go off by themselves."

It's too late to worry about that now, besides, it is just another thing we will have to deal with until this country can get settled." Justin saw the change come over Jessie's face as he took control of himself.

"First thing in the morning, we will go see the major. The shooting happened outside the fort; this is a matter for the state marshal."

"I don't know," Justin responded. "I've never met someone as fanatical as this major. He's not listening to anyone who doesn't say what he wants to hear. I'm afraid he's going to harm those boys."

"That will happen over my dead body and a lot of others," Jessie stated, the scar turning a purple-red. "We will leave in the morning at first light. I have to go and face Belle now," he said, turning and walking slowly, trying to decide what to tell a wife who would not sleep tonight.

As he stepped back in the door, Belle's heart almost stopped beating when she saw Jessie's scar purple-red. She went to him immediately and put her hand on his arm. "What's wrong? What did Justin tell you? It's about the boys isn't it—where are they?" she demanded.

Jessie took her by the arm and led her back to the table, making her sit. Turning toward the bedrooms, he shouted, "Race!"

Race, hearing the panic in his father's voice, jumped up from behind his desk where he was studying the commissary books. Coming through the door into the kitchen, he saw his ma sitting frozen at the table, and then he saw the scar. Fear gripped his stomach, "What is it Pa, what's happened?"

"I'll explain later. Right now, I need you to go get Ed and have him meet me at the village."

"Ok, Pa, but what should I tell him?"

"Nothing. Just tell him to meet me at the village now!"

Race was out of breath when he knocked on his brother's door, then he banged on the door. Ed opened the door and froze from the look on Race's face.

"What's happening—is Ma alright? Did something happen to Pa, or Jenney?"

"No," Race said, as he caught his breath.

"Then what?"

"Pa said to meet him at the village now."

"Has something happened to Two Worlds?"

"I don't know. Pa wouldn't say."

Grabbing his rifle, Ed yelled at Little Otter, "Stay here. I'll be back." He started to the village on the run with Race beside him. "Is Jake with Pa?" Ed asked Race.

"No," Race answered. He had to run faster to keep up with Ed until they reached the village. Ed went straight to Jessie, and Belle, who had followed Jessie into the village.

"Where is Jake and Hawk?" he demanded.

Jessie saw Two Worlds emerge from his lodge and walk through the middle of the crowd to where Jessie and Belle were standing.

When everyone went quiet, Two Worlds spoke. "You need to tell us what has happened to our young braves."

Jessie moved next to Justin, who explained to everyone what had happened. "We will go tomorrow and get this straightened out," Justin promised.

"What if they are not released?" Two Worlds asked.

"We have to give this a chance to be straightened out without violence, but they will not harm our young braves," Jessie stated with passion.

"We will do as you asked," Red Sun spoke up, "but I will prepare the braves."

"If it comes to that, we will ride with you," Jessie said.

The soldiers at the gate nodded as Jessie and Justin rode through and stopped at the major's office. Jessie knocked at the major's door.

"Come in," the major yelled.

As he stepped through the door, Jessie's hair stood up on the back of his neck when he saw the look on the major's face. He stared at Justin standing next to Jessie with badges pinned to their shirts.

Jessie walked up to the major's desk before he spoke. "You have two young boys locked up for defending themselves against three men about to kill them. The shooting took place in the settlement and outside your authority. I want them released into my custody now."

The major came out of his chair red in the face. "I don't care who appointed you state marshal, but Indians are the federal's responsibility, and those two are Indians who killed three white men, and they are going to be court-martialed and shot before a firing squad. Take your badges and get out of my office, now!"

Jessie felt Justin tugging on his arm as he stopped himself from shooting the major where he stood. Turning, they both made their way outside and mounted their horses without a word until they were outside the gates.

"We don't have long. That major is going to make this happen fast; we only have a few days," Jessie warned.

"I will pick up another horse when we get to the lake and ride until I can reach the governor," Justin said.

"Ok, but if you are not back in five days, I'm going to be leading the way to the fort myself," Jessie replied.

Justin changed horses three times during the night and kept them at a gallop until he came to a small spring-fed creek an hour after daylight. He let the horses feed and rest for a half an hour while he splashed water over his head, refreshing himself to go on. He knew if he didn't get back in time, Jessie, Red Sun, and the others would not be able to hold back Ed and Spirit Snake. If they left for the fort, the men of Tuckertown would be with them along with Dave, Bill, and John.

Water still dripping from his wet hair, he mounted his horse and put him into a gallop that he could maintain all day and into the night again until he reached the Capitol building. It was after midnight when Justin rode his horse up to the steps and dismounted. He headed for the front door where two guards came to attention and pointed their rifles at him.

"What do you want here?" one of them demanded.

"I have to see the governor right now," Justin said with an urgency in his voice that even a guard could understand.

"Sorry, sir but you will have to come back tomorrow."

"It won't wait, I need someone to let the governor know I am here. Just tell him it's Justin Hannah."

"Wait here. I will go get my captain," one of the soldiers said and went down the steps.

It was no more than five minutes when the guard appeared with another soldier buttoning his jacket. Walking up to Justin, he asked, "What is this all about?"

"My name is Deputy Marshal Justin Hannah. Governor Perry knows me, and it's critical that you let him know I am here now. Lives depend on it!"

"I have heard of a special force the governor has put together, and I have heard your name. If you will wait a few minutes, I will let the governor know you are here."

"I'll wait."

Fifteen minutes later, Justin saw Governor Perry approach with the captain right behind him. Reaching Justin, the governor said, "Whatever has happened? Come on inside. Captain, wake up the cooking staff and have them bring coffee and something for this man to eat."

"Come with me." The governor took Justin by the arm and led him inside to his office. "Now tell me what's happening. From what I can see, you have been on the road day and night."

While Justin was explaining the situation to the governor, the captain came in and nodded his head so as not to disrupt Justin's story. The governor held up his hand to Justin, then spoke to the captain. "Get to the fort and bring Brigadier General Paulson here now."

"Yes, sir," he replied then headed out the door.

"I'm sorry, Justin, please finish."

"If I'm not back there with a way to stop the major, you're going to have another war on your hands, and this one isn't going to just be about Indians." Justin was finishing his story when there was a knock on the door.

"Come in," ordered the governor. The door opened, and half the cooking staff brought trays of food and a pot of steaming coffee. They placed it on the table and left, leaving two servers to pour coffee.

The brigadier general opened the door and saw the captain standing there with half of his uniform on. "This better be important waking me up in the middle of the night," he said, half-dressed himself.

"Yes, sir, General, I have been sent by the governor himself to bring you to the Capitol now."

"What's wrong, have we been attacked?"

"No, General, all I know is the governor wants you now."

"Give me five minutes. Go wake Colonel Bane and have my driver get my buggy ready to travel now!"

"Yes sir!"

The captain had been gone less than an hour when the buggy came to a halt at the Capitol. The captain escorted the general and colonel past the guards to the governor's office and knocked.

The door opened, and the governor said, "Keep your voices down and come on into my office."

Governor Perry spoke to the general, explaining what was happening and said, "If Major Stoddard carries out his threat, it will undo everything we have accomplished in the past five years, trying to bring peace to that area." Looking the general in the eyes, he said, "It's imperative that you send someone immediately to stop this execution before it happens. I can't emphasize enough how important this is."

Turning to the colonel, the general said, "You will leave immediately within the hour along with your staff. I will have a letter for you, giving you your orders, before you go. You are taking over Fort Dade and relieving Major Stoddard. Take only what you need, and when you get this resolved, send someone to retrieve the rest of your belongings and family."

"Yes sir, General," he saluted and left the office.

Turning to the governor, the general said, "The colonel is a good soldier and has experience in these matters. He will take care of this problem."

"I sure hope so," Justin said, relief in his voice. He walked into the main salon with the general and the governor.

"How about a drink while we wait on the colonel," the governor offered, nodding to one of his staff. "Afterwards, we need to let this man get some rest, it's going to be a long ride back."

It was late afternoon. Jessie was talking to Red Sun when they saw a rider start down to the lake. They walked toward him from the village, and the rider saw Jessie and galloped toward him.

"Hold on there, soldier," Jessie said, taking hold of the bridle. "Tell me what's happening." The knot grew in Jessie's stomach as he listened to the soldier.

"Mister Tucker, the major is going to court-martial the two boys in the morning and then put them in front of a firing squad the next day at ten o'clock. It ain't right, Mister Tucker, but there ain't nothing any of us can do about it."

"Who sent you?" Jessie asked.

"Nobody, I snuck out early this morning. The others will cover for me until I get back."

"Ok, come to the house and get some food then a bit of rest before you start back."

"I wouldn't mind some food, but I need to eat it on my way back," the soldier said, relieved now that he had delivered his message.

Jessie knocked on Sara Mae's door. She answered, looking at the soldier with surprise on her face and asked, "What can I do for you, Mister Tucker?"

"Can you fix something for this soldier, something to eat on his horse while he's traveling?"

"Of course, you can come in or wait here."

"I'll wait here, thank you."

Jessie went back to the village to find Red Sun and let him know the news the soldier had brought. Standing next to Two Worlds, Jessie listened as Red Sun spoke to the braves.

"We have stayed out of this white man's war, and we have enjoyed many years peace where we are now. But this new soldier in charge of the soldiers has decided we should no longer live in peace because two of our braves defended themselves against bad men who wanted to do them harm. We will go to the fort when it is time and plead with the new leader to set our people free." Drawing himself to his full height, he said with determination, "We will not sit by while they take our sons' lives. We will not come home without our braves."

The moon was pushing the sun behind the lake when Jessie left Ed and the other braves, who were dancing their "dance of war and a good death" around the fire. The fire would burn most of the night. He walked to the lake, waded in clothes and all, to sit next to Two Worlds who was chanting to the ancestors for wisdom for what was to come.

"Grandfather of grandfathers, I have fought a lot of battles of all kinds, but never have I been willing to give not only my life but my son's life also." Jessie waited for an answer until the chanting stopped and listened as Two Worlds spoke slowly and with more passion than he had ever heard from this man of peace.

"I will be joining my ancestors soon with happy thoughts," he said with passion, "but if I was younger, I would gladly go to my place in the stars now, to save my people. Still, the ancestors show me no sign of tomorrow!"

Jessie stood on the porch, dreading opening the door to face Belle. Suddenly, the door opened, and she was standing there, frightened and trying to calm herself. "Well, are you going to come in or stand there while I give you my opinion?"

"Belle, I don't know what I can say to keep you from being part of this."

"I know what you, Ed, and the others are going to do. I hear the drum! I lost you once, Jessie. I don't want to lose you again, but I won't try to stop you." She stepped forward, hiding her tears against his shoulder as he held her tight in his arms.

Jessie saw the light through the barn door as he made his way, holding a lantern above his head. He stepped through the door to find Franklin and Jeremy saddling their horses.

"What do you two think you're doing?"

"We'uns part of this family too, Mister Jessie, and we'uns going with you to save them two boys no matter how foolish they be."

"Franklin, ever since Justin brought you and Sara Mae here, you have taken care of this family."

"Yas, sir," Franklin interrupted, "that's what I intend to do today." He picked up his rifle and leaned it against the stall.

"Franklin, I don't know what's going to happen today, but I need to know you will be here to keep taking care of my family, I'm counting on that."

"Mister Tucker, as much as I wants to go to make sure you and them boys come home safe, I will do what you asks, you knows that."

"I know," Jessie said, "but right now I could use some help getting my horse ready while I get ammunition from the storage room."

As Jessie was leading his horse through the barn, heading for the village, Race came running through the door.

"Wait on me, Pa, it will only take a minute, and I'll be ready. Franklin, get me my horse; I'll get the saddle."

"Hold on there for just a minute," Jessie said and held up his hand to stop Race. "Son, I am proud of your courage, but you are not a fighter, and someone has to be here with your mother. The ranch has to go on no matter what happens, and you are the only one that can do that. You would make me proud if you would do that."

"I can fight too, Pa," Race pleaded.

"Yes, you can, son, but that's not what I need you to do this time."

As Jessie headed to the village, he saw Belle standing on the porch in the shadows. She thought he couldn't see her tears, but he knew they were there, and it fueled his anger. Riding into the village, he saw the war paint the braves had so meticulously painted themselves and their horses with. They each said goodbye to their families, knowing they may not return.

Jessie heard the sound of horses in the dark then watched as John, his son Frank, Bill, and Dave rode into the firelight. This time, they were wearing gun belts and rifles in their scabbards.

"You didn't think you were going to have all the excitement by yourselves," John said, looking at Red Sun, then Jessie.

Looking at Jessie, Dave said, "This is our country. We fought for it, and no damn Yankee is going to come here and take it away from us. So, save your lecture. We got a long way to go—let's get to it!"

They had been riding for an hour when the sun started its day, shining its light on the group of men that was no less than a small army. The sun had risen halfway to the top of the tall pines, and they were within an hour of the fort when they saw a buggy and a small group of men riding beside it. They all stopped when they recognized Justin as he broke into a run, coming at them.

Bringing his horse to a halt in front of the group, he spoke to Jessie. "I knew this was what I would find if I didn't make it back in time."

"You are in time to fight with us if it is your wish," Red Sun said to Justin.

"There will be no fight. The governor and the brigadier general in charge of the army have sent a new commander with a letter to remove the major at once and release Jake and Hawk."

"The major is court-martialing them this morning with the intent of putting them in front of a firing squad," Ed cried out.

"That's not going to happen," Justin said as he waved the soldiers to them. The buggy stopped at fifty feet before the assembled men. The soldiers stared at the fiercest group of men they had ever seen.

"Drive on, Corporal," the colonel instructed. Jessie saw the uncertainty in the soldiers' faces as they slowly came forward.

Colonel Bane and Captain Amos stepped down from the buggy as Jessie dismounted. The colonel took Jessie's hand and said, "I have been anxious to meet the man Governor Perry speaks so highly of." He saw the badge and looked up to see badges pinned on the other men. "Mister Tucker, you can take your men home now, I'll put a stop to this tragedy."

Ed and Spirit Snake rode up to the colonel. "We will go home when our sons ride next to us," Ed said.

Sensing the anger in Ed's words, the colonel didn't argue. "Then let's get going," he said and walked to his carriage with Captain Amos.

Men and women coming and going along the road from the fort to the settlement grabbed their children and ran to get out of the way. The group of painted braves and men with the sun reflecting off their badges followed the buggy with soldiers inside and soldiers riding alongside. When they got closer to the fort, one of the escort soldiers rode forward to stop the soldiers inside from closing the gate and the bugler from sounding an alarm.

"Open those gates," the soldier yelled. "The colonel is coming through."

"Are you sure?" one of them asked, looking at the group behind the buggy.

"Unless you want your ass in the brig, you'll get these gates back open. Now!" he said, as the carriage approached.

"What about that bunch behind him?" he asked.

"Don't worry about them, just worry about your ass. Now move everyone out of the way."

Another soldier turned and yelled, "Clear the parade grounds. Officers coming through!"

The carriage drove through the parade grounds as soldiers stopped and stared, not sure what was going on and what were they supposed to do. One of the privates was standing next to the barracks door and yelled inside.

"Sarge, you better come outside. You're not going to believe your eyes."

As the sergeant stepped outside, he took one look and yelled to the corporal who was standing and staring.

"Corporal, get the soldiers to arms now!"

"Sergeant, those Indians are from the Double T Ranch, so are the other men. They are here about the two young men, and they are with the colonel."

The carriage stopped in front of the major's office, and Colonel Bane and Captain Amos stepped out, taking a quick survey of the soldiers. They followed the escort soldiers through the door along with Jessie, Justin, and Ed, while John and the others sat their horses, lined up side by side with the braves. John smiled to himself as he watched the whole fort turn out to stare at the fierce looking Indians with their painted faces and bodies along with their horses. They weren't carrying bows and arrows; they were wearing what looked to the sergeant like civil war side arms and repeating rifles. The Indians sat straight, their faces mysterious and unreadable, watching the door Jessie went through.

The major sat behind the desk in the staff meeting room and waited for the lieutenant to bring the prisoners in and place them at a table in front of him. Jake and Hawk looked around, and each wondered where his pa was. Justin said he would get them out, but how can he, they asked themselves, seeing the two guards at the door with rifles as the lieutenant stood next to the table.

"This court-martial has begun!" Major Stoddard announced.

"Lieutenant, did you see these two Indians kill three white men?" the major asked.

"Yes sir, ambushed them and shot them in cold blood."

Looking at the two young braves, the major said, "The penalty for Indians killing a white man is death."

"We only defended ourselves, they were going to kill us for no reason," Jake protested.

"Quiet, there is no reason for Indians to kill white people. You will be taken before a firing squad and—"

The major never got to finish his sentence before the door opened and four soldiers walked in. They told the guards at the entrance to stand down. The major came to his feet demanding an explanation when the colonel walked through with the captain, Jessie, and the others following.

"Colonel! You are just in time to see how we deal with savages," he smugly promised. The colonel walked up to the major and stopped. The smugness left the major's face when he was handed an envelope.

"Those are orders from Brigadier General Paulson relieving you of your command immediately. I will be replacing you."

"You can't do that. I'm in the middle of a court-martial here. These two Indians killed three white men."

"Major, if I have to put you under house arrest, it will not look good on your record. This court is dismissed now. Captain Amos, get those handcuffs off the prisoners."

"You're going to regret this, Colonel, when I get to Fort Houston and give my report," the major threatened, turning red in the face as his anger at this intrusion intensified.

"Captain, escort the major to his quarters and see to it that he and all his belongings are ready to travel first light tomorrow morning. Escort his lieutenant to his quarters. Lieutenant, you will escort the major back to Fort Houston."

"We thought they were going to shoot us before you could get here," Jake said as they stood before Jessie, still confused as to what had happened to them.

"No one is going to harm you now. It's time to go," Jessie said. He took the boys by the shoulders and turned them toward the door.

"Is it over, Paw Paw?" Hawk asked.

"Not yet, but soon," he answered, looking at Justin. The look on Justin's face overrode even the strain of his ordeal riding hard to Tallahassee, and they both knew it was not finished yet.

Jessie knew Justin blamed himself, and it would have to be Justin that finished this. Jessie walked outside and heard the war cry from Red Sun and the other braves as Spirit Snake rode alongside Hawk, giving his hand. Hawk took it and swung up behind him. Justin brought the spare horse he had taken with him to Jake and handed him the reins. The young brave straddled the horse in one motion. As they turned to leave the fort, the soldier that had taken the chance and brought him the news of the court-martial, rode up and handed Jessie the belts and holsters that belonged to the young braves.

Taking the holsters, Jessie then held out his hand, and when the soldier took it, Jessie said, "Thank you for this, and I won't forget the chance you took to bring me the warning."

"It wasn't right what he was doing, Mister Tucker."

"No, it wasn't. You did something to stop it, and for that I'm grateful. This year, when we have our cook-out, I will see to it you drive the colonel."

"Thank you, Mister Tucker." Jessie released his hand and rode to catch the others.

They were out of sight of the fort and Jake and Hawk were riding between their fathers. Hawk looked at Jake and grinned, holding out his hand. Jake, seeing the scar across his palm, reached out and placed his palm against his, saying, "Brother." Ed and Spirit Snake looked at one another and rode a little taller in the saddle, filled with pride.

The moon still reflected its's light off the lake when Justin rose from his sleeping furs. The long-awaited sleep had given him back most of his energy. White Dove remained silent as she watched him dress. Fear crept into her heart as he buckled his gun belt. Justin removed the pistol and checked the bullets before placing it back in his holster. As he picked up his rifle to leave, she reached and put her hand on his leg, stopping him.

"I want my husband back, and our children want their father back."

She spoke in a soft whisper, but the words resonated in his heart, and he realized this wasn't just about him. "Tell the children I will be back to play in the lake with them by the time the sun warms the water."

"I will," she smiled and removed her hand.

Justin walked to the lake to get his horse when he saw Spirit Snake leading his Marsh Tackie. Walking by Justin, he said, "You didn't think you would go alone, did you?"

Justin stopped when he saw Red Sun leading his horse toward his lodge. He continued northeast around the barn and shook his head when he saw Ed and Jessie sitting on their horses waiting.

"I was wondering if you were going to get here before the day is gone," Jessie said, breaking the building tension.

Looking around at the men waiting, Justin said, "You don't have to do this. It was my mistake, and I can finish this."

"I don't recall anyone blaming you," Jessie said. "What part of this do you think don't belong to all of us?"

"Ok, then let's finish this," Justin said and spurred his horse into a gallop.

The private placed the last box of the major's personal things in the carriage, where the lieutenant was waiting.

"Where is my escort?" the major asked the captain. "I should have at least four soldiers to accompany me. I am a major and deserve more respect than this."

"Respect is earned, Major. It doesn't just come with those bars on your shoulders, and since you have shown no respect for what these people go through every day, you are getting what you deserve."

"I'll be putting your attitude in my report when I see the general," he threatened as he stepped up into the carriage.

They were four hours from the fort when the lieutenant rounded a curve and brought the carriage to a halt. He felt fear build in his chest almost taking his breath away, looking at death sitting on horses blocking the roadway.

Justin was off his horse first, walking straight to the side where the lieutenant sat. He grabbed him by the arm and pulled him from his seat, and when he hit the ground, Justin's anger released itself on that man. He kicked with all his strength, catching him in the stomach, almost lifting him off the ground and heard the wind leave his lungs as he tried gasping for breath. Justin knelt on one knee, taking a hand full of hair and turned the man's face where he could look into his eyes. "I gave my word you would not get away unscathed, and I always keep my word." He brought his fist down breaking his jaw.

The major was watching in horror as Justin released his anger on the lieutenant. He didn't see Ed approach his side and was shocked as he was pulled from his seat. He cried out when he fell on his back, looking up into the face of anger. Ed dropped down, putting his full weight on his knee as it landed on the major's chest, taking all the air from his lungs. Pulling his pistol, he placed the barrel between the frightened man's eyes and waited until the major got his breath, so he would be sure to understand what he said. "How does it feel knowing you're going to die?"

"Please, Mister," he gasped between short breaths, "I was only doing my job."

"You were going to shoot two innocent young men for being born who they are." Pulling his gun back, he fired it next to the major's head.

"Please!" he screamed, "don't kill me!"

"I'm not going to kill you, but if you ever come back into this country, they will bury you here." Ed brought the gun barrel down across his head, leaving a bleeding gash.

Riding back, Jessie watched Justin let go of his anger a little at a time until he saw him riding relaxed in the saddle. As the barn came into sight, Jessie rode next to Justin. "You have to let this go now. We don't want to bring this to the lake."

"I know," Justin answered back. "I'm good now."

Eight

THE FREEZE

The cold came early this year, it had been in the forties and fifties for the previous two weeks and the quarters were busy getting ready for the yearly hog killing. The young boys were filling the fifty-gallon steel drums with water; other boys were hauling armloads of firewood to build fires under the three drums. They would dip the hogs into barrels of scalding hot water, which helped to remove the tough bristles of hair.

The men left at daylight and headed for a swampy area two miles away, where they had scouted and found several passels of hogs feeding on acorns. It took two work wagons and four catch dogs, which were trained just for catching wild boars, to bring back twenty-five. It had become a yearly thing. After a couple of cold fronts had come by early this year, the crops were in, and it was time to prepare for winter. That was when the hogs were ready to butcher. Troy and Leroy had made special scrapers just for that along with a spreader bar with hooks.

The two wagons pulled up next to the drums, half full of boiling water. Troy and Leroy each reached into the back of the wagon and grabbed a hog by his two hind feet. They dunked each dead hog into the drum head first, then Leroy grabbed another one and lowered him into the third drum. They would stay submerged five minutes in the boiling hot water, then they were removed and hung on the rack. The boars would be gutted, their insides dumped into number two wash tubs and carried to the creek. There, the women would start the process of cleaning everything that could be eaten, especially the intestines to be made into chitlins, one of their favorites. The men made short work of scraping the hides with the new scrapers.

The heads would be cleaned and used to make head cheese, another favorite. The fat from the body would be boiled down for lard and lye soap. It was a joyous day with the women singing by the creek and the men laughing at themselves at the mistakes they had made all year and how long it took them to get over them.

They would smoke and salt cure enough pork to last all year. The smell of fat cooking and pork being fried to eat, while the cleaning was going on until after dark, added to the feeling of plenty for the coming winter. The meat was cut into portions and hung in the smokehouses, and fires were built to start the smoking process. Some meat was packed in wooden crates and salted layer by layer.

They would smoke and salt enough pork for Race to sell to John, Leo, and the others. People within five miles around were hearing about a closer place than the fort to get supplies and now depended on the commissary at Tuckertown for all their needs.

By the time the meat was put away, the quarters were full of music with fiddles, guitars, and harps. Two of the young men had been practicing together for weeks so they could play with the others. Hailey's feet couldn't keep still, and Troy smiled at her when she started pulling him around in circles until his feet began moving along with the music. He saw Hailey's smile turn into laughter as he felt the small hand of Jasmine take hold of one finger, dancing with them till the music got too fast for her to keep up. He reached down and lifted her into his arms. He had never felt this happy before and kept dancing even after the music had stopped.

───❦───

Two weeks earlier, a wagon pulled up with a man, his wife, and their three kids, ranging in age from three to seven. They surprised Race when they came walking in and asked, "Is this the Tuckertown store that people are talking about where you can buy supplies?"

Race sat behind his desk and just stared, surprised anyone knew about the commissary except the ones that lived close to the ranch. Jenny, hearing the strange voices, came from her small office and smiled when she saw the woman standing there frightened by it all. She looked in awe at the dresses and clothes Jenny had insisted Race order along with pots, pans, knives, and mixing bowls.

"Hi, I'm Jenny," she said, walking up and introducing herself. "I don't think I have met you yet."

"No Ma'am, we have only been in this area for about a year now, and this is closer than Dade or Brooksville. Some folks from Fort Dade said you had a store here."

"Yes, we do," Jenny said with pride in her voice. "It is somewhat limited now, but we can order most anything you need. It might take a while, but we can usually get it," she said with a smile.

"My name is Wanda, and these are my children," she said shyly. "The oldest there is Ralf, and this is Dwayne and their sister Marylin."

"Nice to meet you," Jenny said. "I have some hard candy on the counter I bet you would like, so why don't you come with me while your mother looks around."

The man walked to where Race stood behind his desk waiting. "My name is Carmine Jenkins, and I have a small farm about two miles north of here. I grow potatoes. This is the first year, and we had a good crop, and I was hoping I could trade you potatoes for some supplies."

"Certainly!" Race came around the desk with his hand out. "My name is Race Tucker, and everyone here will be excited to buy potatoes. Did you bring any with you?" Race asked, hopefully.

"I have ten bushels in the wagon," Carmine replied.

Race walked to the door of the storage room at the back, stuck his head through the door and said, "Raymond, open the back door; there's a wagon coming around, and I need you to unload it." He walked back to where Carmine was waiting and watching Jenny show his wife new bolts of cloth. She had sent the happy kids out with their candy to play until the adults were finished doing business.

"Let's take a look at those potatoes," Race said, leading Carmine through the door and stopping at the wagon. Looking in the crates of potatoes, he gave a great big smile, turned and asked, "How many bushels can you grow?"

"I'm only planting ten acres now, and I'm getting eight to nine bushels an acre, but I intend on adding two to three acres a year. I've got forty acres, and when I'm finished, I will have at least thirty-five acres planted with potatoes."

"Where are you selling them now?" Race asked.

"Well, this being my first crop, what I don't trade you, I'm going to try Brooksville. I don't know who is buying and how much they can handle; otherwise, I may have to haul them to the East Coast where they can be shipped."

"Mister Jenkins, I will buy all you can bring me for now. It will take that much to feed all the families that are moving into this part of the country."

"Well, I can be back in a couple of days with the rest if you are sure."

"I'm sure," Race replied, excited. It was one of the things he had been asking about every time he sent an order to Tampa.

After Raymond unloaded the wagon and it had been reloaded with twenty-five-pound sacks of flour, axes, nails, a hammer, wash tubs, iron skillet, blankets, and yards of new material, they left Tuckertown happy. Wanda and the children smiled and waved goodbye to Jenny.

"Well," Jenny smiled at Race, "I think you might want to add on some more space. I don't think they will be the last new families we will be getting. Looks like the word is out about Tuckertown."

It was a couple of weeks until Christmas, and Belle was excited, waiting for Race and Raymond to finish loading her list of supplies into the carriage. Jenny picked out several different kinds of hard candy to take to the kids. It had been a month since Leo had brought Bonnie with him to get supplies. Jenny walked out to where Belle was waiting by the carriage.

"I'm ready, Ma when you are."

"I'm waiting for Race to finish and your pa to get here."

Jenny saw her pa coming from the barn, so she climbed up in the driver's seat and waited on her ma. Race had the supplies loaded by the time Jessie rode up next to the wagon. Belle stepped up into the seat next to Jenny, and they started out.

Jessie was chilled even with the fur coat he was wearing. It was early in the season but looking at Belle and Jenny who both had a blanket wrapped around them and were huddled together, it gave Jessie an uneasy feeling. He had experienced this kind of early cold, and it usually meant an extreme winter. He was concerned about the orange trees and the fruit they were growing. It was their first harvest this year, and he didn't want anything to happen to them.

Jenny stopped the carriage in front of Leo and Bonnie's house. Bonnie opened the door, concern mixed with happiness on her face.

"Get down you two before you freeze your toes off."

Belle and Jenny gratefully got out of the wagon and into Bonnie's warm kitchen. The boys and their wives saw the wagon and gathered up small bowls of food for the visitors.

After two cups of coffee and a warm bowl of soup, Leo suggested, "Let's take a ride and check the grove."

Riding between rows of trees, now taller than a man, Jessie saw round green fruit close to the size of his fist. Some already had color showing. "How long before they are ready to pick?" Jessie asked Leo.

"Another month to six weeks at the most if this cold front coming down doesn't freeze them. If it only freezes the oranges and not the trees we can survive, but I've got a bad feeling, Mister Tucker. If what I think is coming comes, we could lose the trees and will have to start over again," Leo said, the worry plain in his voice.

"What can we do?" Jessie asked.

"Fires! Mister Tucker."

"What do you mean!" Jessie asked.

"We have a little over a hundred acres of trees planted, and half of them are producing oranges this year. The only way to save them is to gather enough wood to place fires all throughout the grove, but me and the boys can't cut and haul enough trees to build the fires that we will need to save them all."

"How much wood would it take to build enough fires to save the trees and oranges?"

"We would need fires every fifty yards and some wind to blow the heat through the trees," Leo answered, sounding defeated.

"How much time do you think we have?" Jessie asked.

"As fast as it's turning cold, I would say we have two maybe three days before the freeze gets here, and it's going to be a bad one, Mister Tucker."

Jessie was silent on the way back from the groves until he reached Leo's house. Before they dismounted, Jessie spoke with conviction. "Leo, bring every wagon that will hold a load to the lake in the morning."

"Whatever you say, Mister Tucker," Leo replied, not understanding but trusting Jessie. "You have enough time for another cup of coffee before you head back?"

"Sure," Jessie said. His mind was racing, but he didn't want Belle to see it and worry him until he told her of his concerns.

Jessie felt the wind getting colder as they got closer to the lake, and Belle and Jenny were hugging each other wrapped up in the blankets they had. As they reached the valley and Jenny started down to their house, Jessie rode close to the wagon.

"I'll be home later. I'm going to see John and won't be gone long."

"You stay out here after dark, and you are going to freeze," Belle said with worry in her voice.

"I'll be fine, I won't be long." Jessie turned his horse and put him into a trot.

It was still early in the evening, but the sun didn't stay long this time of year. John had shut the mill down, and the men were putting away tools and cleaning the saw blade, getting it ready for tomorrow. John saw Jessie leaning forward into the wind, riding his horse toward the mill.

John didn't like what he saw and started walking toward Jessie until he reached up and took the bridle, stopping the horse. "Get down and come into the house and get warm; you look like you're going to fall off if you don't."

"I need to talk to you," Jessie said, his voice shaking from the cold.

"You're not going to talk to anybody if we don't get you warmed up—you just sit still." John started for the house, leading the horse with Jessie bent forward over the saddle. John opened the door with his arm around Jessie, and Myra jumped up from her chair so fast, she knocked it backward. She almost ran to John and Jessie.

"What happened?" she asked with a shaky voice.

"He's OK, just cold. I think he's been riding for a while and got a bad chill."

"Well, sit him in front of the fireplace. The coffee is still hot."

Everyone sat in silence until Jessie had finished most of the cup of coffee. Turning to John, he explained where he had just come from and the problem they had with the grove and the coming cold front.

"Why you come to me?" John asked.

"I need all the outside slabs you cut when you square up the logs," Jessie said.

"As you can see, we burn day and night to keep them from building up on us, but there are still a lot of pieces around the outside that hasn't been thrown on the fire yet," John replied.

"I have Leo and his boys coming in the morning with wagons, and on my way home I am going to stop by the quarters and get men from there. I will bring all the wagons I have."

"The way this temperature is dropping every day, I would say you only have a couple of days before hell is going to freeze over,"

John said solemnly. "Jessie, you need to send as many men from the quarters here now to start pulling what slabs haven't burned yet from the fire. I'll send for my men and get started. Tomorrow, I'll start sawing as many logs as I can, and maybe we can warm that grove, so we can all be eating oranges this spring."

Jessie finished his coffee and was halfway out the door when he felt John's big coat covering him like a blanket. He turned to protest.

"I don't want to hear a word, Jessie Tucker," John said as he shoved him on out the door, closing it firmly behind him.

John was out the door before Jessie was out of sight, buttoning another coat as he headed for the barn.

"Where are you going?" he heard Myra yell after him.

"To Frank's and have him get the men together and then to Dave's and Bill's. I'll be back soon, keep the coffee warm."

Ed met Jessie before he reached the quarter, and he turned his horse and rode alongside him. "Ma told me where you were going, but she didn't say why you would go there now in this cold. She's worried about you Pa, and why are you wearing John's coat?"

Jessie explained to Ed what Leo had told him and what they had to do by the time they reached the reverend's house. He banged on the door with his fist.

The reverend opened the door and looked wide-eyed at Jessie in his oversized coat, at first not recognizing him. "Please come in, Mister Tucker, Mister Ed. Lord almighty, what has happened to bring the two of you to my door this time of evening?"

Jessie quickly explained to him what was happening. "Reverend I need you to ring that bell and get every man in the quarters here now!"

"OK, Mister Tucker, come with me to the church, that's where they will all come."

Reverend Ellis stepped inside the church, walked to the bell tower and taking the rope, he rang the bell twice, then waited several seconds and rang it twice more. He was starting to ring it for the fourth time when the people began filling the church. Ed thought some were wearing everything they had. They were wrapped in blankets or quilts, looking confused, and asking each ether what was going on. When the last group arrived, they shut the door behind them, and the reverend walked up behind the pulpit and held up his hands for quiet.

"Mister Tucker asked me to bring you here, so please be quiet and listen."

Jessie removed the coat and stepped forward to the pulpit. "As you all know by now, we are having an awfully cold winter, colder than normal. I have a hundred acres of orange trees planted that's bearing fruit for the first time, and if we don't do something, they are going to freeze, trees and all. We have a way to save them, but it's going to take the effort of every able body here to do so."

Troy's enormous presence filled the room when he stood and spoke, not only to Jessie but to everyone in the church. "Mister Tucker, you tell us what it is you need from us, and it will happen. We're waiting!"

Jessie explained his plan to the crowd and outlined what he was going to need from them in the next two days. He told them people would have to feed the fires all night and day if necessary.

"Mister Tucker, we will be waiting at Mister John's place come daylight. In fact, we will go now if there is something we can do tonight," Troy finished.

"There is," Jessie replied. "John needs men to help his crew pull slabs from the fire that haven't burned yet. When you go, take wagons with you and load what you can tonight; there will be more wagons in the morning."

"The wagons will be loaded, Mister Tucker, and if that's all, we'll get started now." Troy turned, leaving the church with everyone following him.

As Jessie and Ed rode toward the village, they saw smoke coming from every lodge and a bonfire in the center of the village. Several braves sat on stumps close enough to keep warm and talk about how this was going to be colder than years past when animals died, and creeks had thin sheets of ice along their edges. They stopped talking and stood, staring at the riders coming into their village until Jessie sat up straight showing his face. Slipping from his saddle, he walked to the fire and opened John's massive coat to let the warmth of the fire surround his body, bringing him back to why he was there.

While Jessie warmed himself by the fire, Ed explained what was happening and where they would need their help. Red Sun spoke up, saying, "We will be there."

Riding back to the barn, Ed noticed Jessie sitting straighter in his saddle from the warmth of the fire and John's heated coat. "What do you need from me?" Ed asked. "You seem to have everything under control."

"Son, there is only one who is in control here, and he's talking with a cold breath right now. You need to be at the mill coordinating the wagons. John and his men will have their hands full, cutting as many slabs as they can."

"I got that covered, Pa, and I will come with the last wagon." Ed turned toward home where he had a warm meal waiting.

Franklin and Jeremy waited in the barn wrapped in horse blankets, warming their hands around a small fire made in a scooped-out place in the dirt, waiting for Jessie. They both jumped to their feet and walked as fast as they could when they heard Jessie opening the door. Jeremy took the reins when Jessie stepped down and led the horse to a stall, removing his bridle and saddle before feeding him.

"Mister Jessie, we have heard what's going on with everyone helping with the lumber to keep them trees alive that Mister Leo gots planted from this here freeze coming, and Mister Tucker, it's coming. All you have to do is look at how thick the fur on them squirrels and rabbits and the foxes I've seen lately. I didn't hardly recognize them, they were so big in their winter coats. This is one time, Mister Tucker that I insist me and Jeremy gets to do our parts."

Facing Franklin, he put his hand on his shoulder and said, "Franklin, this is one time I have no argument. You and Jeremy have the wagons ready to go daylight tomorrow. Now, let's go home and get warm—it may be our last chance for a while."

Two of Leo's boys met a wagon train halfway to John's sawmill, packed as high as could be loaded and tied down. Bill was in the lead and pulling alongside JRs wagon, he stopped. "Where is all this scrap lumber going?" Bill asked.

"Pa is waiting on the wagons, and he will tell you the different places to unload," JR replied.

"Are there more coming?" David asked.

"Yes," Bill answered, "this is just me and Jessie's two grandsons. John's two younger boys are driving his wagons, and there will be more men right behind us with the wagons from the quarters as soon as they are loaded. John and his crew have the saw running to cut as many slabs as they can by tonight, then he will bring the boys and his crew to cut young scrub trees that will burn."

"Mister Tucker got here early this morning, and he's helping Pa and Todd load the other wagon with lightered knots to start the fires under that green lumber, but they will see you coming," David added.

Leo saw the wagons in the distance and waved to them. As they came closer, Leo pointed toward the tree line where the northwest freezing winds would be coming from. Meeting the wagons, he told the drivers Jessie would show them where to unload.

"Start unloading your wagons on this front row first wherever you see a pile of lightered knots. They will be spaced about every fifty yards or so apart down the line of trees. Unload half on top of the lightered and the rest next to it for later to keep the fires going through the night. We will work our way every fifty yards apart all through the grove and let the wind blow the smoke and heat through the trees. We hope we can keep the fires going until this front blows through and the temperature rises. I will stay with you and help." Jessie explained. Pointing at Jake and Hawk, Jessie said, "I want you to go with Leo and Todd and help them find lightered."

It was getting dark when Leo saw the wagon loads of scrap lumber and what looked like Red Sun and all the braves from the village riding alongside the wagons. Leo met the wagons at the edge of the grove holding up his hand.

Jessie came riding up next to Leo and asked, "What do you want with these wagons?"

"Unload them toward this end of the grove, because the wind is going to come from the north through those pines, it will be blowing the heat and smoke throughout the rest of the trees. So, we will build the biggest fires there."

Looking up, Leo saw several more wagons in the distance coming from a different direction and turned to Jessie, confused.

"They are the rest of the men and women from the quarters and village, bringing food. It's going to be a long night," Jessie stated.

Leo's wife and the wives of his sons met the wagons carrying the women from the lake and insisted they all come inside as they helped bring in pots of food to be warmed up for later. Several women had brought coffee pots and bags of coffee. Some of the women from the village had never been inside of a white man's house, and they stood just inside the door not knowing where to go or what to do. Belle recognized the awkwardness of the village women and led Leo's daughters-in-law to where they stood and introduced them to each other. Then she led them to some chairs against a wall where they could sit and watch. Belle knew this was all new to them, and they were waiting to be told what was needed of them.

David's wife spoke up, saying, "We need to go bring chairs if we are all going to stay here."

The women from the quarters responded, "We can do that," and headed for the door with David's wife. The village women stood up to follow.

Small fires were built, surrounded by different groups of men, laughing trying to keep the tension down. The men had stretched short pieces of canvas from tree to tree in front of their fires to make a barrier from the north wind. They were all waiting for the word to light the main fires, but Leo insisted on waiting for the temperature to drop below freezing before firing the timber. Most groups had pots of coffee hanging over the fire to keep hot. Tonight, they weren't interested in warm coffee.

Every hour, Leo would pick a leaf from a tree at the far end of the grove away from the protection of the pine forest, bend it in between his fingers and watch as it opened slower and slower with each hour. Watching the bright cold moon, it was an hour after midnight, when Leo picked a leaf from one of the trees, and it snapped between his fingers. The men heard him and shouted the message from group to group across the grove.

"Light the fires!"

The men began pulling branches from the fires they were standing around and headed for the piles of wood closest to the forest. They worked their way through the grove, lighting fires as they went until they all met at the far end. They watched, fascinated by the rising lights, and it didn't take long before the sky was full of sparks, disappearing only to be replaced by an endless supply.

The men let up only long enough to eat when the wives brought hot food and coffee to the grove. Everyone had gotten caught up in saving the orchard; the sound of men yelling back and forth to each other could be heard everywhere over the crackling sound of green wood burning over hot coals. Red Sun and the other braves moved up and down the rows of trees, feeding wood on the fires without rest. Wagon after wagon had been unloaded—it had become a personal goal for each man—there would be no stopping until the danger was over, and only Leo could tell them that.

Throughout the night, men kept throwing slabs from the mill to keep the fires going. The temperature had dropped a couple more degrees by two in the morning. It was still an hour before daylight when Leo found Jessie feeding one of the fires. Jessie heard the sound of desperation in his voice as he spoke to him.

"Jessie, we can't let up on the fires! This freeze is not going to let up until maybe tomorrow sometime. I don't think we are going to have enough wood to keep the fires going the rest of the night and tomorrow. We probably have enough to get us through the night and maybe a while in the morning, but not tomorrow. If this freeze don't let up by noon, we will run out of wood, and within four hours after the fires are out, we're going to lose the oranges and most likely the trees too."

"We are not going to lose these trees! We need more wood—we'll get more wood!"

"Frank! Troy! Red Sun—over here!" Jessie shouted. Less than a minute later, they all came hurrying toward Jessie with questions on their faces, followed by Bill and Dave. "What's up?" Bill asked as he walked up next to Jessie.

"We are going to need more wood, lots more."

"We loaded everything at the mill that wasn't burned," John exclaimed.

"Did any of you bring an ax?" Jessie asked.

"We all did," John said.

"So did we," Troy added."

"We brought no axes," Red Sun answered.

"We are going to have to cut timber and keep feeding the fires until this is over. Red Sun, you can have the braves keep the fires built up." Jessie decided.

"I'll take my men and start now," John said. Bill and Dave followed John.

"I'll do the same," Troy agreed, and he turned to find his men.

It was mid-afternoon, and the winds had died down to a gentle breeze when Leo walked to the far end of the grove away from the protective tree line. He picked a leaf from the tree furthest from the fires. He folded the leaf and watched as it unfolded in his fingers, and a huge smile came over his face.

He turned and yelled as loud as his voice would carry, "It's over, we've done it!"

Bill had just finished cutting a small tree when he heard Leo yell but realized the men further back in the woods didn't hear Leo. He yelled to the other men, "Leo said it's over!"

The quiet was suddenly overwhelming, then Jessie heard the yell all through the grove and woods as the axes stopped. Men gathered at the tree line on the edge of the grove, and they were so covered with smoke and soot, you could hardly tell one from the other. All Jessie could hear was men's laughter as they pointed and laughed at each other, shaking hands and patting each other on the back, Red, Black, and White. Jessie's heart swelled as he realized, there was no more "them!"

Nine

THE WEDDING

*I*t was a beautiful spring morning, and Jenny decided to go for a ride. She asked Jeremy to get the carriage ready with her trusted Molly. Jenny packed her bag containing her blanket, pens, diary, paint, and brushes along with her roll of art paper ordered specially from Tampa. Hugging her ma goodbye, she climbed into the carriage, took the reins and flicked them gently across Molly's rump.

She hadn't gone far when she heard Jeremy call out, "You be careful, Miss Jenny!" Jenny smiled as she waved her hand without looking back.

Jenny traveled less than half an hour when she turned off the main road to Fort Dade and drove perhaps a hundred yards to reach her favorite spot. A small, clear, spring-fed creek wound through red gum trees lining its banks on both sides. Unhitching Molly from the carriage to let her graze on the rich grass along the creek, she shook open her blanket and laid it on the grass in the sunshine between the trees.

She always sat for a while when she first reached her spot, looking out across the hills dotted with small oak stands and pine forest reaching past the horizon. Each time she came here, Jenny felt like the world was right, and she always had to make herself leave.

Frequently, Jenny sat and watched small herds of deer and sometimes hogs, running with their short legs, going to feed on acorns under the oaks, and she thought if she had a house built right here under the trees, she would happily live here forever. She quietly removed her paint and paper from her bag and began drawing an eagle that had landed above her on a limb, proceeding to eat a rabbit as she drew him.

Jenny was putting the final touches to his feet, which were wrapped around the arm size limb and holding the rabbit until he finished his meal. Then he disappointed her when he spread his huge wings, lifting off with no effort and soaring over the trees. Jenny gasped, startled when she heard someone behind her clear his throat.

Turning around, at first, she thought she was having an illusion, seeing a man she had seen a dozen times in her daydreams. Jenny stared, not sure if what she was looking at was real.

He removed his hat, revealing a mass of black hair, and spoke in a deep, mesmerizing voice.

"I am sorry to startle you. My name is Captain Amos, Walter Amos," he corrected. "I came from Fort Dade, and I am on my way to see Mr. Tucker. I saw your carriage, and then I saw you. I don't mean to be forward, but you looked like an angel sitting here in the sun. I haven't seen anyone come close to being as beautiful as you are. I'm saying too much—I apologize—I should shut up and go away. I just had to see you up close," Walter stammered.

"You have no reason to apologize," Jenny said and smiled, laying her painting on the blanket and trying to calm herself so she would not sound like some silly girl. She started to rise, and the captain stepped forward and took her elbow, helping her up. They were face to face, six inches apart. He could hardly breathe. Stepping back, Jenny brushed the hair from her face, her every move making him feel faint. It took all the control he had to keep from reaching and touching her again.

"What are you doing out here so far from anywhere? Where is your husband to protect you?"

"You've never been to the ranch before, have you?"

"No," he answered a bit embarrassed, not knowing where he was and telling this woman where she should be. "I'm pretty sure I am on the right road to reach the ranch."

"Yes, you are. You're less than half an hour away, and if you help me with the carriage, I will show you."

"I have made a fool of myself, haven't I? What is your name?"

"Jenny Tucker," she said nervously. "I have no husband."

"I should have asked earlier and not made a fool of myself."

"How can a man make a fool of himself when he tells a woman she is beautiful?" she asked, looking him in the eyes. "There are not a lot of men in the valley that tell a country woman she is beautiful."

"I will tell you every day if you would allow me," he said, looking serious.

"What about your wife—do you tell her how beautiful she is every day?"

"I've never had a wife, only a career."

"There must have been women where you were stationed before?"

"There were, but I didn't have time for a wife."

"And now?" she asked.

He turned with a smile to give his standard answer, but the words froze in his throat. Looking at Jenny's eyes waiting on his response, he knew the words he spoke now could change his life.

"Until today, my life had no meaning… beyond this uniform."

"I think we better get you to the ranch before you forget why you're out here." Jenny teased.

"Well, I'll get the carriage ready while you gather your things." Helping her up into her seat he said, "I can drive you if you would like."

"It's not often a girl gets driven home by a gentleman," she said softly, sliding to one side of the seat.

Tying his horse to the back of the carriage, he stepped up onto the seat, and Jenny handed him the reins. He flicked them gently across Molly's rump, and they headed to the ranch.

Jessie, Red Sun, and Justin along with the other braves were sitting at the village discussing finding more Andalusian cows to add to the herd of over fifteen hundred head. They all stopped talking when they saw the carriage come to a halt before it got to the barn, trying to see who was sitting with Jenny.

Even more puzzling, they didn't know any man in this area that Jenny would let ride with her. They were astonished when they saw that Jenny and the mystery man were laughing.

"It is a soldier," Silent Stalker spoke up.

"How do you know?" Jessie asked

"He has on a uniform," Silent Stalker answered.

"It has to be someone from the fort she recognized," Jessie said, a question in his voice.

No one spoke as they watched the soldier step down from the carriage, untie his horse and mounting him, start toward the village. Jenny waved goodbye and scooted over, taking the reins and heading for the barn.

As he reached the edge of the village, they all recognized Captain Amos who had come to Fort Dade with the colonel. The men stood and waited as he approached them and dismounted.

He walked up to Jessie, held his hand out and said, "Good to see you again Mister Tucker." Then he turned and walked up to each man, shaking hands and greeting all the braves who were standing there a bit confused. They were still not used to someone taking their hand and pumping it up and down, then turn it loose and then do the same to the others. He had no idea who each brave was. The last time he saw them, they were painted.

When he finished shaking everyone's hand, he turned to Jessie and said, "I have been sent here with a significant request from the governor."

"Well come sit and tell us what you have in mind."

"Would you like some water?" Justin asked.

"No thanks," the captain answered.

"Well tell us what is so important you had to have my daughter bring you here."

Looking a bit meek, he said, "She didn't have to bring me here. I met her back a ways, next to a small creek."

"Yes, we know where she goes," Jessie interrupted.

"Well, I stopped to talk to her and asked to drive her home, and she said yes. That's all."

"OK," Jessie said, "what is it you are here to tell us from the governor?"

"It's a request. The governor wants you to set up a hunt."

"I've seen the way the governors and their friends hunt, riding down the river killing everything that moves. You are talking to the wrong people. We kill what we eat and use for clothing. Tell Governor Perry that I appreciate everything he has done for the people and me, but you need to find them another paddle boat to take them down a river."

"I'm not sure what you are talking about, but I will relay your message to the governor."

"Captain, you're a good man, and we would like to see you here more often. We appreciate the way you helped to free our young braves from the court-martial," Jessie said. "Would you like something to eat before you head back?"

"No thanks, but there are a couple of things I want to look for at the commissary that they don't have at the fort or the small stores at Dade.

"Sure, take your time, and if there is something you need, Jenny can order it for you."

"OK, thanks," he said, leading his horse toward the commissary.

They all looked at Jessie and laughed. Justin said, jokingly, "The way that soldier was almost running toward the commissary, you may have a new son before long."

"That would be alright with me, as long as she stays here," Jessie answered. "Now let's get back to talking cows."

Jenny sat behind her desk listening for the door to open. She brushed her hair one more time and straightened the new dress she had changed into.

Race was totally confused at Jenny's actions; he had never seen her this excited and nervous, and she wouldn't talk to him about what was going on. Captain Amos stepped through the door, and Race saw Jenny almost running from her office.

Trying to maintain her composure, she crossed the room and told Race, "I'll help him."

Race, at first confused, looked at Jenny's new dress and understood what his sister was up to. Jenny frowned at his grin.

"Can I help you, Captain?" she asked quietly, her eyes never leaving his.

"Well, I'm not sure, but you could start by calling me Walter. I'll even take this military shirt off if it would help you remember my real name."

"I'll remember your name, Walter. You don't have to take your shirt off for me to remember that. Maybe you should just look around in case you see something you need."

"Yes, that's a good idea," he responded.

Race sat behind his desk smiling at what he was seeing. Jenny was taking the soldier down each row, stopping every now and then to explain something to him. He had never watched anyone fall in love and wondered if this is how it happens. Then a fearful thought crossed his mind. What if she fell in love and got married and left him here by himself? He wasn't sure he could do this without her. But he knew from the look in her eyes, he would have no say so, and it frightened him a bit.

Jessie and Ed sat their horses, watching and listening to the men behind the plows as they urged the mules on. This would be the last plowing as they built up the heap rows while the women followed planting tobacco seedlings. The plowing started late this year after waiting out the worst freeze they had ever dealt with. The ground stayed frozen longer than usual, and everyone was a little concerned how the crops were going to turn out this year.

Turning the horses, they rode to the sound of hammers banging on red-hot iron as they approached the blacksmith shop. The shop had been expanded with an outside corral next to the shed where they could keep the horses and mules to be shod. The shed had been extended to accommodate another furnace for Leroy who now had his own apprentice, working the bellows and keeping the coals hot. Everyone who watched Leroy hammer out some fine work said he would be as good as his pa one day.

Jessie and Ed sat fascinated, watching them work, and they waited until Troy had finished putting the final touch on a broken plow and laid his hammer aside. Seeing them, sitting outside the shed, he walked over and shook hands with Jessie and Ed. Ed was always amazed at the size and strength of Troy's hands.

"What can I do for you, Mister Jessie or you, Mister Ed?"

"I understand John and the others, including Leo, are bringing pieces of equipment here to have you fix."

"Yas sir, Mister John brings his large saw blade that gets too hot sometimes and warps. I straighten it out for him so he can keep cutting them boards for houses with all these people moving down here. I had a wagon last week that came from the commissary. Mister Race sent him here for me to fix a split axle or he wouldn't have made it back home the way it was."

"I understand," Jessie said, "but you are going to have your hands full just keeping this ranch going. I know John is hiring on people all the time as there is a bigger demand for lumber than ever before, so sooner or later, John and the others are going to have to have their own blacksmith shop."

"Yas sir, I understand Mister Tucker; Leroy and me are at least two weeks behind getting all these things repaired and Mister Tucker we are using up all the spare iron we have. I am already using some of the older plows for iron I need to fix what I can."

"Troy, I will get you iron—all the iron you need here within two weeks, if not sooner."

"That sure would help, Mister Tucker."

"Troy, you have the biggest heart of anyone I know, but you can't keep fixing everyone's equipment coming into this country, using our material for free. I don't care if you're fixing things for other people, but you can't do it for free. If people are going to bring you things to fix, you are going to have to charge them."

"Mister Tucker, you know I don't knows nothing about charging no white man for fixing something. I knows Mister Dunkin on the plantation, he charged people money for bringing things for me to fix, buts I'se don't knows nothing bout what he charged. They was white people, and it weren't none of my business. I'se just fixed what he brought me."

"I'll take care of the charging," Ed spoke up. "I want anyone, other than Bill, Dave or John, bringing things here to be fixed to come through me. If anyone brings something here to you, make sure he has talked to me first."

"Yas sir, Mister Ed," Troy answered, walking back to a piece of hot iron waiting on him.

Riding back to the house, Jessie spoke to Ed, "Jake and Hawk want to go on the cow hunt this year in the swamp to hunt for Andalusian cattle."

"I thought you had enough cattle, you didn't have to hunt them anymore," Ed commented.

"They're going to be gone one day, and we better get what's left while we can. There are more and more cow hunters coming into this country, and if we can get a large enough herd, we can raise our own and won't have to fight the heat, mosquitoes, and long drawn out drives to Tampa." As they reached Ed's, Jessie started for the village and at the last second, he mentioned, "Oh, by the way, we may be losing your sister to that captain at the fort."

"Wait! We can't lose Jenny, she holds this place together with her bookkeeping. Race is good, but he has his hands full, and he's not as good with the books as Jenny. Who does this captain think he is? How does he know Jenny? Why would you say that Pa? You're just kidding with me. Right?"

"Just saying," Jessie answered, turning his horse toward the village with a big grin that he tried to hide from Ed.

The mornings were still chilly, weeks after the hard freeze, and everyone was readying themselves for a two to three-week cow hunt in the swamps; they only hunted the Andalusian cows now. Jessie was trying to add three to four hundred head each year until he no longer had to look for cows but could raise enough of their own to ship to market. He had heard there was a railroad coming this way, possibly through Fort Dade.

Hawk and Jake were going on their first hunt, and they were excited, riding back and forth between the village and the barn. Jessie was tying his gear behind his saddle, placing an extra box of 44s in the saddlebags. He walked around his Marsh Tackie, checking the chinch belt, the loop holding his whip, and the rifle in the scabbard. Finishing, he walked to where Franklin was checking the ropes and Jeremy was harnessing Dolly and Preacher, who were standing and waiting patiently. At their age, they had been through this routine many times.

Franklin led the horses and wagon outside where they would start their long trip. Jessie walked over to where Belle was standing on the porch waiting with the half cup of coffee he had not finished. It was always hard on her, the waiting and praying no one would ever ride into her yard and tell her something terrible had happened to Jessie. She fought that feeling of fear for days each time Jessie went on the drive.

He would never know that. She handed him his cold coffee, watching the excitement in his face as he turned the cup up and drained it. He gave it back to her with a smile, and when she reached for it, he took her hand and pulled her to him, kissing her hard on the lips.

He pulled back and said seriously, "I'll be back soon, and if that soldier comes around after Jenny, you tell him if he's thinking of taking her off, he had better bring the whole army with him."

"When she looks at him or when he looks at her, you know you have either gained a son-in-law or lost a daughter," Belle said, just as seriously.

"She is a woman to be proud of now. I know that every time I look at her, but I'm not sure I could stand the thought of losing her right now."

"There is no right time, Jessie," Belle spoke softly.

"I know," he said taking Belle in his arms. "I just don't want it to happen now."

"It will happen when it happens, but not before you get back, I promise," she assured him, giving him a quick kiss. "Now they are waiting on you," she said as she pushed him from the porch, then waited until he was out of sight. She didn't feel the tear that ran down her cheek until she tasted the salt on her lips.

Jessie and the others didn't reach the edge of the swamps until late evening. It was after dark when they heard Sara Mae yell out, "Food's ready when you are."

The next morning, Sara Mae brought a large pot of coffee and hung it over the men's fires just as they were waking up and grabbing their cup. By the time the cups were filled, the fire was waist high, giving off enough light for the men to saddle-up and finish their coffee before it was light enough to set out on the hunt in the swamp. While they were finishing their coffee, Jessie spoke to the group.

"We have two new cow hunters with us for their first time, so Spirit Snake and Warrior Spirit will take Hawk with them, and Red Sun and I will take Jake with us."

Within an hour after daylight, they could hear the whips and the dogs barking deep in the swamp where Silent Stalker had seen a large herd feeding in a wetland on the edge of a thick forest of hardwood. It was a swampy, dirty creek full of large alligators.

"They are a mixed herd, but most are Andalusian," Silent Stalker said.

"That's fine," Jessie said, "we are selling any cows that aren't pure Andalusian to the fort; we will fatten them up first. Let's go get them!"

Jessie, Red Sun, and Jake came across forty or more cows that looked like pure Andalusian in some marshland. Jessie sent Red Sun to the left around the marsh to cut them off from the woods behind them and Jake to the right to push them out of the swamp and into the open pasture, still a mile away. The cattle spooked as soon as they saw the riders moving and started for the swamp where they were more adapted to the surroundings than their pursuers.

Red Sun kicked the Marsh Tackie into a run to cut them off with the dogs who were already out front, and he saw them turn toward Jake. Jessie spurred his horse and whistled to his dogs when he saw the wild cows turn back across the marsh, and had his whip going, cracking it quickly over his head. The dogs were nipping at the cattle's heels, turning them toward Jake who was trying to outrun them to the forest. Jake saw five or six break free and head into the woods.

Cutting across in front of the herd he entered the woods where had seen the cows go in. Pushing his horse harder than he should, he wanted to find those cows and get them back to the herd.

Hearing the two dogs ahead of him, he kicked the Marsh Tackie in the ribs, urging him on across the opening. The fast, little horse stopped suddenly, throwing him over its head. Jake flipped in the air and landed feet first in a mud hole.

Confused and dazed, he was trying to figure out why his horse would throw him. His horse had never come close to acting up or trying to throw him. Shock brought him back to reality when he realized his legs were sinking, and he couldn't make them move. Panic set in when the harder he tried, the faster he sank.

Somewhere in the back of his mind, he heard the stories of soft sand that would swallow you and your horse. He leaned forward as far as he could stretch but couldn't reach solid dirt and only felt himself sink to his waist. Realizing he couldn't get out on his own, Jake began to yell.

"Paw Paw, Paw Paw! Grandfather, Grandfather!" He could hear the rifle cracks of the whips. "Hawk, Hawk—help me!"

Making one more effort to free himself, Jake sank even further. The quicksand was up to his chest now. The realization that he was going to die here came to him, and nobody would even know where he had gone. For some reason, that thought bothered him more than the thought of dying.

He gave one more yell, "Hawk, Hawk!" as he raised his hands above his head as if that could somehow help.

Hawk came flying by Spirit Snake, kicking his horse in the ribs, laying low over his neck reaching back and hitting the Marsh Tackie with his coiled-up whip like a man gone mad. Spirit Snake kicked his horse in the ribs harder than usual, and in three leaps, he was running full speed trying to follow Hawk who was still kicking his horse at a full run. Spirit Snake uncoiled his whip and whirled it around his head cracking it three times.

Hawk never slowed up when he passed Jessie and Red Sun who were heading for the woods where Jessie had seen Jake follow some cows. Panic surrounded Jessie's heart and stopped his breath as he kicked his horse into a full run into the area he had seen Hawk go in.

Jake pulled his chin back to keep it out of the wet sand and watched a vast white cloud floating by. Now isn't that odd? He thought. It looks like an elephant I saw in a book once. Somehow, he found peace in that idea. Then he chuckled to himself, as he thought, how funny, my last thoughts were about an elephant.

Jake felt something hit his head, and he cried out, "Ouch, that hurts!"

"It's going to hurt worse than that if you don't grab that handle."

Jake twisted his shoulders until he saw the whip handle lying close to his hand and Hawk staring at him intently. He lowered his arm and grabbed hold of the handle—it was the greatest feeling he had ever felt.

"You can't pull me out. I'm too deep and stuck too tight, the sand feels like a million fingers holding on to me."

"He doesn't have to get you out by himself."

Jake and Hawk smiled in relief when they heard Jessie's voice.

"Jake," Red Sun spoke calmly to him, telling him, "Tie mine and Jessie's whips around your chest."

"Mine also," Justin urged.

"Mine too," Warrior Spirit added.

"I will come out and help you," Hawk said and stood up to take a step forward. Spirit Snake caught him around the shoulders, pulling him back.

"It's not your bravery we need right now. It's your wisdom, or we will be trying to get you both out."

"But, what else can I do, Father?"

"You can help when needed!"

"Sorry, Father, just tell me what to do—Jake is sinking."

Red Sun took over the conversation. "I have seen this happen in the Everglades, and the older ones showed us how to remove someone. Now, Jake, we are going to begin to pull the whips, and you will have to tell us when it is too much. When we began to pull, you twist and turn as much as possible and try to move your legs up and down; it will help loosen the grip the sand has on you."

As the four men began to pull, Jake thought they were going to tear him apart, and he yelled out.

"You have to help," Jessie said. "You have to try to wiggle; let's try it again."

Jake tried with everything he had and managed to move slightly back and forth. Feeling himself move, he kept at it until he was exhausted but saw the top of his chest.

Keeping the pressure on the whips until Jake was ready to try again, the men waited. It had taken half an hour to get Jake above his waist, but he was moving now. Jessie and Red Sun reached out, each taking a hand while Justin and Warrior Spirit kept tension on the whips freeing him of the death trap and onto solid ground.

Exhausted, but relieved, Jake sat up slowly and tried to remove the wet sand from his hands and arms without much luck.

"There is a small creek not far from here," Justin informed them.

Jake sat in the creek naked, feeling vulnerable as Jessie tried to rinse the sandy mud out of his clothes. Hawk waded in and sat next to Jake.

"Are you alright? That was nearly your death day."

"Yes, I know. How did you know I was in trouble?" Jake asked. It was a question he had been wondering about since Hawk showed up before anyone else.

"You called me!"

"No one else heard me," Jake said, wonder in his voice.

"I heard you," Hawk repeated.

Jessie walked by the boys and dropped Jakes clothes by the edge of the creek. "They are good enough to wear until we get back to camp."

"We will go help Big Cypress and the others bring in what cattle they have. That will be enough today."

While they moved what cows they had rounded up, Red Sun rode alongside Jake, who still wondered what had happened and how he wound up in the quicksand almost losing his life. He didn't want to be afraid of the swamps, but he didn't want to disappear with no one even knowing what happened to him. It took a moment to realize Red Sun was riding next to him. "Grandfather, what did I do wrong?"

Red Sun took a moment to answer. "When you are in the woods, you need to remember the animals know the woods you are in much better than you do. You should learn from the animals and use that when you are making choices of where to travel safely. If you see a trail going around an opening that you think would be easier than through the woods, remember they chose that way on purpose. It would be wise to let them lead you through. You do not belong in here if you fear." Red Sun turned away to join the others.

Jessie and the others sat around the fire, sipping on the last cup of coffee, while Sara Mae finished cleaning up and putting things away she wouldn't need for breakfast in the morning. Mister Tucker had told her earlier to get things ready to move tomorrow.

The Crackers Tuckertown

Jessie stood and spoke to the others. He could see they were tired and drained, chasing ornery cows through thickets and brush, leaving them scratched and worn out. By the end of the day when they brought in what they had rounded up and pushed them into a shallow valley with plenty of grass and water, they were exhausted from the back-breaking work.

"We have well over four hundred cows and calves. Most of them are Andalusian with some yellowhammers mixed in. I think we have added enough this year; our herd is getting bigger and bigger, and it won't be long before we can raise enough of our own. Then we won't have to hunt these ornery creatures anymore. Tomorrow, we will move what we have to the salt marshes for a couple of weeks before we start the branding."

With all the men The Double T Ranch had working, it was pretty straightforward with the dogs working the cows, as well as any pro, nipping at heels and reinforcing that with a growl now and then. The men only had to crack their whips occasionally to keep them moving. They were within a half a mile of the marshes when Silent Stalker, who always rode out front, came around the end of the hardwood forest pushing his horse hard. That was not a good indication to Jessie. He spurred his horse to a gallop and saw Red Sun doing the same, riding along the tree line until they both pulled up next to each other and waited for Silent Stalker to reach them.

"What makes you ride so hard?" Red Sun asked.

"There is another herd of cows on the other side of the trees headed for the salt marshes."

"How far away are they?" Jessie asked.

"They will be there about the same time as ours."

"Are they branded?" Red Sun asked.

"Not that I could see. I don't think those cows are from a ranch," Silent Stalker replied.

"We can't let them get mixed in with ours, or we could have a serious problem with the other cow hunters," Jessie said. "I will take Justin with me and see what we can do to stay out of a mess. I knew this was going to happen sooner or later as more cow hunters try to find some of that gold on the hoof."

Jessie waved at Justin as he rode toward the front of the herd that Big Cypress and Warrior Spirit were already trying to round up. "We need to stop these cows until Justin and I get back."

Jessie and Justin rounded the edge of the hardwood forest where they saw a herd of yellow hammers, he guessed was close to two hundred head, and he could tell they had not taken much time to fatten them up along the way. Counting three men working their whips with four working dogs, Jessie and Justin moved around the herd as the two outside men fell back to the third man.

Justin said to Jessie, "These men are professional cow hunters, not ranchers. I would bet good money from the way they act, all of them had fought in the war."

The three men turned and faced Jessie and Justin, spreading out about three feet apart.

"Yep, just as I thought. These men know what they are doing, they've been soldiers in the war," Justin whispered.

"What do you want?" the man in the middle asked the two strangers as they came to a halt in front of the three men.

"My name is Jessie Tucker. I own this piece of land, and I have a small herd of around four hundred head headed for that salt marsh at the end of these trees. They have not been branded yet. If our herds get mixed up, it will cause problems neither one of us needs."

"I understood this was still open range. We just spent most of four days going around another rancher that isn't letting anyone bring their cows through his land anymore. Hell, Mister, I guess cow hunters are becoming a thing of the past. Carpetbaggers are buying up land while it's cheap and even talking of putting barb wire around their land, so we can't cross it."

"Where are you taking your herd?" Jessie asked.

"We have always taken them to the stockyard in Tampa. He has always been fair with us, pays in gold," he replied, smiling for the first time.

"Well, Mister...?

"I'm Hampton, and my two brothers there is Arnold and Buster."

"You need to slow down and let these cows put on some weight if you're going to get good money for them," Jessie informed the men.

"We don't even know how much they are paying this year," Arnold spoke up.

"We don't even know if they are still buying," Buster added.

"They were buying last year, and there's no sign of them not buying more, but you're not going to get more than twelve to maybe fourteen dollars a head if you don't slow down and let them feed and fatten up."

"Mister," Hampton insisted, "we don't have time to wait on a bunch of cows to get fat. We all have families and kids at home with no one there to protect them, so I guess we will take what we can get. It should be enough to supply us until we can round up more of these yellowhammers next year."

"Men," Jessie said, speaking to all of them, "I can move my cows into another pasture for a few days so yours can get to that salt marsh, which looks to me they need."

"Well, Mister, I appreciate that, but are you going to have this placed closed off by next year?"

"No, there will always be a corridor through my land for independent hunters like yourselves. This country is being built by people like you. I have also heard rumors of some ranchers fencing off their property, but as long as possible, I'll never put a fence on my land. The exception will be my groves if cows get in and eat my trees."

Jessie looked around at the cows still slowly moving forward. "How many head did you say you had?" Jessie asked Hampton, who seemed to be in charge.

"Right at two hundred, best we could count. They'll be counted again when we get to the cattle yard."

"I will make you an offer," Jessie said. "I will give you eight dollars a head and put them in with mine."

Justin could see all of them trying to put the numbers together in their head and spoke up, "That's sixteen hundred dollars."

"How are you going to pay us sixteen hundred dollars?" Buster asked, his mouth open in disbelief.

"I have the money if you want to sell them or you can take them on to Tampa where you might get a couple more dollars apiece for them." He didn't have to wait long for an answer.

One look at each other, the brothers nodded to Hampton. He rode up next to Jessie, reached out his hand saying, "Mister Tucker, if you can show me that much money, you have a deal."

Reaching out and taking his hand, Jessie said, "I have the money. Let's take these bunch of cows and get them to the marshes. Justin, tell Red Sun to keep bringing our herd and let them mix." Turning back to Hampton, he said, "When we get this herd settled, you can follow us back to the ranch and get your money."

Jenny felt anxious as she gathered the items she was taking on her ride this morning and was glad to see the carriage ready. She carried her things and loaded them quickly behind the seat. Then, she left Franklin and Jeremy totally confused, watching her put Molly in a trot—not a hello or goodbye!

Jeremy was even more confused when he saw Franklin smiling and shaking his head. "What you smiling at? This is very confusing!"

"Lawd, Lawd, Miss Jenny done gone and fell in love with that soldier man."

"Well what we gonna do if he takes Miss Jenny to the fort and keeps her there, and we won't get to see her anymore?" Jeremy sounded distressed as he was asking Franklin for answers.

"We'll just have to wait and see how Mister Tucker handles this one. Jenny is his baby," Franklin said seriously.

Jenny became more and more anxious as she got closer to her turn off, straining to see ahead of her, doubt clouding her mind, wanting to feel excited, unsure until she saw what she had been looking for. The horse was feeding along the creek bank, but she saw no one as she slowed Molly and turned off the road. Jenny's heart almost came out of her chest as she spotted a head of black hair lying in the grass.

Not wanting to seem too anxious, she brought the carriage to a halt fifty feet from where she could see the shape of his body lying in the foot-tall grass. Stepping as quietly as she could off the carriage, she began to slowly ease forward until she was standing looking down at the smile on his face, his eyes still closed.

"I have been coming here every day waiting for you to show up. I was going to give you one more week, and then I was coming to see you anyway. What took you so long?" As he opened his eyes, she took his breath away with the way she looked at him. "That's a lie," he added, looking at her. "I would have come here every day for the rest of my life if I had to."

"I wouldn't mind that, if I had a home here to wait for you in," she said as she knelt, leaned forward and kissed him on the lips.

Looking up into her face with the feel of her lips on his, Walter said, "I always thought love was something you chose to do when it became time to find a wife and start a family. The way people feel about their families, I didn't realize love was something that took over your mind to the point you can't do your job. I have people wondering if I have for some reason lost my mind. I can't concentrate on my duties; the colonel is demanding to know what's happened to me, and I don't know what to tell him—that I am so in love with a beautiful woman, I can't think of anything else. I take care of my duties for the day, leave and don't come back until dark. The only way I can see to solve this is to marry you, build a house where we sit now with a large window looking at this view. I think that would explain things to a lot of people."

She spoke softly as she ran her fingers through his thick hair, "I have waited, loving my family that includes everyone at the lake, the village, and the people in the quarters. My brothers, who have watched over me since I was born, sometimes too much, but always with love. I don't think I can give that up, Walter." She leaned down and kissed him again.

"I would never ask you to give all that up. I've seen how special that place has become to a lot of people."

"It's too far for you to ride to the fort every day, what if they sent you somewhere else?"

"I have reached the point in my career that I can retire at any time I want. Since I saw you sitting in the sunshine, thinking you were an angel and the want started, I have thought of nothing else."

"What would you do? Other than farming or hunting cows, there's not much else to do in this country. You certainly don't look like a farmer," she giggled at him. "I don't want to spend half my time waiting for you to return from cow hunting or taking a herd to Tampa, like the other wives do, including my mother. She has gone through the horror of a missing husband. I don't think I could live my life waiting to see if you're coming home in one piece, just coming home and start all over again the next year."

"Maybe I'll start my own mercantile store in the growing community of Dade. That's part of my training when I was a junior officer and in charge of supplies for all the forts in North Florida," Walter suggested.

"That's still too far away. Why not help Race and me? It is already getting more than we can keep up with, and more and more people are moving into this part of the country."

"Does this mean if I build you a house here and stay close by, you will marry me?"

"Of course, you silly man. You knew that the first day you stopped here." He reached and pulled her around and into his arms.

They spent the rest of the morning walking the land, planning where to build the house, the kitchen, and bedrooms. They talked about how they would put in real glass windows, she would pick the color of the curtains, where he would build the barn and the smokehouse until they both realized it was already afternoon. Walter stopped her and turned her to face him.

"We need to go and talk to your father, I don't know how long I can do without you now."

"I'm afraid it will have to wait, he's off on one of their cow hunts and probably won't be back for two or three weeks."

"I don't think I can wait that long to see you!"

"Instead of waiting here for me, the ranch is less than half an hour away, and you wouldn't be waiting here wasting our time."

"I won't be able to come see you every day, but I will be there every chance I get."

"I'll be there waiting for you, but I think I had better be getting back before they send out a hunting party for me."

"I can drive you home again if you would like."

"I will be fine. Molly knows the way home with her eyes closed by now."

Captain Amos put his shirt back on over his undershirt, and he wondered if she had noticed. He stood next to his horse until the carriage was out if sight before he mounted his horse and started the long ride back to the fort. The more he thought about the fort, the less he wanted to be there. Riding up to the gates, he had his resignation letter written in his mind.

Captain Amos went straight to his office to write his resignation, but before he could get started, a soldier knocked on his door, informing him the colonel wanted to see him as soon as he returned.

"Have a seat, Captain," the colonel stated and waited. "I have a letter here from the governor, stating he was misrepresented last time he asked about a hunting trip. He has sent a letter to Jessie Tucker, and I'm sure you wouldn't mind delivering it to the ranch," he said knowingly.

Does everyone know? The captain wondered to himself.

The colonel stood up and handed the captain the letter. "I would like you to deliver that tomorrow."

"Yes sir, and there is something I need to talk to you about."

"Later when you get back," the colonel dismissed him.

Race knew the captain was there before he walked in when he saw Jenny frantically trying to rearrange her hair as she headed for the front of the store. Meeting her at the door, Walter pulled her around behind a shelf and kissed her.

Stepping back, still holding her hand he said, "I have to talk to your father."

"I know," she smiled, "and I think he knows what it's going to be about."

"That too," he smiled, "but I have a letter from the governor that I need to give him."

"He's not here now. They are at the branding pens, where they will be at least another week or more, but he comes and goes, and maybe you could wait here until he gets back," Jenny said playfully.

"You know I would love to, but I need to find him now," he said, putting on his official voice.

"Don't pull that official stuff on me," she laughed. After explaining to him how to get to the branding pens, which were more than two hours away, she pulled him back behind the shelf and kissed him. "You better get that official letter to father or they may put you out of the service," she teased, pushing him back out the door and watching until he was out of sight.

"Get that silly grin off your face, Race Tucker. You wait until it happens to you!"

Captain Amos had been riding for more than an hour and a half when he saw the gray smoke rising toward the clouds and guessed it came from the branding fires. He continued, turning toward the trail of smoke. One of the braves working the branding tapped Jessie on the shoulder and pointed to the rider a quarter of a mile away.

Jessie stuck the hot branding iron to a cow and then handed it to the brave and started toward the rider, recognizing him as he rode closer. The captain rode close and dismounted, dropping the reins and greeting Jessie.

Letting out a small chuckle, Jessie said, "Captain I know what it is you want to talk about, but I have a bunch of ornery cows to brand so there might be a better time to talk about this than right now. I'll be back at the ranch in a couple of days, and then we can talk about you and Jenny."

"Mister Tucker, Jenny is certainly one of the things we need to talk about, but that's not why I'm here." He reached into his saddlebags and took the letter from the governor, handing it to Jessie.

Jessie put aside the humor as he opened the letter, read a short section of it and put it in his hip pocket. "Thank you, Captain, I will be getting back to the governor in the next few days, right now I have work to do. If you go back by the commissary, tell them I will be back at the ranch in a couple more days."

"I would be glad to, but I'm cutting straight from here back to the fort, and I still want to have that talk with you soon," he told Jessie, mounting his horse. He turned and started the long ride back.

It was still an hour before dark when the men heard Sara Mae ring her dinner bell. Scattering the hot ashes, they headed for the creek to clean up and get some of that cow stink off them before sitting down for the evening.

All the men were curious when Jessie took his bowl of stew and biscuit and walked a ways from the others. He sat on a piece of log, pulled out the letter and began reading it.

"…The incident you spoke of was with a different governor. Just shooting animals for pleasure while riding down a river on a boat is not what I had in mind. I understand the Indians do a winter hunt for food and hides when the animals have their thick winter fur. That is when I would like to go on the hunt, hunting as they do. I will send my own staff to set up a camp and bring anything you deem necessary. I hope this clears up the misconception, and I will expect to hear back from you." Sincerely, Governor Perry

Jessie had been back at the ranch less than a week when he was in the barn and saw the rider coming from the direction of Fort Dade, but he couldn't recognize who it was. When the rider was close enough, Jessie realized it was the captain without his uniform on. Jessie stepped outside and gave a quick wave to let him know he was there.

"I couldn't tell who you were out of your uniform," Jessie said as Walter dismounted and shook hands. "Looks like you have come to have that talk."

"Yes, I have, and before I talk to anyone else, I wanted to talk to you to let you know my intentions. As you can see, I am out of uniform because I no longer have one. My resignation went through a week ago. I am no longer in the army. Jenny and I have talked about what would happen if we got married, and I can promise I will never take her away as long as she wants to stay here. We have picked a place to build a home where she goes to draw and write."

"We all know where she goes," Jessie chuckled. "At this point, everyone at the ranch knows what's going on, and they are all happy to see her walking around smiling. I think we should finish this conversation with Belle and Jenny.

Jessie and Walter headed for the commissary and stopped by the school room on the way. Belle and Jenny had Franklin and

Jeremy install benches with small desks that Jeremy had designed for two people to work together on. Most of the Indian women and children had stopped coming sometime back when they thought they knew enough about the white man's words and adding numbers. Most of the students now were kids from the quarters and from the families, John kept hiring for his mill. The mothers, who had never been taught to read or write, attended with the children. Belle was determined to keep the small school room open as long as someone wanted to learn.

Belle heard the footsteps coming down the wooden walkway along the building. She recognized the sound of Jessie's footsteps along with someone else. It sounded like they were coming her way and stepping to the door, she saw who was approaching. Belle turned and told Jenny she should dismiss the class for now. As she told the students they could leave, Jenny heard the two sets of footsteps, and her heart started beating fast. She knew it was time, and she did all she could to compose herself, but her heart was still racing when they stepped through the door. Jessie smiled at Belle, and she knew all was well and smiled back.

Walter walked over to Jenny and took her hands. "Are you ready?" he asked.

Jenny was unable to speak; all she could do was nod her head.

Walter turned and looked Jessie in the eyes, speaking to both Jessie and Belle. "I have asked Jenny to marry me, and she has agreed. I will build her a home, and we have discussed what I might do in the future. But before, I um… I would like your blessings." Not knowing what else to say, Walter stopped and waited for their answer.

"We have all waited for the right man to come for Jenny but always with the dread of losing her. I am happy we are gaining a son instead of losing our daughter," Belle answered.

"Father, I have talked to Walter about working here and helping Race and me, as we are becoming more and more depended upon by the folks around us. More people are moving closer to the ranch than Brooksville or Fort Dade, and they need supplies too."

"I know," Jessie replied, grinning. "Race and I have already talked about that. I think you and Race are right if you can convince Captain Amos to be part of this," Jessie said, pleased.

Walking over to her father and pointing her finger in his chest, she stated with an I know you are messing with me look, "He's not a captain anymore, and you know that."

Pulling her to him, Jessie said, "He can be anybody he wants to be as long as he doesn't take you away. You have always had your mother's and my blessing." Walking over to where his future son-in-law stood, Jessie held out his hand. When Walter took it, Jessie said, "Welcome to this family, Walter Amos. Have you two set a date yet?"

"No sir, I want to build our house first."

"Then let me offer a time. You don't have to use it, but after the cattle drive to Tampa and before the winter hunt, we have our yearly cookout. Everyone will want to be here for the wedding. Just something to consider," Jessie offered.

This year, the cookout had a special meaning, and everyone was excited as they came together again. This time it was a much happier occasion as they all greeted each other.

Jessie stood looking at Belle in the new dress he had bought along with his suit in Tallassee, and his heart said she was as beautiful as the first time he saw her. As she was finishing her hair, Jessie walked over to her and wrapped his arms around her waist.

"Do you know how much I love you, Belle Tucker?"

"Yes, I do. I count on it every day, and I can't tell you how happy I am knowing that. Why else would I love you so much," she teased. "Now you better let me finish so I can go help Jenny. She can't be late for her own wedding."

Jessie felt the excitement as he watched the women from the village carry food to the picnic tables. He listened to the sounds of laughter from children playing in the lake and the noise of conversations from all the families around the lake. Leo's family and the new men and their families, John had hired for his lumber business, mingled and shared stories. Jessie watched as Sara Mae looked over Franklin and Jeremy, making sure their shirt tails were tucked in. She had sewn them both a new pair of cotton pants and a white shirt for the wedding, and Franklin and Jeremy had cleaned and shined their work boots the best they could. Sarah Mae looked beautiful in a new dress she created from material she had picked out herself in Tampa during the last cattle drive.

Jessie smiled, watching the three of them, Sara Mae between her men, walking proudly to be a part of this family. Walking through the crowd, he saw two of the men from the quarters slowly turning the yearling calf over the dying coals, the meat would be done by the time the coals died out.

Jessie found the reverend and pulled him aside. "Reverend, could you get someone to ring the church bell twice when Belle sends someone saying they are ready?"

"Yas sir, I will go myself. You just let me know when."

"Thanks, Reverend."

Jessie walked toward the village where Woman of The Wind was dressing Two Worlds for his part in the two ceremonies.

Colonel Bane was more than happy to perform the ceremony and looked forward to the festival. Jenny had asked Two Worlds if he would give her and Walter the blessing he had given Ed and Spirit Snake.

Ed happily agreed to be best man and helped Walter dress for his wedding. Walter wore his best dress suit of black wool that he saved for special occasions. Ed, seeing Walter fumbling with the black bow tie, stood behind Walter and made a perfect knot. Now he watched as Walter paced the room mumbling the words he wanted to say at the wedding. They were waiting for word that everyone was ready.

The reverend stopped by and told them, "I'm on my way to ring the church bell, and Mister Jessie said to tell you to bring Walter to the lake."

Looking at Walter, Ed said, "It's now or never," and he chuckled as he put his arm around his shoulder and started for the door.

Little Otter and Little Moon were excited as they helped Belle get Jenny dressed. The wedding dress was made of fine white cotton and delicate lace that Sara Mae had brought from Tampa. The dress had a form-fitting bodice and high lacey collar. The skirt was flared with lace trim on the bottom and enhanced Jenny's figure. Sara Mae and Belle made the dress together, driving Jenny crazy, measuring her over and over until they thought it was perfect.

The twin sisters had never seen a white man's wedding. Belle let the two young women comb and fix Jenny's hair, adding small feathers from quail and small yellow sunflowers that were still blooming. When they were ready, Belle sent Little Otter to let Jessie know. When Little Otter returned, she told Belle that Jessie was sending the reverend to ring the bell to let everyone know it was time. She added that Walter was waiting.

The ceremony would take place under the arbor Franklin and Jeremy had made for this special happening. It was covered with lace Sara Mae had bought with the dress material, and the women from the village had decorated it with flowers and strips of fur with feathers that fluttered in the breeze.

Belle beamed with pride as she walked with Jenny, holding her arm. She could feel Jenny's grip getting tighter and tighter, and she patted Jenny's hand to keep her calm. Belle smiled at Woman of The Wind as she led Two Worlds to his place, a chair next to the arbor.

The crowd found places to sit on the benches that had been made for the occasion, and Ed waited with Walter under the arbor. When Walter saw Jenny walking with her mother, his knees went weak with the thought she was going to be his wife.

Belle stopped at the edge of the crowd where Jessie was waiting to walk Jenny over to Walter. Jenny stepped close to the man she had loved and worshiped all her life and gave him a hug, whispering in his ear, "Thank you, Daddy, I love you."

Jessie knew if he didn't say something, he was going to cry. Stepping back, he started toward the waiting husband with Jenny on his arm, and when he swallowed the lump in his throat, he leaned down and whispered, "I'm not really giving you away. I'm just loaning you to Walter, but you will always be my little girl I brought from Georgia."

Looking up smiling, she squeezed his arm and said, "I know, Daddy."

Stopping in front of Walter, she reached out her hand, and as Walter took it, Jessie willed the tears back. Somehow, he managed to find his seat next to Belle who was wiping her eyes.

After Colonel Bane finished speaking about the gift of marriage and the duties that came with it, he asked for the rings and instructed Jenny and Walter to say their vows. Ed gave Walter the ring he would place on Jenny's finger, and the two people she considered sisters handed Jenny the ring for Walter. As they placed them on each other's fingers, they said the precious words they had prepared for each other. The colonel pronounced them man and wife and offered his congratulations.

Jenny and Walter thanked the colonel warmly and turned to Two Worlds as he rose from his chair. The women from the village also rose and came forward. Jenny's heart fluttered when she saw the robe made from the red wolf. Ed turned Walter, so he faced Jenny, and as they stood almost touching each other, the women wrapped the robe around the two of them.

Standing close to Jenny, wrapped in the robe, Walter felt he had stepped into another world, listening to Two Worlds as he shuffled around the couple chanting and calling on his ancestors for their blessings. When Two Worlds finished, the women removed the cape, folding it for Jenny and Walter to take on their marriage trip.

Jenny and Walter stood arm in arm as the people, one by one, came by to wish them well. They thought about staying for the meal, but what they really wanted was to be alone in their new home. Everyone pretended they didn't see them as they slipped away to the barn where Jeremy had the carriage waiting.

A week after the wedding, Race and Jenny sat down with Walter and planned out the future of the commissary. Race would still handle the ordering of supplies for everyone at the lake and extra for the families that were moving into the area. Jenny would always keep the books, and Walter was helping her set up for all the different operations at the ranch.

Walter would work with the quarters to find buyers for the tobacco crops and with Leo for the oranges, and he would make sure they had everything they needed to get to market.

The country was changing now with railroads being rebuilt to pick up freight closer to the suppliers. More supplies were needed up North and the farmers provided as much as they could grow.

Ten

THE HUNT

In January, the chill persisted with constant cold fronts coming through, one right after the other. Jessie talked to the braves, and they agreed to his request to take the governor hunting this year for their winter hunt. That would mean staying out in the woods for several days. Everyone had been waiting to get started ever since a messenger came from the fort, informing them Governor Perry was there preparing for the hunt and would be coming in a couple of days.

Hawk and Jake saw the wagons coming from the fort and jumped on their horses to ride out to meet them. They both wanted to see what the new governor they were taking hunting looked like. They were both impressed with his full head of hair and the black beard that covered his face, protecting it from some of the cold. There were eight soldiers from the fort, including the sergeant and two privates who had been there when they had the boys locked up. The privates kept their grins to themselves watching the other soldiers staring at the two young men with headbands of earned feathers. The young braves were riding around the wagons trying to satisfy their curiosity about what was in them, and they pulled to a stop, staring at the most beautiful horse they had ever seen.

They both came off their horses and eased toward the big stallion. "I wouldn't touch him if I was you," one of the soldiers called out, "that's the governor's hunting horse, and I am the only one allowed to handle him."

Neither Jake nor Hawk paid attention to the solider as they walked up and began to stroke the stallion's cheeks, both talking to him at the same time. The big animal looked first at one then the other and stood perfectly still.

The soldier who had warned them not to touch the governor's horse dropped back next to the sergeant and asked, "Are they wild? What are we supposed to do if they if they attack us?" The soldier hadn't seen the boys when they shot the three men.

The sergeant informed him, "Everyone that saw the fight can't stop talking about how fast they were with those pistols they wear. You are safe here. Just don't even think about bothering these people unless you want Governor Perry to stick you in some shit hole fort for the rest of your short career, now get back where you belong."

Jessie and Red Sun walked out to where they wanted the governor to set up and waited on the wagons. As the wagons stopped, the governor got out with a big grin on his face, excited about going on a real hunt just like the Indians.

"Jessie, it is good to see you again, and I hope this is not putting you out!"

"Everything is fine, and you can have your men set up your camp where they are. Let me introduce you to Red Sun, the chief of this band. It is he who gave permission for your hunt with his braves."

Turning to the chief, the governor held out his hand. The Indians were becoming used to white people shaking their hand up and down and then turning them loose. Red Sun held out his hand until the white man got through pumping it, then he spoke. "You are a friend of Jessie's and helped our people stay here. We will take you on the hunt with us, and you can kill many animals for us to use."

"Thank you, Chief. I am looking forward to the adventure; now if you will excuse me, I will go and let the men know what to do."

"Are they all staying?" Jessie asked with concern in his voice.

"No, no, when they are through setting up my camp, only the lieutenant, two of the soldiers, and my personal aid will stay. The others will return to the fort tonight," the governor answered.

"When they are through setting up camp, they can build their own fire, or they can join the braves here. When you are ready, I would like for you to come to the house and have supper. Belle has fixed a special meal for you."

"Thank you, thank you," the governor said and smiled as he turned toward the wagons.

Belle sat on the front porch listening to the drums in the village. Over time, she had learned the different sounds and rhythms of the drums, the celebrations, the call to their ancestors in times of sickness and death. Tonight, sounded very different. She heard the fast-paced, upbeat rhythm of the excitement of the coming hunt. Belle sat and waited in anticipation for the celebration to end and see Jessie coming home with a smile on his lips and that certain look in his eyes. It made the hair on the back of her neck stand up and goosebumps cover her arms, every time even after all these years.

Governor Perry and his group sat outside of their small camp watching and listening in fascination as Jessie and the other braves kept rhythm on the drums. Two Worlds did a slow dance around the fire that lasted for over an hour, calling on their ancestors to watch over their hunt. As the moon rose above the treetops, the drums went silent, the fire burned down, and the ashes were scattered for the night.

It was just turning daybreak when Jessie walked to the village, a smile on his face and an air of anticipation, sipping on his cup of coffee. He joined the governor who was sitting outside his tent on a chair in front of the fire drinking coffee with his personal aid behind him.

"Can I offer you a chair and more coffee?"

"Thanks, but I think we should join Red Sun and the others; there are things to talk about before we start out."

"Of course," the governor said, and rising with his cup, he followed Jessie to where the braves were loading the horses with supplies for the next three to four days.

Jessie steered Red Sun, Justin, and the governor over next to the heat of the fire while they talked.

"Governor, the four of us will hunt together for the larger animals: deer, coyote, red wolf, and bear. Silent Stalker and the boys have scouted a large swampy hammock less than a half days ride north from here where we will set up camp. Franklin will send a wagon every day to carry the animals back to the village, so the women can start their cleaning and curing of the hides. Governor Perry, if you want, you can have your wagon follow us to camp. The other braves will hunt the smaller animals: the fox, rabbits, and turkeys. We should be back in three to four days."

"Great, can't wait to get started," the governor said.

Jessie and the others reached their campsite before noon and did some scouting where they would hunt the next day. The soldiers set up the governor's sleeping tent and built a fire for the coming night.

Later, as they sat around the fire discussing the hunt, Justin asked the governor, "Just out of curiosity, what kind of gun are you going to hunt with?"

A big smile came across his face, and he said to his aid, "Bring me my rifle."

Taking the soft, beautifully designed long leather case from his aid, he untied the leather straps and opened the end flap. He took hold of a beautifully carved stock, pulling a fifty caliber Hawkins from its case and handed it to Justin. Justin just held it and stared. It was a true Hawkins, a legend with the mountain men, and more of a myth this far south. He never imagined seeing one, much less be holding one as beautiful as this.

Justin looked up at the governor with his eyes full of questions.

"It was presented to me by a Hawkins representative on a hunt in Wyoming a few years back. It will drop a buffalo in its tracks. I can say that for a fact," he said and smiled.

"You have hunted large game before?" Justin asked.

"I have tried to go somewhere every year for the past fifteen years. No gentlemen, this is not my first hunt." He reached and took the rifle back from Justin.

"That's a beautiful rifle but a bit overkill for deer and wolves," Justin remarked.

"This is not the gun I will hunt smaller game with. No gentlemen, I will use my new model 1885 .45-70 single shot designed by an innovative gun designer by the name of John Moses Brown. Everyone will know that name one day. I understand there will be bear hunting on this trip, and gentlemen, I have hunted the grizzly. You only get one shot at a charging bear, and it had better stop it, or you've got serious trouble on your hands," he laughed. The men sitting by the fire listening to the governor began to form a different opinion about the man they first met.

The four men, led by Red Sun, had followed Silent Stalker's and the two boys' tracks. The signs they left told them what to expect ahead all day. They let the governor do the shooting and were impressed with his hunter's patience and skill. The first day when they caught up with Silent Stalker and the boys, they had seven deer and six beautiful, winter, thick-furred red wolves tied across two mules. They saw small packs of coyote in the distance but didn't pursue them.

Jessie lay still trying to understand what he was hearing, then he realized it was more of a feeling than a sound that had awakened him. Rising, he wrapped himself in one of his sleeping furs and followed the faint sound that became a chant he recognized. Red Sun was singing his death chant—was he expecting his death? Red Sun had been on this hunt every year, and Jessie had never seen him do this. Recognizing the importance of this moment, Jessie turned and left as silently as he had approached.

The four men sat around the governor's campfire, sipping hot coffee and waiting on daylight to get started. Silent Stalker and the boys had started ahead a half hour before when Red Sun spoke.

"Today, we hunt the bears. They will be in the hardwood hammocks, and the brush is thick; that makes the bear a better hunter than we are. We will not just be hunting the bear—the bear will hunt us before we are done—today will be a dangerous day." Turning to Governor Perry, he said, "Today is the day to bring the big gun."

Red Sun insisted on leading the way, following the trail Silent Stalker was leaving with their horses' hoof prints and broken stems on brush that told Red Sun what he was following. They were more than a mile into the hammock, following an old trail, and the scrub oaks were thick. The only fresh tracks were the scouts' horses ahead of them when Red Sun came to a sudden halt, coming out of his saddle and pulling his rifle from the scabbard on the way to the ground.

Jessie and the others did the same, moving forward where Red Sun squatted over a track.

"Bear," he announced as they approached. They all looked in awe at the size of the huge paw print. "We hunt on foot now; stay behind me and watch closely. He is not very far ahead of us."

Moving slowly and silently, they followed forty to fifty feet behind Red Sun, watching and stopping when they saw him kneel-down on one knee, leaning his rifle against his shoulder. Red Sun felt his heart slow to barely a beat, his breath caught short in his chest when he saw the giant paw had stepped on the fresh tracks of the horses. He realized the bear had back-tracked behind Silent Stalker after they passed.

Red Sun was still holding his breath when the six-hundred-pound bear broke through the brush thirty feet in front of him in a full charge. Red Sun was just bringing his rifle from his shoulder when he heard a loud boom and saw the top of the bear's head explode. The massive bear went nose first into the ground, somersaulting and landing three feet away. With his last instinct, he reached out, covering Red Sun's moccasin with a huge paw, quivered once and lay still.

Red Sun was still on one knee staring at the massive form that lay at his feet. He slowly turned, looking over his shoulder, and saw the smoke from the black powder trailing from the barrel of the fifty caliber Hawkins. Jessie and Justin stood with rifles still to their shoulders staring at the governor, who had a small grin on his face when he spoke to Red Sun.

"He was almost as quick as a grizzly!"

Rising slowly to his feet, Red Sun walked to where the governor stood, lowering the Hawkins. Jessie and Justin stood on each side of the governor, keeping their rifles to their shoulders, scouting the brush, ready to fire in case the bear wasn't alone. Before Red Sun spoke, he heard the scream above him and looked up to see the osprey circling.

"That osprey started screeching just before the bear attacked you, Chief," said the governor.

"You heard the osprey before the bear attacked," Red Sun said surprised.

"That's what alerted me. Something spooked the bird, and that usually means something's happening we don't see yet, but you better pay attention, because it's going to happen. In the wild, I've found it happens fast when it does."

"Only a true brave and warrior could have saved my life today." Reaching for the governor's hand, he pumped it up and down like the white man does when he is happy with you.

Red Sun let go of the hand, walked past the men, and reaching his horse, mounted him and turned toward the hunting camp.

"He's leaving," Governor Perry said and started for the horses.

"We will give him some time," Jessie stated, watching Red Sun ride away.

"Certainly," the governor agreed, understanding at once what Jessie meant.

Jessie and the others sat around the fire the next morning, drinking coffee and waiting for daylight. Red Sun told the men they would hunt in the morning for more bear, then go back to the lake in the afternoon. "After the morning's hunt, we will have enough meat and furs until next year."

"You think we will find more bear today, Chief?" the governor asked.

"Yes, Silent Stalker and the young braves have scouted an area where the bears feed this time of year. It is not far from here. We will be back with plenty of bears when the wagons arrive to carry the animals to the lodges."

As the men gathered their hunting rifles and checked the loads, the governor saw Red Sun next to his horse. He walked over to him and asked, "Chief, are you sure you are alright? I have seen men who could never hunt again after a close call like yesterday."

"Because of the power of your spirit, I have a new life today, a gift only the great spirit can take now. Ride with me today as a brother warrior. I will give you more bears to test your bravery on."

"Wonderful! It would be an honor, Chief."

Perry felt he was riding as a real man now next to Red Sun. He was not a governor this morning; he was a warrior riding with fellow warriors. This had become an experience as no other hunt had been, and he felt full of life.

Red Sun had been following Silent Stalker's path for an hour, and the sun was climbing over the treetops when he saw a small broken branch and slipped from his horse. The others did the same. They would go from here on foot. Jessie realized his nerves were on edge. There would be no putting that six-hundred-pound image away for a long time, and watching the others, he knew they were seeing the same picture he was.

Using the horses to pull the three dead male bears into a clearing to be picked up, they joined Silent Stalker, Hawk, and Jake. "Governor Perry killed all of them with his Hawkins," Red Sun said, awed by the power of the big gun. Perry was the only one Red Sun would let shoot this day.

As the hunting party reached the village that evening following Silent Stalker, the women met them and walked alongside Perry's horse, dancing, chanting, trilling, and smiling. He remembered the women of the western tribes trilling with their tongues when they celebrated, but he had never been honored as profoundly as this.

It was real, and he knew it was about the bear and the life of their leader. Feeling as proud as he had ever felt as a man, he sat up straighter in the saddle.

The morning sun warmed the day, while Jessie sat with Red Sun as the governor walked through the village to where Two Worlds sat by the fire in front of his lodge. The ancient shaman sipped warm broth from a gourd that one of the women had brought him. Jessie smiled when he saw the governor squat to speak with Two Worlds, then rise and walk to each brave, shaking their hands and thanking each one. Perry was mesmerized by how the women had staked the hides to the ground, laughing as they worked together, scraping them and getting ready to cure them.

Seeing the massive hide of the bear that almost took their leader stretched between two young trees, he walked forward until he could reach out and run his hand through the thick black fur. He would never forget this hunt and the people of Tuckertown. Perry smiled when he remembered the letter in his papers.

Jessie walked with the governor when he told him he needed to speak with Race before he left for the fort. He stopped for a moment to say thank you and goodbye to Belle. They walked on to the commissary and saw Race putting firewood in the heater as they walked in.

"Good morning, Governor," Race greeted him with his hand out.

"Good morning, young man. I believe I have something you have been waiting on. A few weeks back I gave the postmaster general your letter and here is his reply," he said, smiling as he watched Race trying not to seem too anxious. Race tore the letter open, looked up at Jessie wide-eyed, and handed his father the note.

"What does this mean?" Jessie asked, reading the letter.

"You have been added to the list of U.S. Postal routes between Brooksville and Fort Dade. You are officially listed as the Tuckertown Post Office, signed by the postmaster general and Governor Perry."

"Congratulations!" The governor reached and shook Race's and then Jessie's hand. "I won't be governor forever, but I hope I have made enough friends here to get an invitation back again."

"You will always be welcome here, and I know the people of the village will be disappointed if you don't," Jessie responded.

The governor listened to the trilling of the women and became lost in the hunt again as his carriage started its way back to the fort.

It had been almost three months since the governor had been back from his hunting trip, and he was in the middle of a meeting when they were disturbed by a knock on the door. His aid walked in excusing himself, walked to the governor and informed him a wooden crate had been delivered.

"Why are you disturbing me right now?"

"I thought it might be important; it's from Tuckertown, sir."

The Governor's heart began to race in anticipation. "Bring it inside right now!"

Two men brought in the box and set it next to a table where three men sat, confused by the governor's actions in the middle of their meeting. Turning to his aid, he started to say something, when he saw two workers coming through the door with small tools in their hands.

Working very carefully, they removed the lid, and Perry's breath caught short when he saw the thick black fur. Turning to his smiling aid, he commanded, "Get everyone out of here. Close the door behind you!"

Before the door closed, he was on one knee, leaning over the box. Inside, was the thick black fur of a huge bear. The sight made his heart race, and he could feel the excitement of the hunt start as he reached and touched the claws. The claws were attached to a beautiful, thick fur collar from the winter fox. The governor stood, lifting the hide from the crate, surprised it didn't weigh as much as he expected and slipped his arms through the sleeves of the coat. He stood tall and let out a deep breath as it settled over his shoulders.

Governor Perry felt like he had just stepped back into a different, more primitive world when he slipped the antler tip buttons through the slits that held it closed. Then, out of the corner of his eye, he saw it, and his heart went wild. Perry reached and lifted the headband with a single feather hanging by a narrow strip of leather and recognized it as the one Red Sun had worn. Slipping the band over his head, he walked to the closet and opened the doors with their full-length mirrors. He stood staring at the huge bear and with a small smile, in the blink of an eye, he brought the Hawkins to his shoulder and fired.

Eleven

RAISING CANE

Jessie came awake slowly and felt Belle in his arms. He lay still, not wanting to lose her to the coming morning. He smiled as he smelled the slight scent of smoke in her hair and remembering how the night had ended, he became aroused again.

It began the day before, long before daylight. Franklin and Jeremy started the fire using the hot flames from the pine stumps, caked with pine sap that everyone called "lightered" wood, and burned the oak logs to create a pit of hot coals. Then they went to get the young Andalusian yearling hanging in the barn that they had skinned and prepared for the yearly cook-out.

Jessie sat at the table and listened to Belle, sometimes talking to him and half the time talking to herself.

"I don't know if this pot is large enough to hold enough blackberries for a cobbler—you did say Bonnie and Leo are coming early right?"

Jessie just smiled to himself knowing she wasn't going to give him time to answer. He just kept drinking his coffee, watching Belle's cup getting cold when Jenny and Walter walked in.

"What is all the noise going on in here?" she asked, smiling at her pa as if she didn't know. Kissing her pa on the top of his head, Jenny picked up her mother's cup and carried it to the stove. She poured hot coffee on top of the half-empty cup, filled another one for Walter and came and sat down at the table, giving Jessie a knowing look. Jenny heard the excitement and a little desperation in her ma's voice when she spoke to her without turning around from stirring the pot of berries.

"Jenny, I am going to need you to help me make the cornbread and cut the corn off the cob for the cream corn, and we are going to need a lot."

"OK, Ma, can I finish my coffee?"

"Sure, honey, but I need you to hurry this morning."

"Ma, we have about six or seven hours before anyone will be eating," Jenny answered back, trying to be patient. She knew it was going to be a long morning as she finished her coffee and rose to help her ma.

Jessie knew he needed to finish his coffee and get somewhere else fast before Belle had him helping her cook. He nodded to Walter and leaving quietly, they walked down by the fire pit, where the calf was already cooking over the hot coals. He left Walter talking to Franklin and made his way to the lake; it had become his daily routine when he was home.

He dropped his pants and took off his shirt and boots before he waded in the cool water. Then he dove and stayed underwater as long as he could hold his breath, swimming back to sit next to the old man. Two Worlds was sitting and puffing on his long stem pipe, listening to the words of his ancestors only he could hear. Jessie always sat and waited for Two Worlds to speak first unless he had a troubling question. Two Worlds waited until Jessie had settled.

"I had a vision last night," Two Worlds stated. Jessie brought all his senses into focus because sometimes you had to interpret Two Worlds' visions. He didn't always explain.

"There was a gathering of great warriors," he said and smiled. "They were from different tribes, but they all worshiped the same great spirit." Two Worlds was puffing small clouds of smoke and still smiling.

"I don't understand," Jessie said, confused.

"Before the sun rises tomorrow, you will understand." The old man stood and walked slowly to his lodge, where food would be waiting.

It couldn't be bad, Jessie thought as he put his pants on and started home to have his own breakfast.

Mr. Francis walked slowly through the quarters as it came alive, smelling the aromas of brewing coffee and fried bacon and that distinct smell of hoecake they had all come to love. Different people came by and walked with him, knowing where he was going. He could barely make out shapes anymore as his eyes turned milkier white every year. Mr. Francis had been around before the others were born. He was the sugar cane syrup maker on every plantation he had been sold to. Mr. Francis couldn't remember anymore how many that had been—it wasn't important anymore, because he knew there would be no more plantations. He couldn't recall if there had ever been a place where he had been as happy to wake up as he was now. Toby joined him and led him into the shed where the plows and harnesses were kept.

"Good morning, Mr. Francis," he heard the men call out.

Mr. Francis stood as straight as his old body would let him.

"You men gots the mules harnessed to the sleds?"

"Yas sir," they all answered together.

"Well, what are you all standing around for, let's get them to the fields and get them loaded. What about the fire under the kettle?"

"Ready to set fire when you say so, Mr. Francis," one of the men said.

"Mules picked out to turn the grinder?"

"Yas sir," a young man spoke up loudly, knowing that the old man could barely hear anymore.

"Mr. Francis, why don't you step right up here on the sled? We are going right by the grinder, and we can drop you off there." Taking the old man gently by the arm, the young man led him to the sled, making sure he was holding on to the front rail.

Troy laid the piece of burlap across the five-gallon bucket they would use to catch the juice as the cane was fed into the grinder.

"Wrap that rope around again, Leroy, just to make sure we don't lose the burlap in the bucket. Then cover it good from that pile of moss, that will help keep out the trash from the cane stalks."

Straining the juice was something they would do each time the bucket was full enough to be emptied into the cast iron kettle. There it would be cooked down to just the right consistency and taste for cane syrup. In the end, that would be determined by Mr. Francis along with the opinion of a couple of older men who had done this several times themselves at other plantations.

Toby stopped the sled next to the cane grinder, to let Mr. Francis off. He and Troy exchanged a nod of understanding, then he drove the mule and sled to the field where half of the two acres of sugar cane had been cut the day before. The cane waited to be loaded on the sled and hauled to the grinder to be stripped of its leaves before being fed into the grinder for its sweet juice.

Leo sat calmly on his stump he used for a chair and sipped his hot coffee watching Bonnie scuttle from one wagon to the other, hurrying everyone. The boys were getting two of the wagons ready to carry everyone on the two-hour trip to the lake.

JR called his two boys to him. "You boys take a bucket each, get water from the creek and make sure all the fires are out."

Walking to where his pa sat still sipping his coffee, JR said, "David and Todd have the wagons loaded; Ma and everyone is ready to start out when you are."

"Well I guess I better finish this coffee," he said and smiled as he turned the cup up and drank the last swallow. Standing and putting his arm around his oldest son's shoulder, he said, "Let's get these women to a picnic before they drive off and leave us standing here."

"If we don't get going, I think they will leave us for sure," JR laughed.

Race and Hawk volunteered to escort Belle and Jenny on a visit two weeks before in their carriage pulled by Molly, the offspring of Preacher and Dolly. Molly had the strength of Preacher and the calmness of Dolly. She had become Jenny's favorite animal. Jenny always used Molly on her small outings in the carriage. Some day's she just needed some alone time, or when she slipped away to write in her journal about all the events of the place everyone now called "Tuckertown."

Belle and Jenny had spent over two hours sitting, talking with Bonnie and her daughters-in-law, by the bank of the spring-fed creek, watching the kids splash and play. The men were clearing land where they were going to build their new homes with the lumber they had begun to haul from John's mill. As it came time to leave, Belle walked to where Leo stood watching his sons cutting trees.

Leo and his sons stopped what they were doing and removed their hats. "What can I do for you, Belle?"

Belle smiled. "Jessie wanted me to be sure to invite you and all the family to our yearly cook-out, two weeks from today."

Myra sat next to John on the wagon seat, watching the younger boys playing chase as they waited on Frank and Dancing Sun to pull alongside them. Frank pulled as close to his pa's wagon as possible without running over his wheel. Myra slipped over to the end of the seat as Frank passed four-year-old Gina and then two-year-old Leslie across to John. He placed them between him and their Grandma Myra. Their second oldest son Todd and wife Sharon rode on the seat behind Myra. Suddenly Myra stood and stepped over her seat into the back.

"Todd, you ride up with your pa. I'm going to sit back here with Sharon." Myra turned to her daughter-in-law and asked, "Are you sure you want to make this trip with the baby not that far off?"

"I'll be fine," she answered, "I'm not about to stay here while everyone else is having fun."

"Not everyone is pregnant," Myra said and smiled. "I'll stay here with you."

"I'm fine, 'Mema.'"

Bill and Martha were loading food in the wagon when John arrived with his family. As soon as the wagon stopped, Martha went to speak with her daughter.

"Good morning, Myra," she said as she walked around the wagon to the side Sharon sat on.

"Hi, Mama."

"Hi, baby, are you sure you should be riding on that bumpy seat."

"I told her I would stay home with her, but she insisted," Myra spoke up.

"You can stay here with me," Martha pleaded.

"Mama, I'm going to the festival. I'm fine, and I'm not going to talk about it anymore." "Lily," she called out to her younger sister, "would you sit here with me?"

"Sure," Lily answered.

Reaching up and touching Todd's shoulder, Sharon asked him, "Would you help Lily?" Picking Lily up, Todd set her next to her pregnant sister.

As soon as Dave and Bonnie saw the wagons coming, they climbed up onto the buggy seat and waited until the others reached their yard, then Dave flicked the reins across his horse's rump and followed them the lake.

Justin sat drinking his coffee in front of his lodge, watching the women feeding the kids and getting the fires ready to cook the flatbread they made from coontie flour. Everyone had come to love the bread. He felt a sense of tension and an undercurrent of power as he watched Jessie head for the lake to sit with Two Worlds, but he didn't know what it meant. Putting it aside, for now, he decided to go and see if Franklin and Jeremy needed help with the fire. He knew Franklin wasn't going to let anyone help with turning the calf as the task had become his pride and joy, but Justin would offer anyway.

"Good morning, Franklin, Jeremy, how's everything going?" He knew the answer before asking.

"Just fine, just fine," Franklin repeated smiling.

"You need a hand with anything?"

"Naw sir, Mister Justin, everything fine here, the beef will be ready when everything else is."

Justin took his empty coffee cup and started around the lake toward the quarters anticipating the day's activity. He walked up on Jessie and Belle's porch and knocked. Belle opened the door and seeing Justin standing there, said, "Jessie is still at the lake."

"Yes, I know. I saw him." Holding his cup in front of him, he smiled and said, "I was on my way to the quarters and ran out of coffee and wondered if you had a cup left over."

"You know I do," she smiled, "hold on, I'll get the pot."

Walking the short distance to the quarters, Justin came to the grinder and kettle set up by the creek. He walked up and watched as the mule pulled a sled load of cane up next to the grinder. Several boys unloaded the sled where the women would remove the leaves from the stalks, using a tool Troy had made in his blacksmith shop. Once the stalks were free of leaves, they were ready to feed into the grinder.

"Mr. Francis," someone yelled, "we're ready to start feeding the grinder, you should be the first one to start feeding cane through."

One of the women took him by the arm and led him to the grinder as one of the men picked up a stalk and handed it to Mr. Francis. Holding the stalk and pointing it toward the opening, the old man smiled as he heard the mule start his circle around and around, dragging a short piece of log attached with a chain to the long pole that turned the grinder. Troy watched everything with a close eye, making sure all the parts he and Leroy had forged worked as they should.

The women who had done this before were showing some of the other women how to use the cane stripping knives, which were working perfectly. As Mr. Francis was feeding the first stalk of cane, Troy saw a drop of liquid fall from the spout onto the moss-covered bucket. He reached and took the tin cup sitting on the frame, held it under the spout, and caught the next several drops. Troy passed it around to Mr. Francis. A smile crossed the old man's face as he swished the sweet nectar around in his mouth and swallowed it— hesitating, to let the taste settle on his taste buds.

"Boys, we'uns gonna make some fine syrup today."

Justin watched as some of the women began to feed several stalks of cane into the grinder and smiled in anticipation as the juice started to flow and fill the bucket. Then he turned and headed back to the village to wait for the festival to begin.

The sun was still below the treetops as Jessie stood talking to Franklin and Jeremy when he saw the wagons with Leo and all his family start down into the valley. "You need me to send you some help?" Jessie asked Franklin before he headed to the house to get Belle.

"Naw sir, me and Jeremy gots this handled Mister Tucker."

Belle stood next to Jessie as he waved to Leo and family, pointing to where he wanted the wagons parked close by the tables under the oaks. That was close enough to carry their food to the tables where everyone would gather for the feast to come.

Leo looked back and smiled, seeing the wonder and confusion on everyone's face as they drove past the Indian village. Even though he had told them about the village, and they had met them the night of the freeze, he knew they would not understand until they saw it for themselves. Belle met Bonnie and hugged her as soon as the wagons had stopped.

"It's good to see you again; I'm so glad ya'll could come," Belle said and called the rest of the women over to her. Jessie talked to Leo while the men removed the harnesses from the mules and led them to the water's edge to drink and eat until they were ready to leave later.

As his sons walked up, Leo smiled and asked, "Do I smell syrup in the making?"

"You do at that," Jessie answered. "Would you and the boys like to see?"

"It's been a long time since I've seen anyone making syrup," Leo said.

"I would like to, Pa," Todd spoke up, "I've never seen how it's made, but I sure love the taste of it with Ma's cornbread or biscuits."

"I would like to go too. I've never seen it made either," Jason, JR's oldest son, said, licking his lips.

"Then let's take a walk," Jessie said, and he started around the lake.

They all smelled the sixty gallons of cane juice cooking as they watched one of the men throw a couple of small logs in the fire pan under the kettle. Jessie smiled and nodded at Troy as he made his way through the crowd of men surrounding the old man sitting in a chair that one of the men had brought from home just for Mister Francis. Stopping in front of him, Jessie spoke, "Mister Francis, you sure got everyone excited around here anticipating what's coming with that smell."

The old man braced himself on the side of the chair to stand up. Jessie put his hands on the old man's shoulder, saying, "Don't get up Mister Francis. You just sit there and make sure these men make it like you tell them," he said and laughed.

Smiling and shaking his head, Mister Francis said, "Old habit, Mr. Tucker, when a white man came around you always stood to hear what he has to say. You don't, they be insulted, and that could get you the whip."

Keeping his hand on the old man's shoulder Jessie said with some sadness in his voice, "You sit where you are Mister Francis. Nobody is ever going to make you stand up unless you want to, cause no one will ever harm you again. I got twenty men here to make sure."

"Yas sir," he said with a smile on his face, "I sure am glad them days are over."

Jessie saw Leo and the boys over by the kettle of boiling juice covered with foam. He watched as Leo picked up one of the wooden paddles and started skimming the foam.

"The little black dots are called tadpoles," Leo explained to the boys. Jessie walked up next to him, and Leo smiled, scooping more impurities from the kettle. "I couldn't help it, I had to do this when I was a young man," he said as he started to hand the paddle to one of the men standing there.

"Naw sir," the young man said, "you keep it as long as you want."

Jessie left Leo explaining to the boys at the kettle what was happening as the foam thickened and walked a ways to meet John, Bill, Dave, and their families as they came past the quarters headed for his place. "I'll catch up with you at the lake," Jessie said as they passed by. Walking back to the open shed covering the kettle, he gathered up Leo and the boys and returned to the village.

Ed walked Little Otter to the village to join her sister and the other women when he saw Justin was back sitting outside of his lodge. He walked over to greet him. "You look really busy," Ed said and laughed.

Laughing back, Justin said, "If I don't get away from here soon, the women will have me busy. I was about to go and greet John and the others."

"Good, I'll walk with you," Ed offered.

Justin and Ed walked to where the men had gathered and shook hands with John and the others. Justin and Ed walked up to Leo, holding out their hands and Ed said, "Good to see you again, glad you could make it." They turned and shook hands with Leo's sons.

An hour later, one of the older boys from the quarters brought a gallon bucket of still warm syrup to where Jessie and the other men had gathered, talking about this year's crop and how much they planned to plant next year. Jessie was talking about how they were building their own herd with the Andalusians from the swamp.

They all stopped talking as the young man walked straight to Jessie and asked, "I'se gots a bucket of syrup Mr. Francis say bring it to you, where you wants me to put it?"

"Just sit it here next to me, I'll take it from here. Have they finished making syrup now?" Jessie asked.

"Naw sir," the young man answered, "but theys got the next round cooking already."

"Well, tell the reverend to bring everyone on down when they finish with the syrup."

"Yas sir, I wouldn't miss eating some of that cow Mister Franklin cooking over them hot coals," he said, grinning.

"Whew, I can't wait to pour some of that on my cornbread," Big John laughed.

"I don't think I can wait," Jessie laughed, wiping a finger across his shirt and sticking it into the bucket of syrup and into his open mouth. Suddenly they were all wiping their fingers and laughing as they tasted the fresh made warm, golden liquid.

It was late evening when Jessie saw Reverend Ellis leading men, women, and children around the lake laughing and singing. Some had little ones sitting on their fathers' shoulders, all carrying pots and dishes of food to add to everyone else's. He saw that two of the men were carrying fiddles and a couple of guitars, and he heard someone blowing on a mouth harp. Then he heard something that would make him smile every time it crossed his mind. He listened to the women down by the lake watching kids play. They started clapping their hands and joining in gospel songs the women and men from the quarters were singing as they went to meet them.

Belle left the group of women and walked to the village where she was met by Waiting Owl.

"We can go now and take the food; Woman of the Wind will come when Red Sun brings Two Worlds and the other braves." Waiting Owl motioned to the other women, and they began to gather the food they had cooked and followed Belle to the lake where the others were waiting. As they were placing the food on the table, Bonnie walked up with her daughters-in-law to greet the women from the village they had not seen since the freeze.

It had been many years since Red Sun had seen his father this excited. Two Worlds emerged from his lodge with a spring in his step and a smile on his face. He was followed by Woman of the Wind, smiling as she adjusted his headdress of feathers and fur and the soft cape of red wolf hides that covered the back of his decorated leggings, above his new moccasins. All the braves stood looking in awe. Some of them had never seen him in his ceremonial dress, and they knew something special was going to happen as Two Worlds, with Red Sun and Woman of the Wind by his side, started for the lake.

After everyone had eaten their fill and started gathering around the men with their fiddles and guitars, they started playing a lively tune. The people were smiling as they wandered around talking in small groups. As the women covered the left-over food, Franklin and Leroy finished slicing the meat from the calf, placing it in a large pan, for anyone wanting to take some home.

The sun had started its descent as the moon was working its way across the sky. Red Sun and the other braves started lighting the fire around the ten-foot-high pyramid they had built of small logs, placed around a large piece of dried oak trunk set two feet in the ground. The pyramid had pieces of lightered knots surrounding the oak trunk, with larger limbs as big as a man's arm. It was eight feet across the bottom and had smaller pieces of lightered wood in between the smaller limbs to start the flames that would light up the night for hours to come.

As the sun disappeared and the half-moon reflected what light it could across the lake, Belle excused herself from the other women and passing by Jessie who was talking to Two Worlds, she told him, "I'm going home to change clothes; you should come soon."

"I won't be long," Jessie told her as she turned for the house.

It was only a few minutes later when John saw Jessie leave Two Worlds and head for his house. John left the other men who were gathering around the music, cutting Jessie off. Realizing John was coming at him, he stopped and waited.

"I won't hold you up long," John said, as he stopped in front of Jessie.

"I've got all the time we need John, what's up?"

"I had a strange thing happen last week when I went to the Brooksville land office, to get a permit to cut that stand of timber just north of me. He told me that he couldn't give me one for that area because it was private land. Was I surprised," John continued, "when he showed me the books, and there was your name on it along with the land my house and mill sits on, also Bill and Dave's farm. I know you have been buying land with the money you get from those cows, but just how much land do you own? And why did you buy the land we all built our homes on, and what are you going to do with it?" John stopped, waiting for Jessie's answer.

Looking straight into John's eyes, Jessie started to explain. "I have been buying land since the second time we pushed a herd of those yellowhammers to Tampa. The ranch now owns thirty-two thousand acres from just to the north of us to the Withlacoochee River."

"I understand you buying land for your homestead and to farm or raise your cattle, but I don't understand you buying the land from under us," John stated, a question in his voice.

Jessie didn't hesitate. "I bought all the land around us because with the carpetbaggers moving down and buying or taking over homesteads that have not been registered, it wouldn't be long before some landgrabber comes here with a lawman and tells you that you are on his land and wants you off."

"Jessie, I have trusted you with my life, and I trust you now, but what are you going to do with the land we are on. Does Dave and Bill know?"

"John, no one will ever be able to touch this land we've had to fight for, to have a place to raise our families. Any time you want to buy however much land you want, it will be there, and this was the only way I knew to make sure no one ever took this land from us. I have seen no reason to say anything to anyone until now."

"Land prices are going up quickly now, how much are you going to want for the land where we live?" John asked.

"It will be the same price I paid for it," Jessie answered. "You and the others know me well enough to know I didn't do this to make money. You take all the timber you can get from that strand, and I will turn it into grass for cattle, or land for Ed to farm. John, I would rather not say anything to Bill and Dave until it is necessary." Jessie stopped and waited for John to decide how he wanted to handle this.

John stepped forward before Jessie could react and pinned his arms to his sides. He lifted him from the ground saying, "You ever pull something like this again without telling me, I will take you and throw you in the lake for the gators to eat."

"I swear, one day you keep doing this, I'm going to kick your big butt and see if you are too ornery for a gator to eat. Now put me down, or I will call Belle who is probably getting impatient, waiting on me."

"Don't do that," John smiled, letting Jessie down. "I would rather fight a gator than have her mad at me," he chuckled as he turned and headed for the lake.

Belle felt nervous as she placed the lamp on the dresser, walked to the foot of the bed and knelt in front of one of her most prized possessions. She opened the lid of her cedar chest and removed the top tray, then laid it behind her. For a moment, Belle hesitated to move the quilt that covered memories she wasn't sure if she or

Jessie were ready for. Closing her eyes and bowing her head, she said a small prayer. "Lord, don't let this be a mistake; I think he is ready now." Lifting the quilt out of the way, she caught her breath and waited until her heart slowed and her resolve strengthened before reaching and slowly lifting the blue and green plaid kilt. She laid it across the bed and then added the sash of the same colors. Belle looked down, and her heart began to beat faster again as she sat waiting for calmness. Then Belle reached in and removed the bagpipes. Bringing it closer, she looked for damage from being stored all these years but found nothing wrong. Laying it gently on the bed, she reached and removed his sandals and beret, then added the fine white cotton dress shirt she had made.

Jessie smiled as he opened the door, wondering what Belle was going to dress him in, maybe the new suit he bought in Tallahassee. She might be wearing her pretty dress he had brought back when he got his suit. Stepping through the bedroom door, he froze when he saw the look on Belle's face. As he started toward her, he stopped and stared at the things that were laying on the bed. They stood staring at each other, Belle waiting for Jessie. He stood still, uncertain at what he was looking at and what she was doing. "Belle, what is this?"

All doubt left her as she spoke. "It is time, Jessie B. Tucker, to show your children where they came from, the same as your father showed you! It is time to bring your past alive for them, making it a part of us as it should be."

"Belle, it has been so long; I'm not sure it belongs here. We have a new life now."

"No, Jessie, we only have a new place to build our life. You are the same man who came home to take his family away from the war and still fought as the warrior to protect us and all the others. It is time." She stepped around the bed and began to unbutton his shirt.

Jessie checked his shirt and adjusted the beret over his long red hair. He waited for Belle, standing proudly in the new dress he bought her. She was smiling at him and reaching once more into the trunk, she lifted the sheath holding the sword that had been passed down for generations. Belle placed the strap over his neck and shoulder, so the sword hung down his back the way his father and his father's father wore it. Reaching back over his shoulder, he pulled the blade from the sheath and watched the light from the lamp reflect off the shiny metal. Lifting his kilt, he folded the cloth over the blade then pulled it through, held it up to the light, and put it back in the sheath. Standing tall, he reached and lifted the bagpipes, placing it in his left arm and said, "Let's don't be late for our own party."

Belle reached and took his arm and said with a big smile on her face, "I wouldn't miss this one for the world."

Jessie stopped just outside of the firelight and stood, listening to the different sounds of music from the fiddles, guitars, a harmonica, and the low background of the drums Red Sun and the other braves had carried from the village. Jessie watched in fascination as some people from the quarters were dancing about, keeping time with the music. John, Bill, and Dave were swinging their wives in circles, and Leo and his family were keeping time clapping and stomping the ground. Frank and Ed stood with Justin watching their wives as they danced with the women from the village circling in front of the drums shuffling and chanting.

Belle released Jessie's arm as he reached for the mouthpiece of the bagpipes and began to fill the bag with air. Strange music began to fill the air.

The music slowed and stopped, and everyone stood still, wondering what they were hearing outside of the firelight. It became louder and louder. Leo grabbed Bonnie and went to whirling her around, yelling an old Scottish war cry. Jessie stepped into the light, blowing the pipes with all he possessed. He marched around the fire and heard the fiddles matching the sound of the bagpipes. The drums started a louder beat, and Red Sun felt a hand on his arm and was pulled along by Two Worlds following Jessie. Two Worlds was stomping his feet and chanting to his ancestors. Then John began high stepping arm and arm with Leo, who had left his wife and joined the dance.

Leroy watched in fascination as Troy with his deep voice resonating across the lake, began a warrior's song and dance. He had heard it only once from his father when he was sold. The night before he was taken to another plantation, the warrior's song had gone on until the master came and told him if he didn't stop the noise, he would get the whip. Belle watched Troy's wife Hailey take his arm and lead him to the circle of light where he joined the other warriors.

Justin felt the power come up through his body as it flowed through the people dancing and chanting, each in their own language. In his mind, he saw Jessie walking to the lake to see Two Worlds, and he began to laugh, nodding to himself, and moved into the circle, following Two Worlds around the fire.

The drums became louder as the women began chanting and stomping in a frenzy. The men and women from the quarters started a dance that had been passed down through the generations as the fiddles and guitars were played as loud as possible.

Belle walked to where Race stood with Jenny, watching a father they had never seen before, and she knew watching the expression on their faces, she had been right. It was time to bring the past forward and make it part of their lives now.

Jessie and Belle stood with their arms around one another watching the last of the men and women from the quarters and the village as they gave up the night. Leo and his family had left earlier to make the long drive home. Jessie and Belle knew something special happened tonight, yet neither one could really say what had changed as they started home. Then Jessie thought about the vision Two Worlds had been given the night before, and he smiled.

Jessie stood still as Belle removed the sword and unbuttoned his shirt, then lifted the sash and unwrapped the kilt letting it drop. Looking at his arousal, she then met his eyes as he pulled the straps of her dress from her shoulders and let it fall. Belle's eyes never left Jessie's as he lifted her into his arms and started for the lake.

The moon still reflected its light across the lake as Jessie waded in, where he had sat so many times with Two Worlds. He let Belle gently down into the water—she clung to his neck as he entered her and whispered softly in his ear, "Jessie, don't ever let this end."

The End

About the Author

Michael Calhoun Tucker is an extraordinary storyteller! In his first book, *The Crackers: The Legend of Jessie B. Tucker,* his prowess as a writer comes alive as he weaves the historical facts about the family's legends and myths into a compelling novel. Filling in the gaps lost to history, Michael takes you on an adventure only he could create. Part fiction, part fact, completely entertaining, Jessie B. and his extended family are Michael's story.

Michael's second book, *The Crackers: Tuckertown,* takes you on a new journey as Jessie and the ancient shaman Two Worlds take on the new challenges of post Civil War Florida with its outlaws, carpetbaggers, and a society that is fearful and caught in prejudice following the personal devastation that was brought by the war.

Born and raised in rural central Florida, Michael has lived and absorbed the very fabric of the Crackers. Michael embodies the voices of his Scots/Irish and Creek Indian ancestors in these exciting novels and entwined in his storytelling are lessons of the spirit and the heart, reflecting this complex man and his unique style of writing.

Contact Page

THE CRACKERS: Tuckertown is available
on Amazon.com in paperback and Kindle versions.

To contact Michael Calhoun Tucker, please use the following:

mcalhountucker@yahoo.com

www.michaelcalhountucker.com